West of the War

by
L. J. Martin

Table of Contents:

Dedicated to
the many thousands who died
forging west to find new hope
In a new land

Missouri is a mishmash of secessionists and abolitionists, where a fellow could have one on either side of himself and not know which was which. Quantrill and his Lieutenant Bloody Bill Anderson are running wild across the country and Colonel John C. Mosby is earning a reputation as the gray ghost of the Confederacy and is said to run like a race horse and double back like a fox.

Many of my friends, most all of whom are sixteen years of age or older, have ridden off to join up, most with the south, but a few with the north. Confederate Colonel Nathan Bedford Forrest put out a notice, "I wish none of you but those who want to be actively engaged. COME ON BOYS, IF YOU WANT A HEAP OF FUN AND TO KILL SOME YANKEES." And he got plenty of takers.

At past eighteen I was looked at askance by many for not joining up, and I am not fond of the implications.

But there is plenty of work on the farm. It is fall and the cotton is in. All of us, the darkies, daddy, and me are in the barn picking seed from the fiber, cleaning away the leaves and trash, rolling fiber into bales, and binding them with burlap—when the pounding of shod horses rings through the barn doors. More'n a dozen of them by the clatter. The pounding of hoofs sends a chill up my back, although I've been expecting it. I say a silent prayer it's boys in butternut.

I kick my way through trash to the doors, but my father pushes by me, "Stay inside, Braden, should worse come to worse, beat a trail and don't look back," he commands. And I know he means it as he normally calls me Brad. I can see out, and the worst has come to pass.

Bluebellys.

My daddy keeps a shotgun charged and ready on a high rack over the smaller pass-through barn door, but I'm glad when he doesn't reach for it on the way out into the yard. The odds are insurmountable.

Even the fact he'd been sold rather than whipped had caused some consternation among our darkies, but the ruckus soon settled and we were back to business as usual, growing cotton and lots of vegetables and fruit—stone fruit and melons—which we sent downriver to St. Louis.

But all that seems soon to change.

The distant boom of cannons is rolling upriver from the south, an ominous rumble, where the Union Army is head to head with General "Ol' Pap" Sterling Price and the Missouri State Guard, as fine a group of boys in butternut as were ever bunched up under one command...or so the word has come to us.

How-some-ever, they've had their hands full as many of them are fighting with shotguns and squirrel guns and only one pair of cannon against new Spencers with bayonets and a dozen or more big guns.

I am not surprised that Mr. Lincoln and his cohorts in the north plan to keep those of us below the Mason Dixon line in the fold, as being a cotton grower, albeit a very small one, I am well aware that the south grows two thirds of all the world's cotton production. And that makes the south the fourth largest economy in the world—even without the industrial might of the north. The north won't let that slide away. They run their mouths off about slavery, and I'm sure it's true they won't abide by new territories becoming slave states as they'd lose the majority in Congress...but to me it's clear it's money that girds their good consciences.

My daddy, Rutherford Jefferson McTavish, Rut to his friends, has held me back from saddling up to ride to join the guard, saying I was needed on the place to defend us from the abolitionists who would gladly burn the big house, the barns, and even the nigra quarters, down around our ears, given the chance...and have done so to neighbors.

3

Chapter One

W e've done our level best to stay out of it, but the rumble of cannon in the distance—a quiet ominous growl most often, enough to rattle your backbone at times—means we're in the path of something well beyond the control of some simple farm folk.

It seems the noose is tightening around all our necks.

The big Mo rolls yellow and muddy almost due north and south in our part of the country, except for a big bend, a bulge to the east then back west, that surrounds our home place—a section of rich Missouri bottom land circled on three sides by the river. Eight more sections of the McTavish farm lay to the west rising up to over two hundred feet above mean water level. The black bottomland is crossed by a slough and sometimes two or three, depending on how high the Missouri runs. Pa had tried to grow rice there a time or two, but the water level is too unpredictable, so just two years ago we planted a small grove of pecans as it's said they like their feet in the water.

The little trading post of Arrow Rock is to the south of us, run by an abolitionist son-of-a-bitch whom we know cannot be trusted—he's against slavery but beats his two daughters mercilessly, and one of them has her majority. Our thirty nigras have been with my family since long before I was born when they were but a dozen, three generations now, and my father treats them as fairly as a man who is considered owner and overseer could be expected to, as had my grandfather...we'd only had one occasion to run a man down with the dogs in the last dozen years. Rather than put the whip to him my daddy sold him cheap to a neighbor of good reputation.

Raymond, whose sister and parents are still with us, was a mighty light-footed African who could run like a gazelle and damn near did our red bones in with the chase. He'd heard of others being freed here and there across the state so I guess that put the rabbit into him. Ray is my age, and he and his younger sister, Pearl—as fine a specimen of a female as there is in Missouri, black or white—and I had spent many a hot summer's day gigging carp in the shallows, catching catfish with cane poles, or trapping crayfish.

As we grew older, Pearl had aroused more than merely my interest, but it was a cardinal sin in my family to risk mixing blood. So I concerned myself with other matters, no matter the occasional strain on my trousers.

I had spoken up against my daddy selling Ray, but to no avail. I still considered him my friend, rabbit or not. Then I'd convinced pa to sell to a kindly owner rather than one who'd offered almost five hundred dollars more. Daddy called me a damn fool, and maybe I am, but I'll live with it, and hope Ray will live...period.

Wolfpack Publishing
48 Rock Creek Road.
Clinton, Montana 59825

ISBN: 978-1-62918-950-5

I follow as far as the pass-through and stand beneath the old gun. My pa has at one time or another taken a job as auctioneer, and can talk like no other so I have high hopes that talk is all this will come to.

"And who might you be?" Pa asks, hands on hips, voice not exactly warm and inviting.

An officer in the lead answers, "I, sir, am Captain Alfred P. Doolan, under the command of General Nathaniel Lyon. And you, sir, are a secessionist son-of-a-she-dog and we're here to set your slaves free and to hang you, should you resist. Where's your root cellar as we will relieve you of your stores. And we're to requisition all the mules on the place." Only then do I notice a buckboard in the background.

I can see daddy blanch a little, his back straighten, and his shoulders go back as the red headed Union captain glowers at him. We will not make it through winter without our root cellar being full, and the mules are the heart of the place. Through clinched jaw, he snaps back at the mounted captain, "My....The darkies are all freemen and here by choice."

From near my shoulder, Pearl, the sister of Raymond, the boy who'd run, yells out. "No sur, that ain't right. No matter what this masser says to you, we ain't free."

The captain, too, straightens his shoulders, then turns to a mounted sergeant at his side. "Hang the lying son-of-a-bitch."

Then Pearl pushes by me. "No, no, I didn't mean that there. He been kind to us...is jus we ain't free." Her eyes flare wide, and a fist comes to her mouth, shocked at what she's done.

A half dozen of the bluebelly boys dismount and are heading for my Pa, who is backing up as his gaze cuts from one to another. One of them carries a coil of line over his shoulder.

My stomach knots and feels as if a dozen prairie rattlers are nesting and gnawing there.

When Pearl had pushed me aside I heard my mama scream from the big house, a scream like I've never heard from her. One that floods my backbone with anger and flushes my cheeks. I have to go up on my tiptoes to gather up the shotgun. "Damn you, Pearly," I stammer as I bring the old coach gun down. She looks as if she's about to chew a knuckle off.

Just as the thick-necked corporal with the rope reaches for my pa—a strange hunger in the bluebelly's eyes and ghoulish grin on his wide face—I am into the space between the double doors, cocked and shouldered, my jaws clamped. The scattergun roars, bucks, and billows white smoke, and blows the old boy back into the yard onto his back with a thump that raises dust. A blossom of blood gurgles on his chest from one side to the other. I turn quickly on the captain intent on blowing the head off the snake and sending the body scampering.

Cocking the second barrel as she comes back from the recoil, and as Captain bluebelly jerks rein and spins away, I give him a blast that flattens him face-first across the big gray's neck. The horse side-hops and humps into the other troopers, giving me a moment's reprieve as they have to control their mounts. Pearl dives to the side and to her belly, covering head with both arms as if we're under cannon attack. The doors around me begin to splinter as the troop opens up with Remington side-arms and their big bore cap and balls—and billowing gun smoke, to my advantage, suddenly occludes all seeing. The darkies behind me dive behind bales and into piles of loose bolls and fiber as the barn fills with lead hornets.

It is time for me to abide by my father's wishes and show them my tail, like a bobwhite taking wing, and I do so,

flinging the shotgun aside as it's now useless. I'm deep into the barn, then through the mules stall and into their corral, scattering the four of them, and then I throw the rails aside and hope they'll follow my lead...and am into the corn, now gone brown with fall upon us. The corn cuts at me as I pound between the tight rows, luckily we'd had a good stand, at least a head taller than myself, and I'm near six feet. But I hunker low as the lead continues to fly, cutting stalks to either side, and rather than run straight down the rows—which I figure my pursuers will presume—after a hundred yards I cut to the side. If I can make it another two hundred yards, the first of the sloughs will offer me shelter among the bulrushes then into the water if I must.

There's a fall chill on the land, and I'm dressed in a long sleeve Tartan patterned flannel shirt that's badly frayed from the elbows down, my trousers are ripped and torn above the ankle, and my brogans worn through on the sides are little better...work clothes. They offer paltry protection from the sharp corn or the oncoming cold. But I don't hesitate as I plunge into the rushes then through them and dive deeply into the slough, coming up spitting and sucking air, then turning downstream I let the current help in my escape. I can hear horses neighing and snorting behind me as their sharp shod hoofs sink into the mud and they complain. But the bulrushes hide me from prodding barrels.

Only then do I reckon that I've left my home and family to the hands of a bunch of bluebellys who have the worst in mind.

After a mile or so riding a bobbing foot-thick hunk of cottonwood through the slough and into the main river, I cast off it and swim the two hundred feet to the shore, now lined with a dense thicket of river willows. I know of a high spot in our fields that's a half-mile or a little more from the houses and barns and head that way at a trot. The hell of it is, it's in the center of a half section of cotton stalks and they are almost leafless having been picked and abandoned to the winter, and not tall enough to offer cover to a bony coyote, much less a man. I work my way back, then along a deep slough now gone dry which I know circles behind the rise. I'm up and out of it when I reach a spot where the rise is between me and the home place, and do the belly crawl the last thirty feet to the crown of the little hill where, from a distance, my head appears no bigger than a dirt clod.

The sun is just kissing the treetops to the west, so it will be dark soon. But there's plenty of light in our compound of buildings, as all of them, other than the slave quarters, are afire and flames are beginning to leap twice the height of the barn from its conflagration. And I can see the huge piles of raw cotton next to the barn as they go up in flame. The damn fools have burned a year's worth of work, what will end up...would have ended up...to be more than a hundred bales of fine long fiber cotton. Our yield, we figured, was a bale and a half to the acre, and we had a hundred twenty acres under plow.

Then I'm ashamed of myself as I don't know the fate of what's far more important...my father and mother, and yes, Pearl and the rest of our darkies. It will soon be dark, but the hell of it is I cannot see into the farmyard as the tall corn is between me and that target. I'll have to wait until darkness, and get in and out before moonrise.

I'm not hunkered down in the cotton stalks long before I see the column of men on the road between my perch and the river as they pass across a narrow slough at a trot, followed by the buckboard now piled high with hams, pork bellies, potatoes, carrots, and other goods from our smokehouse and cellars. Then I'm a little surprised to see a column of darkies, side by side, hustling along behind. It seems our slaves now consider themselves freemen.

8

Bluebellys. The rotten no-account bastards.

As soon as they're out of sight, I go ahead and move at a rapid walk. I'm almost overrun by a pair of our hogs, leading a half-dozen shoats, I imagine escaping the heat of the farmyard. Following them, only a heart-beat behind, is our four mules—Molly, Mac, Gerty, and Bean, and I'm glad they run free and are not enlisted in the Union Army. As I near buildings I can see where the mules have stomped the corn down. I guess they did follow me and am now proud I thought to slide the rails.

By the time I'm at the edge of the corn and shuffling through a pile of shucks and can see into the yard, it's almost full dark but the remaining flames give me plenty of light. We have a half-dozen darky cabins still standing and I move to the rear of them, and carefully pick my way between. The bluebellys could have left a small contingent of guards, but I doubt it.

I've got to get into the house, but it's still burning and even if I could get there, everything would be so hot to the touch I couldn't recover what I hope is still there.

As I near the farmyard between house—now a stand of fallen, glowing, and burnt timbers—and barn, still aflame as the cotton will burn and smolder for days, I see a body swinging from the branch of a huge cottonwood that's shaded our house for as long as I can remember.

And not a sign of life anywhere.

I run across the yard and hoist my daddy up by the legs, but from his bulging eyes and slightly distended tongue I know he's met his maker. The side of him nearest the house is blackened and his clothes burned to tatters. Skin off his blistered legs comes off on my arms. I back away, madly trying to get the gore off of me. The bile rises in my throat and heat floods my backbone at the same time. I'm sickened and incensed by the sight and smell of my father's remains.

It's a horrid sight and searing odor that will haunt my dreams to eternity.

For the first time in all her sixteen years, I hate Pearl to the core.

Deciding to cut him down later, I move away, as my mother is yet to be found, and I pray for her survival. I search every nook and cranny, and would poke through the ashes of the house, but it's still too hot to get near the smoldering timbers or still burning barn. Or to what I'm sure no one has found.

Then, over the crackling and occasional roaring remnants of fire, I hear hoof beats and the rattle of sabers.

It's time to turn tail again. My ma and Pearl, who works in the house, have the lines full of clothes and I grab a pair of hot-to-the-touch trousers and two more shirts as I sprint by.

I'm leaving my daddy swinging from a tree to have his eyes picked by the crows; my mama, I'm sure, a pile of ashes in her own home of forty years...and everything I've ever known.

I wish I had the shotgun I'd cast aside, and the makins to charge it. I wish I had my squirrel gun, as I would quickly become a bushwhacker as I know the country...every slough, stump and tall tree of her. But I will have to bide my time until I can kill some Yankees and take a cat-o-nine-tails to that faithless Pearl until her beauty is nothing but a crisscross of festering slashes.

God help my parents, God help Pearl who took the name McTavish then turned brazen traitor and sullied it, and God help the Yankees who desecrated my home and all I hold dear...help them to a rump roast in hell.

I fade away into the darkness, hoping to find the farm vacated by morning, so I can properly bury my daddy and try and find my ma.

I retreat to my high spot and find a small hollow in the ground at the edge of the cotton and sleep.

It's been the most difficult day of my life...I've killed a man, maybe two, and lost all I've held dear.

Morning is a dark one with a sky as flat and gray as slate. I lay on my back and review the previous day in my mind, and only then mount the hill again to see who's now invaded my home, and make out another group of riders, a Union cavalry troop, but this one is followed by an infantry troop of more than three dozen. I watch as they move closer to the river and continue setting up camp where it appears they've spent the night. A couple of shots ring out and I wonder if I've been spotted and hunker down even lower among the cotton stalks, then see a couple of troopers appear, each with a shoat slung over a shoulder. I guess it'll be roast suckling pig for the bastards tonight. Our pigs.

And papa still sways in the breeze. These bluebellys have no shame.

This will be the last time I see my home place for a good long while. As it seems the bluebellys are settled here. The cavalry troop has set up a camp a hundred yards or so downstream from the infantry. They've picketed their horses over graze a hundred feet farther on a line tied from cottonwood to cottonwood, and it gives me an idea.

I've been horseback since I was five, and I don't plan to walk now. And I see no reason to chase our stock all over hell and gone as what the Yankees haven't stolen have flown to the wind. Fire makes critters more than just a little crazy. Besides, my old mare would not be suited for riding into battle as her best years are behind her. I hope she'll find an easy life in the forest.

And I may be crazy as well, but I'm gonna steal me a fine horse, maybe that Captain's gray if'n it ain't shot fulla holes.

11

The willow thicket begins just beyond where the yanks have picket lined their stock, and under the last of the large trees, one of the few live oaks on our place, is the troop's tack, saddles nicely in a row. A few rest on stumps we've left from cutting small oaks for firewood, bridles draped over a low branch.

I have no intention of slipping up on their camp in the light, even though it's a dark day. I'm praying for rain as I'm sure it will discourage guards and keep their heads down.

I fade back off my perch on the crest of the hill and back to my ravine, then down toward the river until I'm inside the copse of river willows. Only then do I risk a look and begin to carefully pick my way through the thicket. When I figure I'm only fifty yards from the horses, I curl up and try and get some sleep.

Waking startled, I rise and realize my gut is gnawing in hunger, and it's made worse by the smell of roast pig and the ring of laughter coming from the Yankee camp. To assuage my gut, I make my way to the river's edge and drink my fill, only to have to drop to my back as some damn bluebelly is thirty paces upstream, and it's plain what he's doing as it sounds like a deluge being sprayed into the river. Downstream of the camp was not a place to quench my thirst.

I work my way back to my sleeping spot and arrive just as a low rumble of thunder rolls down from upriver—at first I mistake it for cannon fire, but the low growing rumble is then unmistakable. Only a few minutes pass before a crack of lightening throws harsh shadows through the willows and in the count of two, thunder rattles the narrow willow stalks and a gust of wind bends them to the south.

Rain follows almost as quickly as the thought comes to mind. I've made a ruck sack of one of the shirts and carried the other one and the spare pants wrapped therein, and pull apart my makeshift sack and pull on the pants and other two shirts. Now I'm wearing all I own.

I work my way to only twenty-five paces from the horses, when another crack of lightening shatters the darkness and I can clearly see a lot of nervous critters pulling at their lead ropes and stomping fearfully. Under the cover of their shrill whinnies and snorts, I move even closer. When the echo of the crack of heaven's fire resides, I hear the soft sound of a harmonica coming from the camp and make out, through the horses legs, three campfires which are surrounded by tents, some of which appear to be canvas and some Mr. Goodyear's rubber coated material.

A little farther away this time, God lights the sky again and I'm pleased to see the horse nearest my end of the string is a dappled gray, sixteen hands if he's a finger, and probably the least troubled by the kettledrums of thunder. He seems a calm sort.

One of the saddles nearest him, and me, is covered by a pack canvas, so I inch forward on my belly and lift the edge. The sight warms the cockles of my heart as it's a well-oiled McClellan and far the better is a pair of saddle holsters riveted to its fenders, and both have a revolver still stuffed therein. Laced to the cantle in back and to the forks in front are saddlebags, and they are stuffed full, and a blanket roll, picket pin, and canteen are still in place. Unfortunately, the rifle boot is empty. I guess one of those new Springfield's is just too much to ask.

I hope the blanket roll not being used means I've kilt the son-of-a-bitch who ordered my pa hung.

At the far end of the string, maybe a hundred feet from where I study the camp, a single picket guard leans against the stump of an oak, his head down, his wide brimmed cavalry hat dripping water. He never raises his head as I—almost flat on my belly in the mud—pull the saddle out from under the canvas and slide it back into the willows. I hope the Remington I pull from the holster and shove into my belt is capped and loaded, as my life could well depend upon it.

Getting the gray loose and under the taut picket line will be another feat altogether. I smile as the rain begins to be a gully washer even as it floods down my back. The picket guard rises and runs for the camp, I presume to outfit himself with a slicker.

It's my chance, and I lift the picket line and lead the gray under and a dozen feet into willows.

Only then do I realize I don't have a bridle or a blanket, but I saddle him none the less. I know how to tie an emergency rig and almost as quickly as I can say it, have a Spanish hackamore tied from the lead rope. The resulting reins are a bit short, but beggars can't be....

And with another distant crack of lightening, I see the guard returning, only this time he's headed for the tree sheltering the saddles as it's the thickest of the trees nearby. And it's only paces from where I'm mounting up. He's a redheaded whelp no older than myself and I'd hate to kill a fella before he's lain with his first love, but not so much as I'd hate to be kilt.

And therein is the making of war, I'd guess.

There's no time to tarry, so I swing into the saddle, give my heels to the gray, and he damn near leaps out from under me. The willows slap and tear at us as he plunges into the thicket. He stumbles a bit and I pray he doesn't fling me face-first into the mud and tangle of stalks. A shot rings out behind me, but it only encourages the gray, and in a half minute we're clear of most the willows and he's pounding like he's happy to be free of the company of Yankees...he must be a fine Tennessee stud, probably stolen from some Confederate colonel as I've just stolen him from a Yankee captain.

Now to find General Price and his butternut boys so we can both, gray horse and I, join up and help to run these damn Yankees back to New York or wherever they hail from.

I'll come back for what I hope has gone undiscovered in the house…someday, not too far off, I'll come back.

Chapter Two

As I ride away, I can hear the call to arms being bugled from the camp. In a half mile I come to a rock shelf and cross it to a six foot stream I know well, then turn down hill, keeping the gray stream-center. They'll never track me in the darkness. After a couple of hundred yards of six inch deep muddy stream, I rein the gray out and onto a game trail through a dogwood thicket.

Knowing I'm being pursued, I ride all night, south toward Springfield. With the light I hear cannon rumble on south, and only pause to rest, water and graze the gray and fill my own belly with some salted meat and hard crackers courtesy of the Captain as they filled half of one of the rump saddlebags—enough to last me a week, if'n I don't give into a gnawing stomach too readily. Near Sedalia I hear the cannon again, only this time to the east, so I head that way, skirting every sign of life as no one knows who is who.

Near the end of the day, after near twenty-four hours in the saddle, I hear gunfire to the east and become extra careful as we pick our way around a field of corn stubble. We are into the Ozarks and the hills, covered in post oak, rise both to the north and south of the field. As I rein the gray around to the north side of the field, I can hear the gunfire receding in front of me, the sounds of a running fight probably between mounted cavalry as it is moving quickly away.

The hill to my left, to the north, is thick with post oaks and underbrush, but not so thick that I don't quickly gig the gray up into the shadows when I hear the galloping hoof beats of a horse coming our way. Before he comes into view, he's slowed, to a trot, then a walk.

I palm one of the Remingtons and wait. Afraid to even breathe. A sorrel colored head appears, then drops to graze. I stay dead still ready for him to be a bluecoat, and sure as hell the front edge of his saddle blanket appears, blue with yellow trim. Then the sorrel takes another step and I can see he isn't mounted. I give heels to the gray and edge him down the hill, moving slow and easy as I have no idea if his rider is walking along behind, or what? As it happens, the horse is alone. And as it happens, his saddle is empty, but his saddle boot is not. I dismount and let the gray drop his muzzle and graze, and move slowly over to beside the sorrel, and slip a fine Sharps muzzle loader carbine from the boot. The sorrel is unconcerned with the theft. I dig into a saddle mounted bullet pouch riveted to the fender and remove its handful of .52 caliber balls along with some more from a pouch on the other side. It is a bonanza for a fellow far more familiar with long arms than handguns. The last thing I do is drop the saddle off the sorrel and give him some freedom, and myself a new horse blanket, but only after slipping his bridle over his ears.

"Thank you, Lord," I say under my breath.

I re-saddle the gray using my new saddle blanket, reversed so the colors and regiment number don't show.

But my joy is short lived. I've barely gotten the hand-tied Spanish hackamore turned back into a lead rope, the bridle adjusted to the gray, the Sharps into the boot on my saddle, and remounted, when the oaks rattle behind me and I turn to see a half dozen riders staring at me. I smile broadly as they are butternut boys.

"Don't reach for one of those weapons, bluebelly," a fellow with sergeant stripes on his sleeve commands.

"Bluebelly. I ain't no damned Yank," I sputter.

"Climb down, slow and put your face in that cow patty down there."

"I ain't—"

"What you are is about to get yourself killed instead of taken prisoner. Now get down if 'n you wanna take another breath."

I decide I can explain later, and quickly dismount, as six firearms are leveled at me.

As I put my face on the ground, the sergeant guffaws, then says, "Funny, that there fine lookin' gray has a U.S. brand, a McClellan saddle, and a Sharps in the boot, but he ain't no Yankee."

The others in the troop laugh. I take offense and yell from my spot flat on my belly. "I'm Braden McTavish from just north of Arrow Rock where my family's farmed for four generations and I stole that gray from a Union troop in the middle of a rainstorm last night...after they freed our nigras and hung my daddy and probably burned up my ma. And I just freed that Sharps from Union possession...and that bridle, which I've been riding without, with naught but a lead rope, trying to find you fellas. You put a bluebelly in front of me and watch me tear out his eyeballs and piss his sockets full, you don't believe me."

The sergeant is quiet for a moment, then smiles and turns to a rider at his side. "The younger's got more than a dollop of piss and vinegar. Take a look in those saddle bags and see what you turn up. You, down there, shut the hell up while we figure out if you're off to a prisoner camp on we hang you right here or whatever."

"I ain't got nothing in those bags but some dried meat and crackers," then it dawns on me. "Right front, just beside the saddle holster, in the little shoulder bag is a packet of letters. I ain't had a chance to give them a read yet. My name, like I said, is Brad McTavish, and you'll see that none of them is addressed to me."

"Reynolds, check it out."

The corporal digs into the packet, reads the first one, and laughs. "It says, happy fortieth, Alfred...."

"Hummm," the sergeant says, then exclaims, "you don't look no forty to me, nor like an Alfred." The sergeant then snaps at the reader. "Dig halfway and read another."

He did so, and laughs again. "It says 'our baby girl has turned eighteen and we wish you were here to celebrate with us...'"

"Get up, McTavish. You ain't home free yet."

I climb to my feet and brush off my trousers as he asks, "Who was the governor of Missouri five years ago?"

"Turstin Polk resigned to take a seat in the U.S. Senate and Stewart defeated that know-nothing Rollins in a special election, who also lost in forty-eight."

"Humph," the sergeant says, then asks, "And who was the other senator?"

"Geyer, and that abolitionist son-of-a-bitch Henderson was appointed to replace Polk when he come south."

A slow smile parts the sergeant's gray mustache and beard. "None of that proves nothing until you do rip the eyes out of some northern pile of dog shit." Then he seems to relax. "So, where the hell you off to, son?"

"I'm lookin' to join up and kill me some more Yanks. I got me two before I run off ahead of the rope. I'm looking to get me two hundred more...maybe two thousand, God willin'."

"And you stole yourself a fine mount. Is that a stud horse? We can't have no stud horse in the ranks, no mares either."

"Hell, I don't know. He's mighty calm for a stud if he is one. Let's see how he acts while I ride along with y'all, if that's okay with you, sir."

"I ain't no sir, wet behind the ears. I'm a sergeant. You get yourself in the middle of our string and we'll get you sworn in when we get back to camp. If we can find a 'sir' what thinks you're fittin'."

"Yes, sir...I mean, yes Sergeant." And I mount up and fall into the middle of the line as they move uphill and into a single column at a canter. I guess I'm about to be a butternut boy.

If I live long enough.

We don't ride a quarter mile before a line of bluecoats pop up fifty yards in front of us, and white smoke and whizzing mini balls fill the air...and the first volley fells three of the six of us.

I am not wet behind the ears for long.

And I've put the gray to a fine test, escaping the ambush alongside the sergeant, who I've come to know as Ira Keeney.

Sworn in a few miles east of the Big Mo and Arrow Rock at a place called Higginsville, I join up with Lt. Col. Lucious St. Alexander, and his cavalry regiment—thanks to bluebelly Captain Alfred Doolan and his fine gift of a sixteen hand gray. In a matter of days we find ourselves victorious in the Battle of the Hemp Bales at Lexington, on the banks of the

Big Mo again. I am promoted to corporal due to the fact the damn gray spooks at the first cannon barrage and, against my better judgment and totally without my permission, carries me at the head of a charge against a larger entrenched force, thus branding me a hero. My charge is instrumental in our capture of Colonel Mulligan and gets me shot through the left side of my butt, making it more than a little difficult to set the saddle.

Damn horse.

My butt is mostly healed by the time we ride against the bluecoats at Wilson's Creek, on a hot August day made even hotter by cannon and musket fire and white smoke covering the battlefield. Again the overenthusiastic gray will not respond to the rein, and gets me out ahead of our line, and I am soon made a lieutenant. However, he gets me shot through—flesh only, thank the good Lord—on my upper left arm.

And again I am healed up when on a cold March day we ride against the Northern Army at Pea Ridge, all the way over in Arkansas. On the first day it looks as if we are again to become victorious as we push the bluebellys back to Elkhorn Tavern. The following day, however, they came back at us like demons from hell. This time the damn gray takes me so far and fast I find myself behind the enemy line, and giving him the spurs he takes me at a gallop up behind a pair of Union cannons and caissons. The boys in blue didn't see me coming, and I am able to put a couple of them on the ground as the gray pounds up, as there were six more, it was no place to rein up. The gray leaps a union cannon like it's a pasture fence, and throws me with his stumble, but I am able to hang onto the reins.

I fire my Griswold and Gunnison .36 caliber four more times, dropping two more cannoneers before I am able to get back in the saddle. I lay so low as the gray kicks up clods on the way back to our lines that I get a mouthful of mane by the time I can dismount. I am made captain as the cannon didn't get back into the battle, even though the Union boys beat us badly, and General Price was wounded.

But we fight on. Crossing the Mississippi, we ride against, and seize the Union supply depot at Iuka, Mississippi. A great victory but a short lived one. When Maj. Gen. William S. Rosecrans counterattacks and again, after charging behind the lines, the gray has gone a step too far and a Union cannon ball puts dirt and limbs in our faces. We go down hard.

It is September 19, 1862, and I am a Union prisoner and my gray—which I've come to love-hate—is feeding the crows among my dead comrades. I find myself limping north among several hundred other Butternut boys...all prisoners.

We are marched to Springfield, Illinois, with the snow blowing down the back of my neck and my riding boots, purloined from a dead Union cavalry man, worn thin, where I am held for four months. In July of 62 the opposing sides worked out a method of parole, but we are not offered it quickly, and it's more than a year eating gruel and mush before they come to me. I am quick to sign my promise to head west and stay out of the conflict for the duration.

It is March of 64 when I walk out of Camp Butler with five dollars in silver in my pocket, hair grown to my collar, twenty pounds lighter and ribs showing, a recycled pair of brogans a size too big, and a coat with enough holes to mimic a Swiss cheese...but I am free.

One of my cellmates is another Irishman whose family originated in Cork, Ireland, as had mine. Ian Hollihan is a big fellow, at least fifteen years my senior, and had served with General Price, but had never gone beyond corporal, having been busted back a half dozen times to private as he is not one to take to kidding, but was one to take to the delivery of knuckles on almost any excuse.

However, I'd come to like him.

We stand free men for the first time in months, and have money in our pockets.

"So, Ian lad, are you off to find some Butternut boys to tie up with?" I ask him as we trudge away from Camp Butler.

"I'm a man of me word, McTavish, particularly since my word got me set free of that prison slop they called grub and since it'll keep me from getting my hide tacked to some Union privy wall. Yoursef'?"

"The word is there's some gold to be found out Washington and Dakota Territory way, so I'll be headin' there...presuming I find what I figure I'll find at my home place. And I don't figure to find much."

He guffaws. "Yeah, lad, I'm sure the trails of Dakota territory are paved with gold. I did my time in California, grubbin' in the mud and having to break ice for the doin' of it. I'm thinking I'll head west and get on with the railroad. Word is they're soon to be hiring for the Transcontinental. And I'm a gandy dancin' som' bitch."

"Gandy dancing?"

"Railroad term. We Irish know how to drive spikes and lay rail."

"Well then," I say with a laugh, "if it's west your headin', we can watch each other's back for a good ways before we part ways."

He sticks out his big paw, and we shake, then I add, "But I'll be having to stop by and pay my respects to the old family place. I still don't know the fate of my ma, more'n two years now."

"Hell, man, that's two hundred miles due west of here...we otta be heading some north."

"Then head out. I gotta go to the home place."

He guffaws again. "And I wouldn't be thinking you fit to travel with if'n you didn't do just that. Check on your ma, I mean. So I'll tag along."

"The McTavish Farm is next to the river and we might just catch a ride."

And with that, we're off, snow still a foot deep, and the road ankle deep in mud. It will be a stroll of something over two hundred miles before I find the home place, or what's left of it, if anything. And I pray some of what was left behind is still to be found.

With the war and all, there seems to be plenty of abandoned and half-burnt places, so we manage to get out of the weather the first three nights. We even scrounge up some turnips and carrots out of one farmer's root cellar and find a bent up tin pot to cook up a soup. I'd kill for a hand full of salt, but until we come upon a mercantile, that's a dream.

Hannibal is just ahead, and if it hasn't been burned out in the fighting, it'll have a general store and maybe even some folks needin' a little work done...of course we're still wearing butternut trousers with yellow stripes down the outside hem so that may cause some consternation. God only knows what the persuasion of a place is these days.

We wake that fourth morning of our trek to a flat gray sky, but one devoid of snow or rain, and are blessed by good luck. We've lain up in a fine timber barn next to a burned farmhouse. I find an apple crate and make a box trap, finding a few grains of corn among the mouse droppings in the bottom of a crib, and damned if I don't trap us a fat rooster. He looks old as Methuselah, and is probably twice as tough, so we don't dare try and roast him or he'd be tough as the rubber on one of Mr. Goodyear's tents. So I boil him, and boil him, and boil him until meat falls off the bone. It is damn near ten at night afore he is fit to chew, but chew him we do.

Of course we are unarmed, so at quite a disadvantage when we step out of the barn just after daybreak and are confronted by five riders in a semicircle. All of them have long guns and they are cocked and leveled at our midsections.

"You boys deserters?" one of them growls. He is out front a little and seems the leader. Red hair sticks out from under his wide brimmed hat, which sports a turkey or eagle feather. By the mishmash of uniforms, I presume they favor the south.

"You want that long gun stuffed up yer butt," Ian growls even deeper.

The old boy who is doing the talking smiles, showing a missing tooth. "You take offense at the suggestion? Being as how we're five and you're two, and we are totin' long guns and sidearms, I'd say you got lots of mouth on you, big fella."

"You damn right I do, and I bite like a swamp gator—"

Ian starts to step forward but I lay a rough hand on his shoulder. "You been a long time wanting a slab of beefsteak, and if that ol' boy puts a hole in your gut you won't enjoy it much."

Ian pulls up. I swing my gaze from man to man and realize two of them are wearing well-worn butternut trousers, just as Ian and I do—thus, it's the south they favor.

So I speak up, and lie as I think the truth might get us swinging from the nearest branch. "I'm Captain Braden McTavish, just paroled out of Camp Butler, on our way to find a unit to join up with. You fellas jayhawkers or redleggers or what?"

"Not your business, Captain. You're not gonna get far on shank's mare. In fact them brogans look like they got about another mile in them."

"My last horse was shot out from under me and I was knocked silly at Iuka thanks to a Bluebelly cannon and I woke up with wrists tied having to listen to the crowing of some Yankee no accounts…who crowed even louder than you. However, if you're worried about my having to hoof it, you fellas could spare a couple of those crowbaits you're forking and ride double. In fact, it seems I'm in command here."

He laughs and shakes his head. "Not likely, Captain. You might outrank us, if you are who you say you are, but that don't cut it out here."

"Then why don't you just ride on and let us go about our business."

He studies me for a minute. "Your business damn sure better be finding some rebs to join up with. If not, I'd be obliged to hang you from that hickory over there."

"How about leaving us a firearm. The next bunch of hooligans we come across might not be wearing reb uniforms, such as yours are."

He studies me a moment more. Then he turns to a man on his flank. "Portman, you got those two Army Colts we took off that last bunch we put under?"

"I do," the man says, but he has daggers coming out of his narrow eyes.

"Give 'em up, and the powder and shot. We can spare it."

He's grumbling like a bear with his leg in a trap, but he dismounts and digs into his saddlebags and comes up with the weapons.

The leader dismounts and grabs them, and walks over and hands them to us, barrel first. "My name is Whittle, Sergeant Jeb Whittle, and you owe me, captain."

"Sure as Grant's a butt-ugly son-of-a-bitch, I owe you, Whittle. I'll not forget this."

He mounts back up as both of us stuff the revolvers in our belts. He gives me a hard look. "Find some good ol' boys

26

and get back in the fray. It ain't going too well, if'n you ain't heard."

"We don't know what's true and what's a damn lie in the camp. You fellas stay safe out there in the woods."

Whittle tips his hat, and spins his horse and they move away at a trot, that becomes a cantor as soon as they're out of the farmyard.

I turn to Ian. "Glad you didn't try and stuff that rifle where the sun don't shine."

"Yeah, me too," he says, and gives me a sheepish grin.

And we start picking 'em up and layin' 'em down. I figure we're a half day from Hannibal, which was four thousand strong, at least at the start of the war. And I plan to walk right in, just like I'm welcome.

Chapter Three

Hannibal is the eastern terminal of the Hannibal & St. Joseph Railway, which would take us due west as far as the Kansas line and the Missouri River, if we had the money and if I didn't feel I had to make my way to the home place—but I do. So after we pay a visit to Hannibal, it's set out southwest to the McTavish farm. If there is such a place any longer.

The farms get smaller and the farm houses closer together as we near Hannibal, and the few field hands, both white and darky, give us a hard look, but none wave us over for a chat as we stomp along a two track that serves for a road. And it gets wider and more worn as we near the river, and see Hannibal's several three and four story buildings on the far side.

Crossing is the next problem as we'll not be welcome on the ferry as we don't have the two bits to spare that they charge for a single passenger. Damn highbinders.

However, there's a darky just a few paces below the river landing, and he's loading up a skiff with a burlap sack, which I would think is headed across the river, so I trot on down and give him a smile.

"Where you off to, friend?" I ask.

He gives me a funny look, probably because I've called him friend, checking me from brogan to hat and lingering on the butternut trousers, then asks, "Well, sur, I'm fixin' to row across and take this here sack of turnips to market."

"We'd be obliged—" I start, but he stops me short.

"I'm a freeman, don't ya know."

"Never thought you for anything but," I say, and give him the smile again.

"Cost you a quarter dollar to ride the ferry, don't ya know."

"I'm sure it does. How about a dime for the two of us."

"Nickel for you, dime for the big fella," he says, and I'm wondering if he hasn't done a spell working with a Jewish tinker.

I hesitate, so he shrugs, and says. "A dime for both, but you gotta take a turn at the oars."

"Done," I say, and stick out a hand.

He hesitates, but then shakes with a hand as rough as his burlap bag.

The river is no easy task as it's a half mile wide and flowing fairly strong. In order to make a landing at Hannibal, we have to keep the bow pointed mostly upstream, and row like hell. We trade off three times during the crossing and at that it's more than a half hour before we dig the bow into Missouri mud.

He's a fair man, and offers us each a couple of turnips, which we gnaw gratefully when not tending the oars.

It's been more'n a year since I've felt good Missouri soil under my feet.

With the war going on, Hannibal's streets are full of horsebackers, drays and beer wagons and the like, and far worse—Union troops—and all seem to be heading our way, down to the Mississippi and the barges and side wheelers docked there.

We don't favor the main streets, and slip to the side, working our way among some smaller businesses and homes.

As we leave the main part of town, I notice a woodyard a hundred paces away, and it seems busy with a half dozen fellas stacking cord wood, so I turn back to Ian, "Are you up to trying to put a few dollars in our polk?"

"Did Saint Pat run the snakes outta beautiful Ireland?"

"I take it that's a yes."

"That be a yes, lad."

I find the straw boss, the only fellow standing with his hands on hips, and sidle up next to him. "You looking for a couple of fellows who grew up with ax in hand."

He eyes me up and down a little skeptically, then looks at big Ian a little more favorably, then back to me. "I'll pay you forty cents a cord."

"And you provide the axes and a crosscut."

"Yep, you break a handle and it'll cost you a cord of wood."

"I guess six bits a cord would be out of the question?"

"That's what I get, delivered riverside, so, yes, from here to the moon out of the question. A cord fetches four or five dollars a thousand miles upriver, if you can get there and keep from getting scalped. You'll find the tools over in that shed."

"There a stone there?" I ask.

"They done been sharpened. Take two axes apiece. If you're worth a damn, you'll dull one before lunchtime. Take a handcart and about a quarter mile up that trail," he points into a stand of trees, "you'll find where we're cutting. You'll haul your own loads back here to the yard. I'll be loanin' you a hand cart for the haulin'."

"You'll pay at the end of the day?" I ask.

"Yep. Anything less than a half cord gets held over to the next day."

By lunch time we'd both discovered how soft your hands could get when all you had to do was walk a prison yard, not to speak of how your back and shoulders had forgotten hard work. But by lunch, we had a cord apiece. We delivered our loads then went back out without eating.

Another cord each took us almost to dark. The wood seemed harder and each hour to fill the carts seemed longer, but we delivered, and as promised, the straw boss paid up.

As I count up the nickels and dimes the straw boss dropped in my palm, I asked, "Is there a rooming house on this side of town?"

"There is, Mrs. O'Mally's, a room to share and all the soup and biscuits you can stuff down...don't let her charge you more than two bits apiece. Soup's generally light on the meat, but it'll fill you up. And it's less than a quarter mile back the way you came. Yellow two story with blue shutters."

"Obliged," I say, and give him a wave and turn to head out.

"We got more work tomorrow," he calls after me.

"Appreciate it, but we're on the road."

"If you're heading west, be careful. There's a Union regiment out there somewhere, and I'd bet they'd be happy to see you two coming."

"Thanks, we'll keep our eyes open."

As he heads back, Ian speaks up. "Damn if that wasn't a whole lot like work."

"Damn if it wasn't," I agree, rubbing my sore back as I do.

Mrs. O'Mally looks as if she's cleaned up, for many years, all the leftovers from the eight places at her table. But she has rosy cheeks, an Irish accent, and only a slightly forced smile.

After settling on four bits for the two of us, Ian and I are first at the trough and take chairs across from each other. The table is set with bowls and spoons only, but with jars of honey and plates of fresh sweet butter down the middle. On either end rests a large pitcher of buttermilk.

Six more boarders filter in.

One—probably a drummer or banker—with a celluloid collar that his neck bulges over, stringy hair pointing every direction under his bowler hat, and string tie, takes a ladder back chair. For a moment, as the chair moans, I fear it might be crushed to the floor. I hope there's a generous laundry tub full of soup in the kitchen as this boy looks like he might require one all to himself. It's funny how fat folks look to have pig eyes. I guess fat settles around eye sockets as well. He looks friendly enough, which doesn't go for the next two to wander in.

Two rough looking fellas in stirrup-heeled boots, linsey-woolsey shirts, and well worn canvas trousers hang their wide-brimmed drover hats but don't bother removing their holster belts and sidearms as they take seats, nor do they bother giving the rest of us so much as a nod or a snarl. They have hung their wide brimmed hats on the rack provided, so they are not completely lacking in manners. However, the smaller of the two has a crooked eye which makes it difficult to tell which way he's looking. It's cocked sideways and up a little as if he's lookin' for forgiveness from heaven above. Both of them have scarred and calloused hands, and although the second one is wide chested with a generous girth, enough that his belt buckle is eyeballing the floor, neither of them

32

appear to have an extra ounce of fat. It's funny how some fellas with big bellies can look, and be, powerful.

Another follows them. A tall skinny fella wearing a suit coat looking two sizes too large takes the head of the table and announces, "I'm Howard Tolliver, nice to meet y'all."

Ian, the drummer, and I give him a nod, however the linsey woolsey boys are whispering to each other and don't so much as look up.

The next is a man of the cloth, with a backward collar and a gold chain and cross. He appears to be a man of seven decades, with gray hair and a matching Van Dyke goatee, nicely trimmed. He and the drummer are the only ones at the table who appear to have shaved this week.

I'm just a wee bit surprised when Mrs. O'Mally exits the kitchen and takes the last seat, as I figured she'd be hard at work in the kitchen and serving.

But right behind her comes two fine looking young lasses about my age, one with a large white pitcher, with ladle handle sticking out, balanced on a hip. The other carries a platter of biscuits, still steaming from the oven.

Mrs. O'Mally makes no bones about who's running the show. Her first verbal shot is at the drummer, "Mr. Ragsnovich, please remove your hat at the table. You two gentlemen from out Dakota way, hang your belts and firearms on the hat rack please. This is not a firing range nor a battleground. And no one touch those spoons until preacher Manley has finished grace."

"Thank you, Margaret," the preacher says, as the two linsey woolsey boys get up and hang their firearms as ordered, but they eyeball her as if she were something stuck to their boots. As both Ian and I have our Colts stuffed into our belts and under untucked shirts, we escape her wrath…however uncomfortable the revolvers may be.

The preacher must be frustrated and without a congregation, as his blessing goes on as long as many sermons I've heard. Finally, Mrs. O'Mally snaps, "Manley, get over yourself. The foods going cold."

He severs a lengthy sentence with a quick amen and the girls start ladling out the soup and passing out a pair of biscuits the size of your palm to each setting. As soon as the light biscuits kiss the table beside our bowls we're slathering on the butter and dripping them with honey.

Damn, if it's not ambrosia, and unlike we were warned, there's plenty of chunks of pork to go with the potatoes, turnips, and onions. And after we've all finished the first bowl, one of the girls returns with a fresh pitcher full and ladles all over again.

About the time I'm halfway through my second bowl, the cockeyed Dakota boy speaks up, and his comments are directed at Ian and me.

"You two. You got on military trousers." He turns to his partner. "Looks to be rebs to me."

Ian, a little unusual for him, says nothing and goes on shoveling it in. So I follow his lead and just keep eating. But ol' crooked eye won't leave it alone.

"Is that right, you two a couple of slave beatin' southern scum suckers?"

I settle back in my chair and eye him a few seconds before responding. I give him a smile, then ask, "You got a name to go with that mouth of your'n?"

"I would be Cornel Proust, and this here is my pard, Horst Gauss."

"Well, well, corny and horse. Old horse there is big enough to eat hay and do his business in the road, and you're ugly enough that you look like horsey has taken his hooves to you more'n once't. But since we are enjoying Mrs. O'Mally's fine table, I'll be waiting until after we've had our fill to meet y'all in the back yard to finish this discussion."

Both of them sit stiff as posts with mouths so tight you couldn't drive a nail between their lips, but I return to my soup.

Ian, to my surprise, turns to Mrs. O'Mally, "Ma'am, that was as fine a meal as I've had in more'n a year. May the good Lord continue to smile on you and yours. When it comes your time may you be in heaven an hour before the devil knows you've gone to your reward. I'll be excusing myself, if I may. I am not accustomed to such language and bad manners as these two gents and my traveling mate have displayed."

This elicits a chuckle from both the Dakota boys, and a bit of a surprised glance from me. Ian gives Mrs. O'Mally a shallow bow, says "pardon me, ma'am," then rounds the table and reaches up and jerks one of the belts with pistol filled holster off the hat rack. The two Dakota boys have been following his every movement with stupid smiles on their ugly mugs, but they fade at Ian's reach for their weapons and both jump up as he grabs a gun belt, but he doesn't pull the weapon. Rather he closes the three paces between them and uses the belt and pistol as a bludgeon, knocking the cockeyed one silly with the first blow and dropping him to his knees.

The other one grabs a spoon up as if it's a knife, and that makes Ian laugh. He feints with the belt and drives a straight jab into the nose of the larger of the two and he reels backward. Ian drops the belt and goes after him, knocking him senseless with a right and then through the kitchen door with a hard left.

He's on the kitchen floor, with one of the young serving girls standing over him with a pitcher half full of hot soup. He starts to rise and she dumps the soup on his face. He bawls like a branded calf and rolls to his belly and crawls on all fours for the back door, probably hunting a horse trough in which to cool off.

But dropping the belt was Ian's mistake, as ol' cockeye is on the floor and dragging the pistol from the holster.

I firmly believe that Ian could knock out a mule with that terrible right hand of his, but he can't get his hammer-hard right to cockeye fast enough, but he can kick and as the boy on the ground is bringing up the pistol, kicks him under the chin hard enough to lift him a foot off the floor.

Ol' cockeye goes down as if he's been head-kicked by a mule.

Ian brushes off his hands and again turns to Mrs. O'Mally. "Ma'am, I'm sorry that had to happen at your fine table. I'm happy nothing seems to have been broken—"

She interrupts him, "Except a couple of hardheads, boyo. And it seems to me they were in need of the breaking."

The preacher is stammering. "I…I…should I…should I go get the town marshal?"

"I believe not," Mrs. O'Mally says. "I believe Mister...Mister...what was your name, boyo?"

"Hollihan, ma'am. Ian Hollihan."

"Of the Cork County Hollihans?" she asks.

"Some of my folk found their way to Kerry County, but yes, way back, from Cork."

She turns to the preacher. "Reverend Manley, we'll hear no more of this town marshal hogwash. This was just a friendly disagreement. If these ill mannered fellas want to cause trouble after they awaken, I'll request Mr. Hollihan's assistance again. He was defending my table and the good nature of my dining room, and that's that. Agreed gentlemen?" The preacher eyes each of us in turn as we give Mrs. O'Mally a smile, nod, and a "yes, ma'am." I have trouble getting the smile off my face.

Then she turns back to Ian. "I'd appreciate it if you and Mr. McTavish would retire before these two louts get their senses. I'll be puttin' them in a downstairs room so as you won't cross paths until breakfast. If they cause a fuss, I'll be puttin' them out in the street and I have just the coach gun to help with the task. Now, good night to you."

"And to you, ma'am." I say, and Ian follows me out and up to our assigned room.

As it happens, Ian and I share a bed with two other fellows, the preacher and the drummer, who look askance at Ian as he takes up a third of the bed by himself. I try it for awhile, then say to hell with it and move to the floor, which is fine as I've been sleeping on the hard ground for days. Fine, except the chamber pot just under the edge of the bed seemingly hasn't been emptied since a use or two and the smell would gag a maggot. I finally get up and find myself downstairs in the sitting room where I roll up in a hoop rug and sleep the sleep of the dead until daybreak.

It's my plan to awaken long before the two Dakota boys might wander in and find me rolled up and ready to be kicked into a tube of mush.

Chapter Four

And I do awaken before the sun.

I presume the privy is out back and as I need the use of it wander that way. To my surprise, Mr. Cornel Proust and Mr. Horst Gauss are nearby, saddling a couple of good looking tall horses. They are rigged up like drovers, both saddles with hemp lariats tied thereon, both with tall leather wrapped horns for dallying. I hesitate, then say to hell with it and pass within ten feet of them.

The bigger of the two stops sucking up the latigo and gives me a hard stare. Then snaps, "You got our names, buttercup, but we didn't get yours?"

I stop, making sure my shirt is propped up over the firearm stuffed into my belt and it's plainly seen. "McTavish, Brad McTavish."

Both of them have sidearms and long arms in saddle scabbards, but seen to have no desire to reach for either.

He looks me up and down, then snarls, "I believe I'll be remembering you, McTavish. You heading west, running from the war."

"My business, Horse Gas."

"It's Horst. Horst Gauss, and you should remember it." He's talking to me, but glancing up at the big yellow house.

"Have a good trip, Horse Gas," I say, with a curl of the lip, then I glance up at a second story window and see why the two of them haven't tried to gut shoot me. Ian is leaning out the window between blue shutters, his sidearm in hand.

Horst turns to me and as he mounts up, says, "You're the one should be worrying about the good or the bad of his travels. Keep your eye out, pilgrim."

I shrug, and walk on, but I don't enter the privy. More than one fella has been shot through a privy door while his pants was on the floor and he was concerned with his business. Instead I walk on to a corral full of stock and admire a fifteen hand gray mule until the two of them ride out and I'm sure they're gone.

I give Ian a wave and get a smart salute in return.

It's a beautiful mule.

One of the main reasons I want to make a pass by the home place, in addition to checking on my ma, is the slight chance there'll be a head or two of our stock somewhere nearby.

In a pasture a half a mile from the house, with belly deep grass and a small branch of the slough for water, pa kept six fine percheron mares, draft stock, for breeding by a Jack he'd brought up from Mexico. Jack, as we'd not so originally named him, was almost thirteen hands, hung like the donkey he was, and could cover the mares. And the mares would throw the strongest mules, normally fifteen or more hands and over a thousand pounds, some of the gelded Johns as heavy as fourteen hundred pounds. The best mule stock in all of Missouri.

We had to stall the mares in a special narrow breeding stall when in season and ready, and had to muzzle ol' Jack as he would teeth-rip the necks and shoulders of the mares while he was planting the seeds of a fine mule. Ma embarrassed me when she took me aside and explained that was no way to treat a female and I told her I had no intention of putting my teeth to a lady...then added...to my wife, should that time ever come.

Pa was known up and down the river for his mules, trained mostly by Raymond and me, right there on the farm.

We'd only had our own work and brood stock near the house when the trouble came, all the other market stock having been recently sold at an auction in St. Louis. Four mules, six Percheron mares, Jack, plus four geldings we kept for riding and pulling ma's buggy. We also kept a few hogs, a dozen or more sheep, chickens, and our darkies were allowed to keep a dozen goats.

And all of them would be prime pickings for either the bluecoats or the butternut boys, should they happen on them. Particularly the draft horses and mules.

But the fact is, I don't expect to see a sign of life at McTavish Farm.

By the time I've finished my privy business and head back for the kitchen door, the sun has turned the eastern sky crimson and a coal oil lamp has been fired up in the kitchen. I enter and see Mrs. O'Mally stoking the fire in the Buck Range.

"Might I fetch a load of kindling for you, ma'am?" I ask.

"Obliged. Bin is just left of the steps."

I bring in an armload and replace what she's taken from a basket next to the range.

"Coffee's a boiling. Give it a couple," she says as she pours flour in a bowl, then adds a handful of lard.

I watch her work until she looks up. "Pour us both a cup, boyo. My hands are a little slippery."

And I do, then ask, "Those two fellas with the loose lips. They from hereabout?"

"Spoon in a teaspoon of sugar, if you please. ...Them boys come all the way down from Dakota Territory, bringing a load of cattle aboard the Lizzy Ann. They got a pocket full of twenty dollar gold pieces from the sale of them and are horsebacking all the way back, or so they say. They won't be anymore trouble." Then she looks up from kneading her biscuits and gives me a grin. "In fact after the Irish education your friend Ian gave them, I imagine they'll be eager to get on their way."

"I imagine," I say, and return the smile.

One of the young helpers sticks her head in the door. "Have you fetched the eggs yet, ma'am?"

"No, Gretchen, please do, and throw some mash to the birds before you come in."

"Yes'um," she says, passes through the kitchen, and is shortly followed by Ian.

"Could I trouble you for a dollop of that coffee, Missus?" Ian asks, and gives me a nod.

"And good morning to you," Mrs. O'Mally gives him a smile as if he's a returning prodigal son. "Help yourself. Biscuits, syrup, fried eggs and sidepork on the table in twenty minutes, boyo."

"Could we work up an appetite by chopping some wood?" I ask, and get a smile to equal the one that Ian received.

In an hour Mrs. O'Mally has a half cord of wood chopped and split, we have bulging bellies from feather weight biscuits, and we're putting shanks mare to good use on our way northeast to McTavish Farm.

We are well fueled by a fine breakfast and make good time. The riverside road is worn and smooth until we turn west on a rough two track, however I'd much rather be aboard one of the stern wheelers or side wheelers that pass us, moving up the Mississippi much faster than we can walk. Should we ride one downstream we'd come to St. Louis, where the Big Mo meets the Mississippi, and we could catch another ride up her to McTavish Farm, had we the coin.

After only a dozen miles and a little more than a half day, we come upon a shanty town near the water, where some darkies are drying fish, carp and catfish, on racks over smoking fires. The odors waft our way and my mouth waters. In times past I would stride over and invite myself to lunch, but it's a new day.

As we pass, I'm surprised when someone shouts my name. "Masser McTavish."

I turn and see a man approaching, his dusky complexion, with crevices deep enough to be shadowed and a shock of white hair, makes me gasp. Then I see as he nears one eye's gone white and know it's Emanuel, father to Raymond and Pearl.

I can't help myself, but step forward and embrace him, then hold him at arm's length. He seems more frail, smaller, and more bent than I remember.

"You look fine, old man. Just fine. Is Raymond hereabouts...or Pearl," I ask, then my mouth goes a bit dry and my jaws knot as I remember my father hanging and doing a slow roast near the burning house.

"Ain't seen them since the trouble at the farm," he says, but I get the distinct impression he's not telling all he knows. "I did hear Raymond took to flight and headed west."

"And my ma? What of my ma?"

"I don' know, Masser Brad."

"I guess it ain't masser no more, old man. It's just you and I and a new time, unless the south proves the victor. Then we'll take it up again, should the law say it's right."

I can see a flair of fire in his eyes, and he says, through clinched teeth. "Ain't never been right, masser, just been the way it be."

I chew on that for a minute, knowing he could be right. "That ain't truly what this war is all about, but that's a discussion for another time. We got to move on, old man. You give Raymond my regards and tell him...should you ever see him again...now that pa's gone, he'll always have a place to put his feet by my fire."

"Ain't no hurry up to leave," he says. "We got a whole tub fulla mud bugs and we gonna boil 'em up. You welcome to pitch in, should you care to."

I turn to Ian who's been standing back watching this exchange. "You want to suck some tails, pardner."

He laughs. "What the hell are you two talking on...mud bugs, suckin' tail?"

"Crawdads. Crayfish. My old...old uncle here, Emanuel, has invited us to lunch."

"Suits me if it suits you," he says, and we climb a small bank away from the riverside road to the loosely constructed ramshackle village of log and bark houses, and planks and other trash picked up on the river bank. Half of Emanuel's door is a Black Widow whisky sign, turned on edge.

Emanuel tells me of his wife's passing; his wife, Annamae, who many times was like a mother to me. She patched up my skinned knees and even chastised me when I did wrong, even more than my own ma. And I could not help but feel my eyes go wet when I hear of her drowning while hiding from a troop of southern boys. Damn, if this war ain't confusing.

As we sit and are each served a large bowl of boiled crayfish and are given a cup of peach wine almost strong enough to be brandy—a specialty of old Emanuel's, as I remember—memories of times past flood my mind. I've sat to many a meal with Emanuel and his wife Annamae, and his children Pearl and Ray, but this time I realize it's different. I'm a guest in his house...he's not a servant, a slave, in mine. He seems to take no notice of the difference, but it continues to niggle at me. Here my family has owned him and his family since long before I could toddle. He was like an old uncle to me, yet he was also chattel, to be bought and sold should it have to be done. He was...he is...like family to me, yet he is not, and he knew the both of it and I guess so did I.

Things are the same, yet things are so different.

We finish and I rise from the table, made of driftwood planks picked up on the riverbank, and I offer my hand. He takes it, covers my hand with the other one, and gives me a sad smile. "You stay well, young Braden. You always think on the fact yer daddy was a fair man, and your mama nursed us like we was her own chillin...no matter what comes of this here trouble."

"Yes, sir," I say, "and you stay well, old uncle. That was a fine meal and we thank you."

He rises from his bench and crosses the room to a makeshift pie safe with wet burlap covering its contents. Reaching inside he takes out a half loaf of hard bread and a generous handful of jerky then wraps them in a rag and returns, handing them to me.

"That'll get y'all a ways," he says.

"Obliged. I owe you."

It's probably the last time I'll see him, and it's likely I'll never see Pearl or Raymond again, and maybe that's for the best.

It's another three and a half days, or more, walk to Arrow Rock then on a couple of miles on to McTavish Farm, so we set out again.

After an hour, Ian sidles up to me. "You ain't said nary a word since those folks shared lunch with us."

"Just thinking on this war, on the right and wrong of it, on the fact I technically own that man just fed us and a few more in that camp, and the right and wrong of that."

"Well, sir, that Army thing…it's all just a pay day to me, a horse to ride, and the company of some fine lads. But you was raised up here amongst all this and I can understand the wonder of it."

He paces me, quiet for a while, then shrugs as he offers, "You know you do what you know to do and you know to do what your ma and da say to do, if you are an obedient son and you damn well owe that to them what brought you into this world and fed you and put clothes on you and taught you to read, write, and cipher and love the Lord. And if all that ain't right, I guess it ain't your fault." Then he nods his head and says with some finality. "You do what you know and what you done been taught."

I nod, but ask, "So, does that make it right?"

This time he doesn't hesitate. "Makes it right in my head…you do what your ma and da said to do, and what the law dictates. The good book says honor your mother and father…your ma and da. That's good enough for me."

I think on the right and wrong of it for awhile longer as we stride west, then decide I'd best keep my mind on the task at hand, on the trail, and on any who might want to bushwhack a couple of old boys in butternut.

There is a good chance I'll be leaving all this behind me, Missouri, the war, the nigras, and all that went with it. And to be truthful, I hope to never look back.

We pass an uneventful afternoon and find a deep dark thicket to hole up, don't bother with a fire as we're down to a few Lucifer's, don't have an ember box, and the night is warm enough. The bread and venison jerky is plenty and we even manage to save a little to get us started in the morning.

And morning finds us wet, not a real rain, but a cold fall drizzle that portends of the winter to come. The leaves are going golden and it won't be long before the forest offers little real cover. We've managed to keep our powder, but not ourselves. If this keeps up we'll have to find a way to get ourselves some winter clothes, even if we have to steal them. I've never filched so much as a piece of hard candy or even a cookie from my ma's kitchen, and don't like thinking on it.

But the hell of it is, an empty gut that's flappin' again your backbone has no conscience.

Late in the day my stomach is keeping my mind occupied, when I flinch at the sound of gunfire, then realize there are no balls whizzing around me...but it's close. Too damn close.

"Whatcha think?" Ian says from right next to my shoulder.

"Other side of these dogwoods...over a dozen or more on each side by the sound of it."

The dogwoods are on our left, south, and there is a creek bed across a meadow on the right. Moving quickly, we jump a snaking split-rail fence that zig zags, separating road and meadow grass pasture. The sound of gunfire seems to be growing closer, so we pick 'em up and lay 'em down, at a dead run for the willow lined creek.

I bust brush, charge on through and find myself knee-deep in the crick, then crash through the willows on the far side, Ian close on my heels.

And come face to face with two bluebelly boys tending a picket line of a dozen or more mounts.

46

L. J. Martin

West of the War

Chapter Five

Both Union boys scramble for a pair of long guns leaning on a tree stump.

"Don't do it, boys," I yell. "We're just a'passin' through." But to no avail as the first one reaches the rifles and I can see he is intent on doing us harm.

No choice. I pull the Colt and put one in his brisket. The other hasn't quite reached the stump and seeing his fellow blown to his back, coughing and rolling in pain, blood blossoming on his shirt front, spins and throws up his arms.

"I got me four children waitin' back home," he shouts, his eyes so wide I can see the whites around his pupils.

"If you saddle two of those crowbaits, quick as a snake, you can likely go home to them whelps someday," I shout.

He spins on his heels and runs for a stack of McClellan's and in no time has the stock bridled and is pulling latigo on the second one.

"Where's your boys?" I ask.

"Over thataway. They done snuck up on a rebel camp and are having at it."

"Now, run like hell, just the way we came." I point, and he takes no convincing, disappearing into the willows and through the creek.

We grab up the two rifles, shove them in the saddle boots, mount, and whip the critters away the opposite direction from the way he's said the skirmish is underway.

We don't pull rein for at least two miles until the sorrel I am riding and the chestnut Ian straddles are lathered and blowing hard.

We have now cut a day off'n our trip to McTavish Farm, and if we can find a river boat captain who'll ignore the U.S. brands on the rumps of our newly acquired stock, what we get for them will go aways toward our passage up the Big Muddy.

We put another twenty miles between us and what must be some angry Union boys, before we pull up on the banks of the Missouri, maybe ten miles upstream from McTavish Farm. We stake the horses out—happy to note that each has a picket pin and rope on the saddle, as well as a canteen, cap and ball box, and rifle boot. To add to our comfort, each saddle is backed by a rolled blanket and an oil cloth to shed water. We are living in luxury.

Another damn rainy day. We're camped by a two acre pond and it's being dimpled by rain. The sky lays flat and pewter gray. It's even darker to the west, the direction that should take us to McTavish Farm by noon, and the occasional crack of lightening is beyond. By the count of seconds I'd say it's over ten miles to the heart of the storm, so with any luck we'll miss it.

We are flat out of grub and carry few coins but, God willing, we'll come upon someone to whom a thin dime is more valuable than some jerky or root vegetables.

The two geldings have grazed well and watered to their hearts content, and don't in the least seem to mind carrying butternut boys rather than bluebellys.

I've been pushing harder than usual as today will be the day I find out what's happening at McTavish Farm…and to be truthful, I have a hollow in my gut beyond that of mere hunger.

We pass a field of corn that's been picked but the stalks still stand. So I turn in the saddle to see Ian dozing.

"Hey, slacker, how about we take a gander in that field and see if'n we can find some leavings?"

He raises his head. "What say?"

"Let's check the corn field for whatever?"

He follows as I rein off the two track and tie my sorrel to the split rail, and wander among the stalks. As I suspected, there's a few withered ears, most with only a few kernels and some badly bug eaten…but we're happy to share. With a half hours work we've gnawed enough to carry us through the morning.

In another two miles of plodding, we come to the biggest impediment to our immediate goal of the farm, and that's the Big Mo. She's about a quarter mile across and running strong enough, even in this harvest time, to threaten life and limb to them hoping to swim. And Ian has already claimed that a quarter foot in deep water, much less a quarter mile, is too much for his feeble skills.

"There once was a ferry near Arrow Rock, five miles or so upriver if'n we're where I think we are."

"How much coin you got left?" he asks.

"I got two bits, and you?"

"Quarter and a dime. You think that'll do?"

"It used to be half a dollar for a man and horse, or six bits for a wagon plus a dime each for driver and each passenger...but we gotta cross so we gotta make some kind of a deal...if'n it's still there."

In a little over an hour we see the ferry in the distance. It's a small one, just wide and long enough to handle a farm wagon and four up, and as the side wheelers run up and down the river, is free of any lines. There's a man on the tiller and two strong negras on oars on each side. If it operates as it used to, there are two stations on the far or west side. They cross to the downriver station, then a pair of mules on the far side drags the ferry upriver to the second on that side, and they row back.

It's over an hour wait for us as the flatboat is heading across when we arrive. I'm surprised to see there are no mules and it's the man on the tiller and two negras who tow the boat at least a quarter mile against the stream before they can launch for the return trip.

As they're tying up, I approach the barrel chested white fella on the tiller, who seems the boss of the affair.

"What's the toll, friend?" I ask.

He gives me a glare from under thick eyebrows, then snarls, "If you fellas are deserters, there ain't enough coin in Missouri to use this ferry."

I give him a tight smile. "Then since we ain't, what's the toll?"

"Still a half dollar for man and horse. So a dollar will do." He furrows his brow, then inquires, "Don't I know you."

"McTavish, my daddy was Rut McTavish from up the river a couple of miles, but on the far side."

"Well, sir, welcome home. Glad to see you ain't shot to hell."

"A dollar is a fair toll, sir—."

"Max Halfcox," he says, and extends his hand. "I knew your pa well and am sorry for your trouble."

I shake with him. "As I said, a dollar is a fair toll, but we've only got sixty cents between us. We've been keeping the bluebellys company over at Camp Butler in Springfield. They don't send you out with much."

Again he eyes me up and down. "Them are U.S. brands and McClellan saddles?"

"And you see we're wearing butternut trousers, what's left of 'em. We got paroled from Camp Butler and we paroled these critters from a Union troop on our way here."

He smiles at that. "I'll tell you what, as the damn Yanks appropriated my mules, if you and the big fella and your two crowbaits will help my nigras with the rowing and the towing upstream, I'll haul you over for two bits each."

"I'm obliged, Mr. Halfcox. We'll do more'n our share."

We're another three quarters of an hour before we wave goodbye to Halfcox and his flatboat, and mount up. I half want to visit the trading post, but it's over a half mile below the lower ferry dock and I'm eager to see the farm.

The trail swings inland a little and we come to a rise where I'm looking down on McTavish Farm, and I'm a bit taken aback to see what appears to be over a hundred acres of cotton, just picked, and the same amount of corn stalks still standing. Someone has been working the place.

We plod on down to the cluster of burned out buildings, flanking a half dozen slave cabins.

A hundred yards before we get to the home place, I rein up.

Two well carved wooden grave markers are nicely placed at the head of two grave mounds, and they've been cared for. I dismount and read,

Rutherford Jefferson

> McTavish
> 1816 – 1861
> Loved Father and Husband
> And the second,
> Annamae McTavish
> 1818 – 1862
> Beloved Mother and Wife

If I had a hat on, I'd snatch it off. But I slowly dismount and kneel between the graves of my mother and father. The name Alfred P. Doolan is burned in my brain, and his mottled face, red hair, and gray streaked beard has come to me in nightmares and I can now see it as plain as day as I close my eyes to pray for my too-soon departed parents.

He, and Pearl, are the reason my parents are under the sod. I wonder who the kind soul was who put them there, who has tended the graves since, as the mounds are weedless and some flowers, now dry, lean against the wooden markers.

Ian has reined away, kindly giving me space, and I appreciate it as tears streak my cheeks.

Then I hear him say quietly. "There's folks down among those trees…pecans it looks to be."

I look up, but my gaze doesn't go to the orchard, but rather to one of the six slave quarters still standing, and the woman who stands in a doorway of the nearest one. Even at a hundred generous paces, I recognize Pearl, and catch my breath, audibly gasping.

Chapter Six

I rise from kneeling at my parents grave, catch the saddle horn and a stirrup, and swing up into the saddle, never taking my eyes off her. Gigging the sorrel into a quick walk, I move directly at her.

She's shading her eyes with a hand, then from only forty paces, I can see the recognition flood her face. She doesn't come running, which would have surprised me, but rather drops back into the darkness of the cabin.

I dismount and move to the open door.

"What be your intention?" rings out from inside. Pearl's voice, slightly lower than I remember.

"What was the cause of my mother's death?" I ask as my eyes grow accustomed to the darkness.

"She got the cough, the winter after the trouble. Her lungs filled up and she went. I done sent for a doctor, but he was off to the war somewheres."

"Who buried them?"

"Who you think. I was de only one hereabouts."

"Who carved the markers?"

"Who you think. I done tol' you I was de only one hereabouts."

"I should whip you raw—"

"I wouldn't be trying it, Masser Brad." She steps forward and I can see she's holding pa's old shotgun, both barrels cocked.

I'm struck dumb, and stand silent for a long moment. Even in a simple gray sackcloth frock, Pearl is even more beautiful than I remember. The light is filtering in through a burlap window covering and gives her coffee colored face a warm wash.

Finally, I get my wits about me. "I hate you for getting my pa hung, but I'm obliged to you for burying them proper."

"I cared for your mama for over a year. She done lost her mind with the trouble. I see'd her run off into the woods, while them Union sons-a-bitches were cleaning out the place and hanging your daddy. But I fetched her back here after they done left. I made her bed in my little house here. I had to feed her and walk her to the privy and listen to her wail and moan for more'n a year."

"Your fault, Pearly," I say.

"Maybe so, but all I done was say the truth of it. And I let my own folks go off without me so I could care for Mama McTavish."

That, too, shuts me up for a moment.

Finally, I turn and look out at the pecans, where two men, who are too far away to recognize, are standing eying us. Two horses are staked, grazing, at the edge of the trees. A fine looking gray and a swayback paint.

"Who's that in the pecans?"

"That there's a rotten bastard and his helper, that be who."

I smile as I've never heard Pearl swear. "What rotten bastard?"

"Cyrus som'bitch Oglesby, from the trading post."

"What the hell is that abolitionist doing in our pecans?"

"That's his corn crop and them bales over yonder is his cotton. He done growed it all on McTavish Farm."

I can feel the heat creep up my backbone. No one at McTavish Farm ever had any respect for Oglesby. He was known to beat his daughters—Hortence and Harriet—and one of them in her majority. And one thing my daddy taught me a man can't abide is a man who'd take his hand to a woman...then I flush at the thought, remembering I'd sworn to horsewhip Pearl should I ever see her again, and here she is, standing in front of me, in the flesh. And there's no question she's all woman, if a negra. Confusing.

So I put the memory away to think on at a later time, and turn back to her. "So you think he's a som'bitch?"

"He done be worse. He let me and your ma live here, but he took liberties wit me, and he hurt me bad. If he hadn't had the law out here with him when he first come, I would'a give him both barrels...but I'd hang for sure. I believe he's in cahoots with that fat sheriff, Scroggins."

Again, I had to think on that. Her words were spat at me, and I felt like I had to backhand my face clean, like I'd walked through cobwebs. So again, I changed the subject.

"Any of the McTavish stock still about?"

"Oglesby done got them all. Four good mules, the mares, and ol' Jack. But I knows where he has them grazin'."

This time the heat runs all the way to the back of my neck.

Ian walks over and tips his hat to Pearl, then turns to me. "I seen that look on you a'fore. What are you thinkin'?"

"I'm thinking of having a talk with an old neighbor who it seems has over-reached a mite."

I move to the sorrel and mount up. Ian starts to do the same but I stop him. "Stay here with Pearl, if you would. I won't be long."

"That look about you says trouble, Brad."

"Maybe, but it's my trouble. I don't want it to get smeared on you."

"I'll ride along."

"No, sir. You'll stay here and watch over Pearly."

He shrugs. "They's two of them."

"I'll be back," I say, and rein away toward the pecans, where the two of them are standing, watching. As I near I can see a shotgun leaning on a near pecan tree trunk, and a half dozen stuffed burlap bags scattered about which I presume are full of nuts.

Oglesby is the taller of the two, but his man is thick through the chest and is holding a long pole, but he appears otherwise unarmed. Oglesby moves over and picks up the shotgun as I near.

Oglesby spits a long stream of chaw as I get close, holding the shotgun casually. "Well, I'll be damned, if it ain't Braden McTavish. I figured the Union boys would'a skinned you and tacked your hide to the wall by now."

I tip my hat and give him a phony smile as I rein up. "Come to pay my respects," I say, and dismount with the horse between him and me. Out of their sight behind the sorrel I slip the Colt from my belt and move just far enough in front of the horse that I can see him over the animal's neck, and can bring the revolver to bear on him under. I'd hate the sorrel to take a load of buckshot, but better him than me.

"That," he says, staring at the revolver's muzzle, "ain't very respectful."

"I don't mind you working the land while I been gone, Cyrus, but I'm back. Thank you for harvesting my crop of pecans…but we'll take over from here on. By the way, where's my stock."

"Out in the same old pasture, McTavish, but they ain't your stock and these ain't your nuts."

"How's that?" I ask, and my jaw knots.

"Nobody paid the taxes and when I did it all became mine. So you can ride on, off'n my land…off'n Oglesby Farm."

I have to use all my self control not to gut shoot him with that remark.

But I merely smile. "What's your man's name?" I ask, my voice as friendly as I can make it, under the circumstance.

"I'm T. C. Humbree, not that it's your business," he says, then he, too, spits a mouthful of chaw to the ground, then backhands the remnants from his mustache.

"Well, T. C. Humbree, I'd suggest you hightail it down the road, off of McTavish Farm."

Oglesby has held the shotgun, mostly pointing at the ground, but is slowly edging it up.

"Keep them barrels pointed down, Cyrus, or I'll have to let the breeze blow through you."

He eyes me carefully and drops the muzzles down.

T. C. doesn't move, so I suggest again. "Humbree, you deaf, or what. I said move on down the road."

He spits again, and looks at Oglesby who says, "Go on, T.C. I'll handle this."

The man heads for the horses, but I correct him. "Humbree, you're gonna march out of here. Leave the horse where he is."

"Do it," Oglesby snaps, and T.C. trudges off.

Just as he does, the sorrel blows, nickers, then dips his head down to graze, throwing off my aim.

Cyrus dives to get behind a pecan trunk, raising the shotgun as he does.

I'm on one knee, still below the horse's neck, and fire. The slug takes him on the side and spins him around as a barrel discharges into the branches above. He goes to his back but still has the shotgun in hand.

The sorrel does not take kindly to the gunfire and spins and gallops away as Cyrus is trying to sit up enough to get a bead on me.

My second shot takes him about second button down on his linsey woolsey shirt and blows him flat to his back. By the time I get to him to kick the scattergun away, his eyes have rolled up and blood gurgles from his mouth.

"You bastard," T. C. shouts and I turn my attention to him.

"I thought you was leaving dust behind on your way out of here. Give Hortence and Harriet my regards...and tell them no thanks necessary."

His eyes grow round as I bring the Colt to bear on him.

"Run, or join Cyrus on the way to hell," I shout, and he turns on his heel and moves faster than a big man should be able.

I look over my shoulder to see Ian galloping after the sorrel, who will be easily caught as he's slowed to a trot.

Moving over the gray and the paint, I pull the paint's picket, untie the lead rope, then give him a slap and he trots away. The gray is another matter as he's a fine looking animal. Two saddles, bridles, and blankets are nearby and I pick the better of them and saddle up and pull his picket and mount up. By the time I'm back at Pearl's cabin, Ian is trotting up.

Pearl stands, the muzzles of her shotgun down at the ground.

She shakes her head. "You done it now. I can't stay hereabout as that sheriff will hang me sure."

"Bring me that lantern from inside," I say, and she turns and disappears.

"He weren't wearing no uniform," Ian says. "Some might consider that murder, even if it were clearly self-defense. We'd best be getting on up river."

"We got a couple of chores. That old boy who ran on outta here has a long ride to get to the sheriff, and a long walk back to the trading post before he can saddle up. We got some time. I got some things to do."

Ian shakes his head, undecided. "You get my neck stretched and that will sure as hell put an end to our friendship, friend."

I smile. "I imagine it would."

Pearl returns and I see she's without the shotgun. She hands me the lantern.

I dismount and hand her the reins to the gray. "Where's the mules and mares?"

"Out it the back pasture, where you done kept 'em."

"Take Ian there and drive them back. Ian and I got to hotfoot it out of here."

"You ain't leaving me here," she says, and her mouth goes tight.

"I ain't taking you upriver, Pearly. You go your own way and we'll go ours."

"You ain't leavin' me here, Braden McTavish. They'll hang me sure for you shootin' Silas Oglesby down like the cur dog he is."

"Was," I say, and can't help but smile. "You can go with us until we catch a side wheeler, then you're on your own. Now take Ian to get the stock."

She nods, and mounts the horse, having to hoist the frock up well above her knees to straddle the animal. I can see that Ian is a little taken aback, as am I, by the sight of her shapely and perfectly proportioned limbs.

"Go," I say. "We ain't got all that much time."

She whips up the gray as a man would, and Ian, looking a little perplexed, does the same and cantors off four lengths behind.

I move quickly to the ruins of the house, pick my way through the fallen timbers and blackened boards and furniture to the stone fireplace. I'm pleased to see cobwebs cover the cobbles on the side in which I'm interested. At least in the near past, no one has found what I seek. Now, if it's just still there. I find the odd square stone I seek and find it stuck tight. That, too, could be good news. I pick up a loose stone that was dislodged by the heat, and strike the square one until I can see it loosen, then cast the hammer stone aside and slip the square one from its place.

It's still in the leather pouch my daddy had put there, twenty-eight liberty double eagles, five hundred sixty dollars face value, and likely worth more than face as gold is dear, now that no one knows if paper money is worth the paper it's printed upon.

I move back to the sorrel and pack my newfound wealth in a saddle bag. Drop to a knee and thank the good Lord and my father for my good fortune, ask him to bless and keep my ma and pa, and move over to where I've set the lantern aside.

Loosening the cap on the reservoir I sprinkle coal oil over the nearest bales of cotton and then break the lantern chimney and light up. The cotton is bound tight so doesn't flare immediately, but when I'm sure it's caught I mount up and head out toward the back pasture. I hate to see good cotton destroyed, but not so much as I'd hate to see it help finance the Union.

I'm not much more than a mile—halfway to the back pasture— before I come upon Ian and Pearl, driving the horses and mules back.

"Let's turn them upstream," I shout.

"I gots to get some things," Pearl yells at me.

"Fine, you go get what you got to get. We'll be leaving lots of track and be easy to follow."

She gives me a look like she wishes she had her shotgun, but gives heels to the gray and moves on around me.

Now, if we can just get far enough ahead that she can't catch us, we'll be on our way to get shed of some of these fine horses and mules, and shed of Pearl.

It's just a hair over forty miles from McTavish Farm to Brunswick, and it's my intention to push the critters straight through. It means we'll stray from the riverside for most the way, and take some real back trails, but it also means we put some distance between us and the body of Cyrus Oglesby…and be too far, too fast, for Pearl to catch up with us.

It was my intent to leave the jack behind, but as we're driving loose stock he's not to be denied and follows, bellowing his dislike for being away from his familiar pasture. And if you've ever heard a big jack bray you understand why I have the urge to drop back and put an ounce of lead between his eyes. But I don't, he's sired some fine mules including the four among our bunch.

At midnight, after I figure we're about halfway to Brunswick, Ian reins over. "I got to have some coffee and we need to blow and water these animals. Next water, okay?"

"Suits me," I say and in less than another half mile we dismount at a little meandering stream lined with good grass.

In minutes Ian has a pot brewing and as we hunker down on our haunches to await its boil, he asks. "So, what's this Brunswick all about?"

"It's got a ferry, as it's across the Mo, and it's got over five hundred river vessels a day tying up there."

"And?"

"And I plan to trade a couple of horses or mules for the fare to get us upriver toward the territories."

He nods. "It's my pleasure to part company at Omaha as I hear they'll soon be hiring for the Transcontinental."

"Good, then I'll only have to worry about your fare that far."

"I'll be a'leavin' first chance."

"Hell no. You hang around 'til I can feed you to the buffalo. I need someone to do the light work," I laugh and he snorts.

"Then it's Benton City, Dakota for you?"

"Fort Benton, Benton City, whatever they call it. That's as far as the boats go."

I can't begin to tell you how shocked I am when a female voice from out of the darkness asks, "Y'all sharing that coffee."

And even more shocked when Pearl walks up, still carrying my old man's shotgun, and hunkers down beside me.

"You can see in the dark?" I ask.

"Like you said, you leave a wide track. A'sides, there's plenty of moonlight." She yawns, then asks. "Did y'all plan to camp here awhile?"

I must be daft, thinking how beautiful this woman is who's carrying a shotgun that could blow me in half if she took a mind to, but it's the last thing I'd tell her...beautiful. Instead, I say, "We're pulling up for Brunswick soon as we finish this pot."

"Thas fine by me," she says, then adds, "I don't fancy no old rough hemp rope stretchin' my neck."

I knew she was tough for a woman, but I had no idea how tough. In fact, it's obvious she's tough as she is pretty. I guess she'll be with us at least as far as a paddle wheeler. Word is there is more than one boat fixin' to make a run at the river all the way to Fort Benton, and it's damn sure easier than saddle sores or a mud wagon.

Dawn finds us only three or four miles from Brunswick, or so I figure. So I rein up again, by a trickle of water and some fine grass for the stock, and we make another fire.

Pearl moves away as I'm heating the coffee pot and returns leading the gray. She has a bedroll packed with some personals and a satchel tied behind the saddle along with a rolled up horse pack that will fit one of our mules, a boot that fits alongside that accommodates the shotgun, and a couple of jugs hanging from the horn tied on with thongs.

She drops the saddle and gear from the gray, not asking for a bit of help, then removes the satchel and comes to where my fire is taking the cold from the morning. The first thing she removes is a pair of trousers and hands them to me.

"These was your daddy's. Might be best you get shed of them what makes you look to be a rebel."

And she's right. I slip behind a bush and change, then stow my butternut with the yellow stripe away.

She removes a slab of bacon, a small skillet, a skinning knife, and a chunk of hard bread from the satchel, cuts six generous slices, and goes to frying. Soon, we're munching bacon and sopping hard bread in the hot grease. It's all a fine compliment to my meager attempt at a breakfast of the mud I call coffee.

Wanting to leave her behind may just have been a foolish mistake.

She cleans and repacks our implements while Ian and I lay back.

"What's the plan?" Ian asks, his hands behind his neck as he leans on a log. I'm flat in the grass, admiring the morning sun, thinking how fine it would be to close my eyes for a few minutes.

"I figure we'll find a spot to leave you, Pearl, and the stock across the river from Brunswick. I'll take the ferry over and see what the attitude of the place is, and if'n there's a boat headed upriver."

"You got the funds for the ferry?" he asks.

And I confess, "I had some hid out at the farm, and dug up some coin while you and Pearl was fetchin' the stock." I don't mention it's over a year's wages for a working man.

"The hell you say," he says, eying me a little suspiciously.

"Yeah, I say. We got enough to stay fed for a while."

"I guess you didn't trust me to help with that chore?" he says, with a little snap to his voice.

"It was a one man job. Wasn't like it was so much I couldn't carry it." I laugh.

"How much?" he asks.

"Enough for us to eat a while. And you know I'll share."

He shrugs. "That's a fine thing," he says, and I can't determine if he's sincere or sarcastic. And he closes his eyes.

It's the first time since we left Illinois I've had an offsetting feeling about my companion, Ian. And it doesn't sit well with me.

Still, I join him in closing my eyes.

I awaken to the sun high in the sky, noon or a little later. Pearl is nearby where our saddles are stowed and is pulling her shotgun from the boot. I watch as she moves over to me, and seeing my eyes open, says in a low voice, as Ian is still sleeping, "I heared some turkey talk out in the woods, and got some personal business out there. I be back. Don't y'all get light footed while I be gone. I gots welts on my...my bottom side...from a'chasing you all last night."

I have to smile at that, and ask, "I'll be happy to rub a little bacon grease on them welts."

"You and most the nice Christian folks I met most my life. You just snooze away, Mister McTavish. I'll be comin' back right soon."

I'm feeling properly chastised as she picks her way across the little trickle of water and disappears into the woods, the shotgun comfortably over her shoulder.

I'm not so taken aback, however, that I can't slip back into dreamland, and do.

My sleep is rudely awakened by the muzzle of a cold gun barrel pressed to my forehead.

West of the War

Chapter Seven

I'm staring into the bloodshot watery eyes of a face I remember from my distant past. Sheriff Oscar Scroggins of Marshal County, Missouri. He's a hard man to mistake, with a full shock of gray hair shooting out from his head over pointed lobe-less ears that, long with age, would shame a mule. His bulbous nose testifies to his enjoyment and overindulgence in corn liquor. His voice comes from deep in his belly and passes through some narrowing of his windpipe that makes it somewhat higher than a large man should be burdened with.

His is almost a squeak. "You just lay there like a slug under a rock, McTavish. You and your fellow here are on your way back to Marshal County to be hung up like the rotten murderers you are."

I have to clear my throat, dry from a hard sleep, as he straightens up and backs away just out of reach. Then I ask,

"Murderers? Since when is a fellow defending himself a murderer?"

There are three with him. One is the guy, I guess mistakenly, I sent hot footing it away from McTavish Farm just before I traded shots with Oglesby...T. C. Humbree. Only this time he's armed, carrying a fine Sharps rifle. The other two, reined up a distance away, I've never laid eyes upon, but they, too are well heeled with both sidearms and long arms. And all have their weapons aimed our way. They remain mounted, while Humbree is walking our way, a crooked grin on his wide face. One of the mounted deputies is obese, the other is missing half an arm. Both, obviously, were not qualified to take up arms in the war.

"Self defense," Scroggins snorts. "Not like I heared it. Y'all get on your feet so we can get you bound up and saddled up for a short meeting with Judge Harrington before I string you up."

"You heard it wrong, Sheriff. Oglesby was stealing my pecans and had a double barrel scattergun...in fact he fired a barrel my way. And I returned fire."

"Item one, McTavish. They were his pecans as he, and I, bought them fair and square, along with the rest of McTavish Farm, from the county at auction. Item two, you see, I was his partner. So you shot a man who was harvesting his nuts and mine and you're a gonna hang for it. Item three, we hang horse thieves, even if you wasn't a murdering som'bitch. Now, get on your feet and turn your back to me."

I can see there's no talking my way out of this, so both Ian and I get our feet under us, and I know we're both thinking of a way out. Before I can fully stand, a blast from back behind me causes me to leap aside and I nearly lose my footing. I can feel the buckshot pass close by me and Scroggins is blown backward, dropping his sidearm at my feet as he goes down. Ian dives behind the log he's been resting upon and I drop to my belly while snatching up Scroggins's sidearm.

All three of his deputies have swung their guns to the forest, looking for the shooter. My shot takes Humbree in the thigh and he screams as he collapses, slinging the Sharps aside, far enough to be out of easy reach.

The shotgun roars again, I guess aimed at the two mounted deputies, but they are a bit out of range and are fighting their mounts, who seem to dislike the discharge of arms. I fire at the nearest, the fat one, but at seventy-five feet I miss. I guess the sound of a chunk of lead passing near, and the peppering of buckshot from fifty or more yards, is enough to take the fight out of him and he gives heels to his mount and, followed closely by his pard, they pound away back toward Arrow Rock. By the look of them I don't imagine they'll stop until their horses collapse under them. I'd guess they were deputized merely for this adventure and are not experienced lawmen.

I turn my attention back to Humbree and see he's crawling to retrieve his Sharps. I move quickly and have my foot on it as he tries to grab it up.

"I guess I should have shot you dead back at the pecans," I say.

"Just doing my good citizen," he says, his voice low and pained. "Fact is, you likely killed me as this leg is broke bad and bleeding."

"You did your good deed, bringin' me this fine rifle. I'll put it to good use."

I look over my shoulder and see Pearl, looking very apprehensive as she's just killed a man, a white man, and a lawman at that. She's biting a bottom lip. Her shotgun is still smoking slightly and hangs loosely at her side as she walks out of the woods. While she approaches, I go to Hunbree's horse and retrieve his bullet molds, cases, powder, and a

71

handful of finished shells from a possibles bag hanging on his saddle horn.

Pearl's already done plenty, but I'm used to asking. "Pearl, could you tend to Mr. Humbree, please. It seems his hind leg is leaking."

She nods and in seconds is pulling his belt off and binding the leg with it, then she walks to her satchel and takes out needle and thread. She turns to me, the bottom lip she's been biting is now quivering. "I don't think his leg dun be broke. I think you got nothing but meat, and outside de bone at dat. He be fine if'n it don't go green."

I don't know if that's good news or bad as he's brought the law down on us and done it so much faster and with much more vigor than I gave him credit. The good news is we can bind him up, get him in the saddle, and send him packing after the rest of the posse without the worry of him bleeding out. Not that it would be much worry to me.

It takes us most of an hour to tie Scroggins draped over the saddle of his horse, to get Humbree situated, and send him after the others, leading Scroggins's body draped horse. By his attitude toward the trailing load, I won't be surprised if he dumps it first chance after he's out of sight.

"Now what?" Ian says, as Humbree and his burden disappear into the woods.

"Same plan, only we're all gonna cross over to Brunswick."

"You got the coin for three of us and a dozen head?"

"I got the coin."

"Then let's get moving. Them old boys are still well heeled and might be coming back."

I have to laugh at that. "They won't be coming back until they round up a half dozen more. Pearl done discouraged them."

"Damn if she didn't," he says, and we both laugh.

Now, to distance ourselves from the law and get on the river, heading to somewhere Ian can tie up with folks planning or maybe already constructing the Transcontinental, and I can put miles and Big Muddy water behind me and get my feet in Dakota Territory.

And Pearl? At least she'll be in country where a nigra woman can run free, and damned if she hasn't earned it.

It takes us just over two hours to find the ferry station across the river from Brunswick, and another hour to wait for its arrival. It's big enough for a coach and four up so it can accommodate the six mares, four mules, our three riding horses, and the three of us.

The crossing doesn't cost a dime, much less a chunk of gold from my saddlebags. I make a fine bargain as I trade ol' Jack, my big donkey, for our passage—as much as he's served McTavish Farm and the six percherons well, creating dozens of fine mules, I'm happy to be shed of the trouble maker. After giving the ferryman a bill of sale, we leave Jack—braying like hell won't have it—tied to a post oak on shore, next to the shack that serves the ferry.

The ferryman, Silas Throckmorton, like the deputy who came along with Scroggins, is a man with a missing wing. His gray hair testifies to his loyalty to whatever side he served, as, at the beginning of the war, he'd have been old enough to stay on the farm. His left arm is off at the shoulder. Midstream, I ask, "Where'd you serve?"

He glances over at Ian who's leaning on the rail, palavering with Pearl, then turns back to me. "I see your friend there still wears the butternut. You a southern man?"

"Served with Mosby. Captured, as a field promoted captain, and did over a year at Camp Butler in Springfield before I was paroled with the swore to God promise to head west. And I don't swear lightly."

"Then I guess I'll tell you I lost the arm at New Madrid, last March. Shot off at the elbow by a damn Yankee, sawed off well above the wound by an over cautious sawbones. Daddy died...made it four score and seven...the Christmas before and as I was youngest of five and didn't get the land, he left me this ferry. We owned them five," he nods at the five black men working the four oars and tiller, "but I always treated the darkies fair and they stayed with me after the damn Union burned our home place, run my brothers and sisters off, and set our darkies free."

I cross over to where my horse is tied to a makeshift picket line down the center line of the ferry and dig into my saddlebag then return. "Can I beg a favor then?"

"And what would that be?"

"An abolitionist son of a bitch who was the sheriff of Marshal County, down river, stole my land and stock while I was away in arms and came to hang me upon my return. He did not live to fulfill the task, but I imagine many of the other Union boys will take umbrage and be on my tail." I hand him a twenty dollar gold piece. "I'd be obliged if'n you'd tell them you saw us pass by on the other side of the river, should they come asking."

"Sounds like you might need that twenty. Y'all hang onto it. I got lockjaw comes to helpin' yanks."

"I'm obliged. I'm headed up to Dakota, Fort Benton if we get that far, to start fresh."

"You might be headed to Montana Territory. Leslies Weekly says it looks to be split off from Dakota and Washington, maybe already has."

I shrug. "So long as there's gold to be grubbed or hides or beavers or some damn thing. I swore to it, and I'm headed west."

"God help you, son. Your mares and mules will be valuable out in the territories. They'll give you a fine start. But It's a savage land you're headin' to."

"And it's a damn savage land I'm leaving. I'm still willin' to hand over this gold eagle, you do right by me."

"Don't insult me son, or even one-armed I'm likely to chuck you overboard. I'm a southern man and I do what I say, when I say, how I say, and I done said it."

"My apologies, sir. I've overstepped my bounds."

"Go west and do well for yourself and proud for the south. Field promotion all the way to captain? Sounds like you already done the south proud."

"I hope so, sir." I look over my shoulder and see the ferry landing approaching, so I turn back to Mr. Throckmorton. "And what are the sympathies of the folks in Brunswick?"

"Put it this way, I would not have your friend wander about in those butternut trousers."

As we unload, I caution Ian and Pearl of the local sympathies and direct them into the woods to lay low and find graze for the stock. With a piece of lead rope I measure Ian's waist and inseam, preparing to see if I can find a seamstress or a pair of ready made trousers rather than those he wears.

One small building near the wharf serves as ticket office for a number of side wheelers, but only two are bound for Fort Benton, Dakota. The Emilie and the Bold Eagle. The Emilie being the only boat over one hundred feet to ever have made the run, and her two hundred ten feet with more than a thirty foot beam. Her captain, a fellow name of Le Barge, must be a skilled river man. She is now in St. Louis, headed back this way in a fortnight. The Eagle, a boat I'm assured has a shallow draft and a competent captain, is due here tomorrow. Only one hundred forty feet in length and thirty four beam, rumored to only draw just a little over thirty inches fully loaded, she should have an easier time of the twisty, shallow at times, and snag filled Big Muddy. If she makes the run as quickly as has the Emilie, the trip will take only a touch over thirty days, rather than the more than two months, probably two and a half, it would take horseback, if we could make twenty miles to the day average...and with winter coming on? I'm worried that coming winter—possible rains and high water—will keep the boat tied ashore somewhere between here and there. Then, come Spring, she'll face a bombardment of ice floes.

But if she's forced to lay up, wherever that may be, it'll be a far piece from a Marshal County posse.

I find a buyer for two of my mares and pocket another one hundred dollars—had to sell them way too cheap—leaving four mares, four mules and three gelding riding horses.

It costs me one hundred dollars apiece for Ian and I, paid with the understanding that if Ian disembarks along the way, I'll be refunded one half the difference of his fare for the rest of the trip. And it's only that inexpensive as we'll camp next to the horse stalls with our bedrolls and not eat but two meals a day each. And it's two hundred dollars well spent if it saves me six weeks and the dangers of Indian country—Indians who I'm assured will dog our trail to steal our stock.

The horses and mules are one dollar per day each for the transportation and fifty cents per day for feed, with the understanding I can unload them nightly and skip the feed if there's graze—as after a week we'll be tying up every night as the river becomes more and more tricky to navigate. So long as I have them back on board one half hour before daylight. With eleven head to feed, it will be well worth the effort. Besides, the feed is only a generous fork full of meadow grass hay, and the Percherons require more.

I ask him why so cheap for the critters, and he smiles and asks, "Them big ol' horses look like they could pull a mountain down."

"They pull, and so do my mules."

He merely nods. "Ever body pitches in on the rough uphill trip to Benton City."

Even at that it seems a proud price to pay, but knowing that it costs ten dollars to haul a sack of flour from St. Louis to Fort Benton makes it more palatable.

I buy a ticket using the name Nolan Byrne, a long lost second cousin of mine back in County Cork who I have corresponded with but never met, as it was the first to come to me. I list Ian as his own name, as none of those after us have any idea who he might be.

Pearl will make out just fine in Brunswick with its northern sympathies.

It takes me four hours to find Ian a pair of black canvas trousers, from a seamstress who made them for another soul who didn't show back to pick them up. And those have to be taken in to fit his waist, which is far narrower than his wide shoulders.

As they've been more than merely fine companions, I find a mercantile and buy us a pound of coffee, a side of bacon, some hard biscuits, and the treat of two pounds of peaches sugared and put up in a crock. Having heard of Dakota, Idaho, and Washington winters I buy two pairs of Long Johns and plan to gift one to Ian.

I track my companions from the ferry into the forest, and find them near a slow creek with every horse and mule staked in belly deep grass, a fine campfire, and coffee boiling.

Ian has cut a willow pole and caught two fat catfish and a half dozen sunfish.

We eat a satisfying meal and are finished before nightfall. Over coffee the subject of the trip on the Eagle comes up. I turn to Pearl.

"I will leave you with a twenty dollar gold piece, Pearl—"

"You ain't leaving me, Mister McTavish."

"This will be a very hard trip...no place for a woman. Even a woman tough as you. You're staying here or going on somewhere else."

"You, sir, are a thankless som'bitch. And that not be a reflection on your dear mama."

I'm taken aback by her forwardness. I start to object, but Ian jumps into the discussion. "Brad, I seem to remember Miss Pearl here saving your hide from an ugly old boy who was eager to see you swing. If I got a vote in this, I vote Miss Pearl goes along to the territories."

That makes me clamp my jaw, "You ain't got no vote." Then I turn back to Pearl. "I'll give you two gold pieces. That's forty dollars, Pearl. More money than you've ever seen."

"No, sur."

"Fifty dollars, and that's my final offer."

Ian shakes his head in disgust, then turns and walks away, saying over his shoulder. "I believe I'll be staying here with Miss Pearl, as you are a sorry som'bitch."

"I done paid a hundred dollars good money for your fare. And I just bought you a fine pair of long johns."

He turns back. "Ain't that something. You got some of your daddy's money. So, you offered her fifty to stay, so I guess it would only take another fifty for her to go. You got enough of your daddy's coin?"

"None of your damn business," I sputter, then spittin' angry, exclaim, "Damned if I don't and how do you know it was daddy's? I lived on that farm, too, don't you know." Fact is it was daddy's money, but he didn't know that.

Pearl's voice softens. "I know I never been much to you, Braden, but I did care for your daddy and for your mama when she woulda starved if I'd'a gone on with my own folk. And if I stay here, them Arrow Rock som'bitches will hang me sure. Seems that is what you aim to have happen?"

My mouth goes dry and I get a flash of my daddy swinging. My mama and daddy cared for Pearl and her family, almost like family, slaves or no, and I'm suddenly flush in the face. I'm confused, and not for the first time. I'm feeling like the som'bitch she called me. Damn, if it ain't a confusing world.

The fact is, it'll be a much more difficult time with a distraction as great as Pearl's womanliness. Should the truth be known.

I rise and dump the rest of my tin cup of coffee in the fire to sizzle and steam, then turn to the two of them. "I'm riding back to town first thing in the morning to buy Pearl a ticket…but you got to sleep in the stable with us. There ain't gonna be no lady-like quarters. You understand."

"Can't be much worse," she says, "than that damn ol' cabin I was raised up in."

That makes my face flush even more. "I'm gonna roll up. I been chastised enough by the two of you."

"And damn if you didn't deserve it," Ian's harsh words whack me in the back like a 'cat o nine tails' as I stomp away.

West of the War

Chapter Eight

The Eagle is secured at the wharf taking on stores and a straggle of passengers—most boarded at St. Louis—when we arrive shortly after dawn. She must have arrived in the dark of night. The small stalls are located on the boiler deck just aft of the two twenty foot by seven foot round iron boilers and on either side of the seven foot by two foot round iron casing that hides the piston that drives the ship. The good of it is the area will be warm in the coldest of weather, the bad is if the boiler's blow—and it's not an uncommon occurrence on steam driven boats—the stock and the three of us will go meet our maker in high and hot style.

At least three dozen cords of cut wood line the hull along either side and block the wind from the open sides of the boat. We're protected from the weather by six foot thick walls...however I'm sure they'll come and go as they are consumed.

I'm concerned as the freight and boiler deck has only seven feet of clearance, and the crossbeams lower the headroom another foot in intervals. At over six feet in height, Ian will likely enjoy many lumps on the noggin if he's not careful, and the Percherons will spend their time with bent ears should they stand full tall.

While Ian and I load the critters via an aft gangplank, I send Pearl on an errand. I'm sure all stores will be two or three times the cost, or more, as we get farther upriver. And lead and powder and other fixins are easy to haul on this wide boat among our belongings. And the two Iron ax heads and fine hunting knifes I've instructed her to buy will be necessities.

The Sharps I've 'inherited' is as fine a weapon as any I've ever handled, much less owned—if you can call the way I acquired it owning. I have a clear conscience as I'd think if a feller tries to load you full of holes with a weapon, taking it is fair game.

She's a 45-90 with a shell the size of my index finger and a chunk of lead in each that would likely bring down an elephant...and from what I've heard of the American Bison, he can be as tough as one. As a youth my father saw buffalo in western Missouri, where the Ozarks meet the prairie, but I've never had the pleasure. I'm sure I'll see plenty.

After we get situated with our bedrolls alongside the stalls, Ian and I return to the wharf to watch the activity and wait for Pearl's return. Just as she comes our way, her arms loaded with paper wrapped packages, she has to jump aside, scattering her packages, as a passenger wagon pulled by a fine set of matching blacks with white blazes on their noses almost runs her down. The wagon is reined up near where we stand. The driver jumps down and extends his hand to a fancy dressed woman, perched amidst a pile of matching tan leather luggage.

And she's not happy. She refuses his hand and steps down on her own, then turns to him and snaps, "That was careless of you. You made that young lady drop her packages and could have injured her badly."

But he's not to be chastised, and snaps back at her. "Damn nigra should give way. Find someone else to haul your bags aboard. I was paid to deliver you and delivered you are." Rudely he spits a gob of chaw on the ground and backhands the dribble from a thick black bushy mustache.

Ian moves even quicker than I do and edges the hack driver aside with a sharp elbow and a, "Stand aside and watch your lip before I split it for you." Being a half head taller and as broad as the driver, the man appraises him with a curled lip and bulging eyes, then reassesses and backs away silently. Ian turns to the lady.

"Ma'am, I'd be proud to help you with your luggage."

She flashes him a smile, and I realize how beautiful she is. Near Ian's age, at least fifteen years older than me, she still takes my breath away with wine colored hair and plenty of it piled on the back of her head, green eyes that seem to pierce to your very soul, skin as smooth and flawless as the fine kid leather on her many bags, and she has other attributes a gentleman shouldn't mention.

Ian turns back to me. "Braden, grab a load here."

I nod. The balance of the seats in the passenger wagon are taken up with fancy matching leather bags and a steamer trunk, another trunk is on the boot at the rear, all of the same matching tan leather and brass fittings.

The lady walks back across the dusty street to where Pearl is trying to gather up dropped packages, and to my surprise bends and helps her.

"Obliged, ma'am," Pearl says, admiring the lady with some wonderment as if she'd just descended from heaven, then moves to and up the wide gangplank, glancing back more than once.

Ian and I have to make four trips, each carrying the end of a steamer trunk that's large enough to have held her husband and two children.

I direct Pearl below with instructions to find our bedrolls and stow her packages, and Ian leads me down to where he offers the lady his arm. "May I escort you aboard, ma'am?" he asks. I have to smile as all I've seen is the rough side of him.

Pearl has returned by the time we top the gangplank. Ian, who's acting like an Irish lord...at least until they top the gangplank and she has to step down to the deck. He's trying to help the process, but steps on the hem of her dress and we can hear it rip as she descends.

"Oh, ma'am," he says, his face coloring. "I'm so sorry. I'm a clumsy oaf."

"No problem. You've been kind. I can find someone to mend—"

Before she finishes the statement, Pearl steps forward. "I have my sewing bag, ma'am. I'll be happy...."

"That's kind of you, young lady."

The boat's purser is almost at a run as he comes to her side; fat, officious, and a little breathless, manages. "You must be Miss Allenthorpe?"

"Yes, Madam Angel Allenthorpe."

"Can't begin to tell you how privileged we are to have you aboard. Follow me to your stateroom," and he spins on a heel and starts away, then turns back to us. "Well, get her bags, you two louts."

I have to smile and snap at Ian, out of the lady's earshot, "Yeah, Lord Ian, get the damn bags, you lout."

"What's a lout?" he asks, not knowing to be offended or not.

"Well, sir, I believe it's a low life...or maybe a bumpkin...and that sure as hell fits a fellow who still has not thanked his pard for the long johns."

"Since you bought Pearl a ticket, I thank you for the long johns."

"And odds are," I say as I pick up the end of a heavy trunk, "you'll be thanking me again most every winter day up river."

Pearl is right behind Madam Allenthorpe and Ian and I take up the trail, him at the front and me dragging up the back, hauling the first of the steamer trunks.

I have heard of Madam Angel Allenthorpe, a celebrated singer and actress. I'm surprised she's not accompanied by an entourage of hangers-on and a full orchestra. But it seems she's alone.

After we get her settled I take a moment to admire her stateroom, actually a pair of rooms, one of which is a smaller necessary room with a toilet scupper through the hull and nearby ladle in a scuttlebutt of water to wash it clean, a dressing table, a cupboard for the stowing of clothes, and a full length reflecting glass. The bed is a four poster and wide enough for four should they sleep on their sides. I'm sure the fluffy covering is filled with goose down. It's just a mite different than our quarters, I think, with a smile.

There are sixty staterooms on the main deck, but I'm sure no more than one other the size of this one. She is scheduled for one hundred twenty passengers plus a crew of twenty. There is a main dining room that seats sixty, a smoking room for men only to one end, forward with a fine view of the river ahead, and a much smaller sitting room for women only aft of the main. The kitchen is on the lower deck and serves the dining room with both a stairway and a dumb waiter.

Miss Allenthorpe has changed into a full length purple silk robe with yellow rope trim tied tight around what I presume is a corseted narrow waist and Pearl is seated nearby, hard at work, while we load the lady's belongings. While we're admiring her lodging, she reaches into a reticule and offers each of us a coin. "Thank you, gentlemen."

Both of us refuse.

"Then I will buy you a glass of champagne after we're underway."

"Not necessary," I say.

"Yes, it is necessary," she says, so I merely nod.

She turns to Pearl. "Are you voyaging with us?"

"Yes, ma'am," Pearl says with a quick glance, still sewing away.

"You're doing a fine job. I bought that dress in Rome, and I believe you've saved it. Are you employed on the Eagle?"

"No, ma'am. I be a passenger," she smiles, flashing white teeth, "going west to find my fortune, don't ya know."

"And you have a stateroom?"

Pearl laughs, as do Ian and I.

"No, ma'am. I be down in de belly of de boat with these two louts." She seems to find that amusing.

Miss Allenthorpe eyes us up and down, then turns back to Pearl. "They seem gentlemen to me." We give her a smile and she turns back to Pearl. "I need a lady's maid to help with my ablutions and such. I hope you're not offended by the idea. If you'd consider the job we can make you a pallet in the dressing room. I'll remunerate you at the rate of one dollar per day."

Pearl looks a little suspicious. "Ma'am. What be remunerate?"

"I'll pay you."

Pearl's eyes are now shining. "Sure 'nuf. I gots to get my satchel."

"And I'll teach you the king's English."

"Yes, ma'am," she says, and I can see she's wondering what that means as well, but the dollar a day has her head spinning.

The lady turns to us. "Thank you, gentlemen. If you don't mind, I'd like my privacy."

And we follow Pearl out and down the ladder to the lower deck, and damned if I'm not jealous.

As Pearl is gathering up her things, I suggest, "So, Pearly...or should I now say, Miss Pearl, I guess you're shed of Ian and me?"

She's silent for a long moment, then, her arms full of her belongings, offers, "Mister Braden, as God is my witness, I will pay you the hundred dollars you done spent on my fare."

"I don't expect that, Pearl. Consider it remuneration," and I laugh, "for caring for my folks. I'm glad for you."

"You ain't seen the end of me, Braden McTavish."

I have yet to correct either she or Ian with my temporary name, Nolan Byrne. So I take the opportunity. "Y'all call me Nolan for a while. It's the name I took in case those Arrow Rock boys check the passenger list."

She nods, and Ian shrugs, then adds, "I kind of like your new name, lout."

"Don't get used to it," I say, only half amused.

With that, Pearl moves away and I can't help but think she's not only moving up the ladder to a high floor, but up to a higher station in life. I smile at the thought. But I'm also a little maudlin, seeing her disappear.

As I'm contemplating getting what I wanted, to be shed of a woman on this difficult trip, four fellows appear near the boilers. I wander over to where they seem to be preparing to depart.

"Y'all mind if I watch?" I ask, and a burly fellow with dirty blond pork chop sideburns and a shiny bald pate, shoulders like an ox, and a raspy voice that's used to shouting over steam engine noise. His shirt is missing the top two buttons, and tufts of blond chest hair protrude.

"You bunked down here?" he asks, looking me up and down.

"Yep. Me and my pardner over there."

"We're short a hand. Peabody done got drunk and throwed in the Brunswick jail. I can pay you a dollar and a half for a twelve hour day, if 'n you prove your worth."

"How about my pardner?"

"Only need one. You want the work or not?"

"How about this. I work one day, my pardner the next. We can save us a half dollar a day fare if we graze the stock when we tie up nights."

He thinks about that a moment as he looks over to where Ian is scratching the ears of one of my mules. "That's fine by me, if you're both willing to pitch in when we're taking on wood, every three days or so."

"I already paid for two meals a day for the two of us."

"We eat down here, but if you paid you can eat topside with the fines. We take a half hour for dinner and a half hour for supper."

"Fines?" I ask.

"Yeah, them fine highfalutin' city folks who had the silver to pay their way."

I laugh. "Well, sir, I never thought myself highfalutin' but I paid for the chow. If we breakfast above can we lunch with the crew then supper above?"

"We can work that out," he says, with a low guffaw. "We eat right good down here. One of the perks of working the boats."

"When do we start?" I ask.

"I'll train you today and you can start in the morning. No pay while you're training, other than lunch."

"Done," I say, extending my hand. "I'm Brad...I mean, I'm Nolan Byrne. That ugly fellow over there is Ian Hollihan."

"Dag Eriksen," he says, and pumps my hand like he's trying to bring up a gallon of water. And it's a hand with a quarter inch of callous and rougher than a dry corn cob.

He wastes no time and yells at Ian. "Hey, Hollihan, get your lazy Irish ass over here if you want to prove your worth."

Ian eyes him with some doubt as he hasn't been privy to the discussion, but then comes over and accepts Eriksen's extended hand. "What's up?" he asks.

"We're working for this straw boss—"

"Engineer," Eriksen corrects.

"For Engineer Dag Eriksen. You and me trading off every other day—"

"Nights," Eriksen corrects. "Least for a while. Y'all's the low man on the totem pole."

I shrug, then add, "We're training today for lunch, but one of us works on the morrow."

"Tonight," Eriksen corrects again. "And you'll help load a barge full of wood today before we drop lines."

Ian shrugs. "The hell you say. And we're making a little coin for this hot work?"

"Yeah, I'm making two dollars a day and you're making a dollar. That's cause I'm the best looking."

"Humph," Ian says. "So it's a dollar and a half a day each, even though you're a sogger."

"Twelve hours, and you'll earn it," Eriksen says, and guffaws again.

"Mr. Eriksen," I say, "you do the trainin', we'll do the learning."

Then he points from one to the other of the rest of the crew. The first is a red headed stump with a mottled face.

"That's Willard...we call him Wheezy." The second has a scar across one white eye and no front teeth, "that there is Alabama." The last is scarecrow thin with long stringy gray hair to his shoulders, "and the skinny fellow is Eustace, goes by Slim down here."

They all give me a nod and disdainful look. I guess Peabody was a friend and they hate seeing him replaced.

The men return to work and Eriksen waves us to follow as he speaks, "We're a mountain boat, shallow draft and fast, and it's a good thing as it's three thousand miles of backbreakin' curves and dangerous snags and sandbars from St. Louie to Fort Benton, and we'll climb to five thousand feet above sea level by the time we tie up there."

"So," I ask, "curves and sandbars?" I shrug. "Is that the worst we'll face?"

Eriksen guffaws and slaps his thighs. "Well, if 'n you don't consider the snags and logs damn near as long as the boat, tornadoes, winds wantin' to upend us, hail big as hen eggs, fire from the heaven that would split us down the middle should we be hit, ten times our number of Osage, Pawnee, Arikara, Sioux, Assiniboine and the damned murderous Blackfeet and Crow who'll gut you, scalp you, and tan your hide to use for a possibles bag...or maybe ass wipe." With that he guffaws again, then waves us along. "Oh, yeah," he adds, "and that don't take into consideration the dugouts, flatboats, Mackinaws, keelboats, and other side wheelers wantin' to run us over or shoot us down if we get close enough to run them over, and willin' to pot shot any man foolish enough to show himself, we get near. And, of course, these two damn boilers could go anytime, y'all don't pay close attention. That would cook the meat right off 'n your bones and make us all fish food."

Ian sidles up beside me and says in a low voice. "Damn if he ain't an encouraging soul."

90

"Let's hope," I respond, "that Dag Eriksen is a man prone to exaggeration."

Chapter Nine

riksen shows us the equipment, the two long boilers with fireboxes below. The openings of the fireboxes face the bow, to catch the wind and make the fire burn hot. The boilers are lined up side by side.

He points to a gauge on each boiler. "You see that go over one fifty, you start heaving buckets of water into the fire bins. Over one fifty is an invitation to join all your bloody Irish relatives in hell."

We both nod, and don't break a smile.

I notice the boilers have an opening at each end and am surprised as it seems a place to leak steam.

"Don't those hatches into the boilers leak?" I ask.

"Yeah, but necessary. There's a good gasket there, but it'll fail over time."

"What's the hatch's for."

"You'll see," he says, and gives me a crooked smile.

At the rear is the steam driven piston encased in a much smaller iron tube, connected via a fly wheel to a walking beam, a metal covered log that's a drive line which swivels off a crank turned by the piston, which in turns spins an axle connected to gear boxes near the wheels on either side of the boat. Gears allow the huge paddle wheels to be sped up or slowed independently, and either one to be reversed so the big boat can nearly turn inside its own length.

He finishes walking us thru the equipment, then gives us a nod. "Y'all can wander the boat for an hour or so...till you see the wood barge draw alongside. Then come a'running."

"Yes, sir," we both say, and head for the ladder. Then I turn back to him. "How long before we take up lines?"

"Soon as the wood's loaded."

Good, I think, as I follow Ian up the ladder to the cabin deck. The faster we get on the water, the sooner we'll be leaving any Arrow Rock posse far behind. I feel lucky so far.

Sixty passengers have boarded either in St. Louie, points in between, or here in Brunswick, and most of them are strolling the deck. We make a full circle, admiring the fine carpentry work, the huge wheels, and the chimneys, which rise sixty feet high, just behind the wheelhouse which tops the ship and is almost an all glass house so the captain can see all obstructions, every direction.

Under the wheel house forward is the main dining room, with a men's smoking room forward of that and a much smaller ladies sitting room aft, then the cabins are back to back to the aft observation deck.

I duck into the main dining room where a dozen people are gathered around a small pianoforte, and where Madam Angel Allenthorpe is plunking a tune while the others look on in rapture.

She glances up, and smiles. "Mister....what was it, Mister Byrne. Are you gentlemen ready for that glass of Champagne?"

I glance at Ian, who's smiling like his uncle has just left him a saloon in his will. He nods, and I return Miss Allenthorpe's smile. "Yes, ma'am, I suppose we could do with a glass."

Having never tasted Champagne, I'm guessing, but my pa spoke highly of it as he'd had a glass in New Orleans.

We move over to the group and give each of them a nod.

"Have you met Captain Johanson?" she asks, and a tall whiskered man steps forward from the group and extends his hand. His is a wrap around beard without mustache, nicely trimmed and gray as a bilge rat. Piercing blue eyes seem to bulge a little as he looks us up and down in turn. She continues, "I picked this boat because of Captain Isaac Johanson, whose long experience on the Mississippi, and one thousand five hundred dollars per month salary, as reported in Leslie's Weekly, was very impressive."

I glance at her as her look of adoration at the captain is a little surprising and I'm wondering if it's for his reputed skill, or his earnings. The man is being paid a small fortune, so her admiration is somewhat understandable.

"You gentlemen are traveling with us?" Johanson asks with a low rumble of a voice as Ian and I shake his hand in turn.

"Actually, Captain, we're in your employ as of this morning. Working for Mr. Eriksen on the boiler deck."

"We don't drink while on duty," he says, and his stoic look turns a little sour. It's all I can do not to smile as river men are renowned for emptying a bottle a shift.

"It would be the night shift we'll be working?"

"Both of you? We only lost one man, last I heard."

"We're alternating nights," I say, again giving him a tight smile.

"Unusual," he says, looking a little confounded.

"We've paid our fare, sir, and probably should be requesting a refund—"

"Not likely," he says, his smile condescending. "Besides, did you bring your own grub?"

"No, sir."

"Engine deck passengers provide their own chow. So if you paid including meals, you're in for a penny in for a pound."

So I continue, "We got stock on board and can save the feed cost, should one of us graze them when you're tied up for the night. We're pay as we go for hay and grain."

"Humph," he says with obvious agitation. "Who negotiated that affair?"

"Your agent here in Brunswick, sir." I'm starting to get a little irritated with the man. But I bite my tongue. Just coming from the Army, I'm fairly used to supercilious sons a bitches being in command. So I add, "We'll be no trouble and we both know how to work."

"You any good with metal. Blacksmith and such?"

"I'm no tinsmith, but I've pounded my share of plowshares, hoes, wagon fittings, and such. I was raised on a farm aside the Big Mo, sir, with forge and bellows. I've been pounding hot iron all my life. And I have cause to work careful around your boat. I saw the Pittsburg blow just below our place, the safe flew two hundred yards up on the bank, and we treated a half dozen at our house for their burns and buried a half dozen more at the end of one of our fields."

He looks a little irritated again, as if I've put a damper on the group's enjoyment. He clears his throat before giving me another glare. "The Pittsburg. That was a half dozen years ago. You were still in swaddling—."

"Hardly, sir. I was well into a score of years."

"All your life pounding iron…or hoeing cotton? All a young life, I'd say, but many farm boys know iron. I was one myself," he says, but he seems to like what he hears and goes on, "You might earn your keep at that."

Ian steps forward for the first time, his hands clasped behind his back. "We never took on nothin' we didn't finish, Captain. You'll be a'beggin' for us to stay on, come Fort Benton."

He laughs low. "That's yet to be seen." Then he turns serious and gives Ian a scowl. "And I don't beg."

"Yes, sir. I didn't mean—" Ian clamps his jaw and gives him a nod, then turns to Miss Allenthorpe. "Now can we beg a glass of that fancy wine?"

"Just one," the Captain says, then he turns to her. "Thank you for the song, ma'am. You sing fine as a whippoorwill."

"Thank you, Captain," she replies. "With a little more variety, I hope. Will I see you at supper time?"

"River permitting, you'll be welcome at my table, me there or not. It's roast duck, fried chicken, and oysters tonight, with all the trimmings." He glances out the tall window. "I see our wood is coming alongside so I must attend to duty. We can get in a few hours on the river before we lose the light."

He starts out, and I have to beg off. "Ma'am, we have to report below. Another time?"

She laughs, which lights up the room. "Surely," she says, as we head out.

"Another song, Madam?" one of the men asks, and I'm sorry we have to leave.

"One more, then I have to retire to my suite," she says, stressing the suite, and I hear the pianoforte tinkle as we make our exit, then the strains of Amazing Grace.

When we hit the boiler deck men are already swinging hoists out over the barge, cranking on geared winches, bringing half cord loads aboard with each long exertion. Eriksen yells on seeing our approach, "Get to stackin' you loafers." And we do. Fifty cords worth.

While we're stacking wood, from pallet to deck, Slim and Wheezy are stoking the fire bins, and the pressure gauges are beginning to crawl up.

A bell on a stanchion at the bow end of the engine room rings at least ten times, its clapper swung by a line up through the overhead.

"We're casting off," Eriksen yells. "Look lively now."

Our journey is about to begin.

I can hear the deck crew scrambling and see the dock lines being dragged onboard as the speed of the side wheels pick up and they bite water.

When Erikson engages the gears and the steam engine exerts, the noise is deafening. The wheels begin churning up water and the bow swings to midstream. The five men on the crew, begin a song barely heard over the engine and gear noise.

"To the West! To the West!
To the land of the free!
Where the mighty Missouri
Rolls down to the sea!"

I felt a surge of excitement roll through me. Ahead of us is gold, grizzly, wild Indian, wilder country, and the spine of the continent, the Rocky Mountains.

Ian moves aft to calm the stock. They are restive, moving from side to side in their small stalls. I note at least two of them try to rear, but the low ceiling keeps them afoot. The noise has made them fearful and Ian's going to try and calm them. I join him as the big percheron mares might just break out, should they try.

I can see the whites of their eyes as I approach and their ears go back occasionally. Not a good sign in horse or mule. After a few moments they do calm, but I'd guess it to be a long while before they are truly at ease, if ever during the trip.

"Who's starting out tonight?" Ian asks.

"You got a coin? You flip, I'll call."

He digs in a pocket and comes up with a nickel, flips, and I call tails and lose.

"You sleep for a couple of hours," he advises. "I bet it'll be a long twelve."

I nod, and find my bedroll and a spot as far as I can get from the steaming, rattling, clattering heap that's the steam engine, while he finds a shovel to clean the stalls, then I try to snooze. But the constant beating of the engine, the stench of burning wood, engine oil, smoke, hissing steam, and clattering gears keeps sleep at bay. That, and the constant vibration of the deck makes my teeth rattle and my ears ring. It seems we'll experience a continuous earthquake so long as the steam engine beats.

And, to my great surprise, the yowling of cats occasionally rises over all other sounds. Why cats? I remind myself to ask Eriksen when I report for my shift.

I think I haven't slept a wink, but when I rise up to Eriksen's shouting in my ear, I realize I must have slept hard.

"This ain't no bawdy house where you can snooze the night away, Byrne. You got to relieve the boys."

"I paid for supper upstairs," I mumble.

"They start serving at five and it's six now, time to go to work. I guess you can eat double at breakfast. You'll get lunch in six or so, come midnight."

I glance around and see that Ian is missing, eating his share and mine I suppose. Damn, my stomach is growling and I've got six hours before a meal break.

I report to Eriksen's station, a small table, more a stand up speaker's lectern, mounted to a post just below the bell, forward. He calls a burly black over and introduces us.

"This is Sam. He's the boss of the night shift, second engineer, to be technical."

I'm a little dumbfounded and I can't help but stammer, "I…I'm to work for a nigra?"

"It's work for him or don't work," he says, and there's no question he means it.

I shrug. Damn, if it ain't a strange new world. Sam, I guess is used to the slight, and scowls and looks away, ignoring me. When he looks back I guess I'm looking a little sheepish, so he waves me along and leads me aft, even beyond the stalls, and I help him secure freight that's been loosened in travel. As we work, he's stoic, silent as one of the boxes we work over. The man pulls his shirt off as he works, and I'm a little amazed by the size of his chest tapering over a washboard stomach to a narrow waist and his vein lined biceps the size of my thighs. The muscles ripple his back like the wake of the Eagle as he moves. He lifts crates that I'd have to lever with a strong pry board, and does it as if they're filled with feathers.

We come to several marked DANGER in red paint, and I inquire. "I guess this ain't cats?"

"Cat's all be in cages, not cases. That be gunpowder. Three tons of it in them cases. I wouldn't be lighting my pipe near here."

"I'd say that's sound advice." And I'm a little more tender with my tying down and wonder about the sixty feet or so separating the powder from the ship's fire boxes.

"Three tons?" I ask, a little amazed.

"Should it go they won't be a piece of dis boat big enough to make markers for our graves…o'course they won't find chunks of us big enough to bury."

"Comforting thought," I say, and he smiles, flashing white teeth, for the first time since we met.

Finally I remember to ask. "What's with all the cats in cages?"

"You gots to feed 'em an slop out their leavings. Dat be another new-man task."

"But why cats?"

"Army buys a few at every fort along the way. They gots terrible rat troubles in their stores. And I hears fast as we sell them more, the wolves and coyotes eat 'em up."

We work a while longer, and I finally comment. "You've got a fine job."

"I be a fine hand, and most the white boys, even if de start out fine, soon drink dem sevs into a stupor. Alcohol don't touch my tongue. The devil's nectar got my daddy hung by the neck even if 'n it tastes sweet as a woman's kiss, but I believe I done learned."

"Any other blacks on board?"

"Yeah, one of the deck hands says he done knows you."

"The hell you say?"

"Yep, Ray be his name. But he didn't call you Nolan?"

"Then maybe he doesn't know me," I mumble, but I'm sure he does. That's a shock. Raymond, my childhood fishing partner, my father's slave, Pearl's brother. It's a family reunion, if you can call it that.

Truth is, I'm looking forward to seeing him.

We stay underway for only another hour, then the boat moves alongside the shore line and roustabouts secure her to some sturdy oaks then put out the gangplank so the passengers can stroll the shore and feel hard land underfoot. As soon as those who want to depart do so, Ian leads the animals ashore, two at a time, and stakes them out to graze, saving me dollars.

When the fire boxes and boilers have cooled some, I find out why the blacks and the new hands have the night shift. Sam, me, and another young fella about my age, Duffy, who's last name is McDuff, begin shoveling the ashes from the fire boxes into buckets. Many chunks of coals still burn bright. We dump them overboard and steam rises from the river where they splash.

When the fire boxes are clean, I learn why the boilers have bolted accesses over two feet in diameter. Duffy opens a valve and the steam roars through an escape pipe to up above the hurricane deck, then it slowly peters out.

I help Duffy unbolt and remove the hatches with only the slightest remnants of escaping pressure and steam, while Sam moves to a scuttlebutt and drains a ladle of water. Duffy hands me a shovel with a cocky grin.

"You the junior man, Nolan. Climb in and shovel the mud into the bucket and pass it out to me." He hands me a pair of heavy gloves.

I stick my head in, and jerk it back. "Damn, it's hades in there."

"Yep, climb on in. We do it damn near every night."

"How come there's mud in there?" I ask, stalling for time.

"They don't call her the Big Muddy for nothing. It's river water we boil, and that's the leavin'. We got to get it out or soon the boiler would fill up."

"You mean I have to get it out."

"Yep, I done it for six months since I been aboard." He gives me an even bigger grin. "Now it's all your'n. Go in feet first."

He pulls a stool over and I manage to get my legs in, then trying not to touch my back to the hot rim, slide on in. Every bucket full I hand him I get to stick my head out and breath cool fresh air until he returns from the rail. After the third bucket Sam meets me at the opening with a big ladle full of water. He's been drinking from that ladle, and most of those I know would never drink from the same glass as a nigra, but I'm proud to at the moment—fact is I shared many a cup and chunk of jerky with Raymond and Pearl—and by God if the water don't taste just like water.

I count seven buckets full of scum, mud, and rust, before I'm able to follow the bucket out. I do believe I'm going to earn my buck and a half a day. If I haven't sweated a gallon of water there ain't a river out over those rails. My clothes will be salt stained from the sweat and I'll have to wash them in fresh water daily or I'll soon smell like a goat.

Next stop we make at a town I'll be looking for a change of shirt and trousers for Ian and me.

The best of the shift so far is lunch. We spoon down all the hot beef stew we can eat, with a fine hard bread and a glass of cool beer which seems contrary to what the captain has preached in front of his passengers.

Now, only another five and a half hours more.

Our last job of the shift is to fire up the boilers again, and by the time the morning sun is beginning to light the sky at our backs, I see we have one hundred twenty pounds on the gauge.

Eriksen reappears, and in moments, the signal bell rings repeatedly. He throws the wheels into gear, the lines are being dragged aboard, and we're heading for midstream.

We have yet to see a mile of straight river as she weaves and bends, and at times almost oxbows back on herself. Still, Sam tells me by the end of the day shift we could be in Kansas City. The good news is I should be able to find Ian and me a change of clothes, the bad is we won't be able to graze the stock and the night will come proud having to buy hay and a palm full of grain for each critter. Still, it's a fine bargain as my percherons weigh two thousand pounds, maybe more, and it costs fifteen dollars a hundred weight for freight. That means I'd have to pay at least three hundred dollars each, were they dead weight. The mules are only nine to twelve hundred pounds, but still the cost would come proud.

Eriksen slaps me on the back. "You did fine, Nolan me lad. They'll be a card game going up on the aft deck. You don't have the coin, I'll loan you four dollars, you pay me back five come payday?"

I give him a tight smile and a shake of the head. "You know how to double your money, Mr. Eriksen?"

He looks interested. "How's that, son."

"Fold it over and stick it back in your pocket."

I get a laugh from him. "Not a sporting man?"

"When I own a gambling house, maybe."

He laughs and slaps me on the back again. "Go get some breakfast. You'll get bored soon enough, then maybe the cards will have a run at you."

"Maybe," I say, and head for the ladder.

Chapter Ten

Breakfast is being served and I don't have time to wash and dry my clothes, so I serve myself from a buffet table laden with fine food—eggs, bacon, ham, biscuits, gravy, fried chicken, flapjacks—and I can see I'm not likely to starve. I load a plate and retire to the deck outside the dining room. I don't want to offend the few others who've appeared for the early serving as I'm sure my stench will overwhelm some tender soul. Breakfast, I understand, will go on for two hours.

I plop down on a spool of line and enjoy the passing fields, now gone fallow and brown with dead foliage, the intermittent forests of hardwoods are almost bare of leaves, and a few grazing cows and horses pick over what's left of the pastures. I'm half way through the mound of food when I glance up and see Raymond pacing my way, two other roustabouts flank him.

He's within five paces when he glances over and sees me, then cuts his eyes away. When he's even, I realize he's going to ignore me.

"Ray!" I call out, but he keeps moving.

"Raymond, hold up there." I rise and rest my plate on the spool and turn back and see that he's paused, looking over his shoulder.

"I gots nothin' to say to you," he snaps his head back and moves on.

Heat floods my backbone, but I say nothing. I return to my seat and my fork, but he's spoiled my appetite. Damn, if that wasn't an uppity thing to do.

I'll have to think on it, and maybe take up the matter with Pearl.

Damn, if my feelings ain't hurt a little. Long as I've lived I don't remember not knowing Ray and I knew Pearl as a baby, still on her mama's tit.

Then again, I think, shaking my head. It sure as hell is a new time.

I stay there a long while after I've returned my crockery to a tray in the dining room, watching the occasional scow or bull boat and even another side wheeler pass. I'm about ready to try and find my bedroll, when I see Madam Allenthorpe, with Pearl a couple of paces behind, heading for the dining room. The famous songstress is resplendent in a Kelly green gown sporting a matching parasol, while it appears she's found some finery for Miss Pearl. The gray smock is no longer and she's finely done up in a deck length yellow dress trimmed in lace, with a bit of lace worked into her hair. She has on white gloves, and damn if she doesn't look as stylish as my daddy told me some of the black ladies—of questionable endeavors—in the quarter at New Orleans were attired.

Madam Allenthorpe pays me no mind, but Pearl sees me as they swing the door aside, and gives me a wave.

"Y'all doin' just fine?" she yells across the twenty feet separating.

"Fine as frog hair," I yell back, and she flashes a grin at me and disappears inside.

If that ain't something. Damn, if Pearly doesn't look like a fine lady.

I decide to take a turn around the deck before going below and getting some rest, and when I reach the aft of the passenger deck, see a group of a half dozen fellas perched on kegs and line spools round a couple of planks spanning two hogshead barrels. I get closer to see a gent in a puff tie and well cut coat dealing faro. One of the four players is Raymond, and one of his fellow roustabouts, and two others are passengers.

I pause and watch a moment until the dealer, a fella with a fine mustache so thin it might have been drawn on with a pen, one gold front tooth, and what looks to be a diamond stick pin in his silk cravat, surveys me up and down.

"You want to join the game, pilgrim?" he asks, his smile tight as the lips of a gopher snake.

"No, sir. Just watching the frivolities."

"My name is Chance O'Galliger, and I'll take fine care of you should you sit in."

"Don't know the game, sir."

"It ain't no hill for a stepper. You'll learn quick."

"Thank you, but no thank you. Looks as if it could be an expensive schoolin'."

"Humph," he grumbles, and turns his attention back to the game.

Ray never acknowledges my presence and seems intent on the cards. So I wander on.

Throwing a couple of buckets overboard tied to lines, I fish up two gallons or more of water, find a spot amid the crates that's fairly hidden, and strip down and scrub myself and my clothes as best I can with a bar of lye soap I borrow from Sam. It seems I'm destined for more baths in a week than I'm accustomed to all summer. I've brought my bed roll into my hidey hole and can stay wrapped in my moth eaten blanket while I work. I rinse my duds as well as possible and spread them on the crates to dry, and curl up nearby in my bedroll, naked and as obviously so as a politician's lie. Which I've learned they do with most every opening of their pie hole.

I am still not sleeping well. Finding a loose board in one of the short walls that alternate between openings to the outside on the engine deck, I've managed to pry it loose and hide my gold coins and my Sharps. It's probably as good as consigning them to the purser and the boat's safe, as if the boat goes down, or blows all to hell, the likelihood of recovering them would be slim to none and slim done rode outta town. I'll have a better chance, if there's any warning of coming disaster, to recover them from the nearness of the loose board.

When and if I get some time to chat with Pearl I hope to talk her into sewing me a belt to wear under my clothes to conceal my rapidly diminishing riches. That is, if it's not beneath her newfound position in life. I sleep until lunch time when the clattering of the engine and gears awakens me and I find my clothes dry. I'm wrinkled, and smelling a little of lye, but dry and not smelling like the pig sty back on McTavish Farm.

I see Ian snoring away nearby and don't bother him. I'll wake him in time for supper should he not awaken himself, as it's his night on the job and having missed my meal when I took the position, don't want the same fate to befall him. Ian is blessed with the ability to sleep anytime and anywhere and I'm jealous of that.

Admiring the passing country and the bite of the huge side wheels in the water, I lean on the rail until I see Pearl and Madam Angel Allenthorpe exit her cabin and head for lunch.

I've positioned myself where they have to pass, and Madam Allenthorpe glances over and flashes me a smile. "Why, Mr. Byrne, or is it Mr. McTavish? Pearl has told me so much about you."

Pearl actually blushes and looks down.

"The bad or the good of it, ma'am?" I ask, and sidle up alongside Pearl with Madam Allenthorpe on the other side of her. I catch a whiff of something Pearl must be wearing…lavender, I think. It's a lot more pleasant than the animalistic farm-work odor I'm used to from the both of us.

The madam continues, "Why, even under the circumstance of your growing up, she says you were a fine friend and a fair master, as were your pa and ma. However, thank God that whole arrangement is coming to a close."

I nod, but offer no opinion. "So, are you ladies off to dinner?"

"We are. I'd ask you to join me but I'm sharing the captain's table and it's not my place to extend invitations."

"And you, Pearly?" I ask.

She glances up. "I be—"

But Madam quickly corrects her. "I will be, or I am, please Pearl."

"Yes, ma'am." Pearl turns back to me. "I will be at another table, and I would be pleased to have you join me."

I'm just a bit amazed. It seems Madam Allenthorpe is doing more than employing Pearl, she's teaching her manners and citified proper speech. I have to smile.

As we reach the door to the main salon, the madam gives me a nod and polite smile and is seemingly apologetic. "I wouldn't correct Pearl in front of others, however you know her past and there's no hiding from an old...old friend."

"That I do. I guess all we country folk could use some civilizing."

"Maybe, as I help Pearl, she'll pass it along." I don't tell her I know the king's English, well taught by my mother, but like most, I fall back into the patterns of those around me.

She heads for a table near a wide expanse of glass window, where Captain Isaac Johanson and a couple of other officers are already seated, and I follow Pearl to another round table that seats eight. We join six other fellows, all of whom, save one, snatch their hats off and rise as Pearl takes a seat. The one who does not is a burly sort, thick with hard-work-earned muscle, dressed in rough clothes. His full black beard, except for a streak of white down one side, extends to mid chest and he's got bushy eyebrows that almost shame the beard. His dark eyes are piercing as he glowers at Pearl, then me, then back at Pearl.

"That tops it all," he says, his voice almost a growl, dripping condescension. He rises, taking with him a full plate of food he heads for the outside door.

Pearl ignores him and turns to the others. "Thank you, gentlemen," she says, giving each of them a smile, then she shocks me a little.

"I'm Pearl Allenthorpe, may I make your acquaintance?" She can't help but cut her eyes my way as she speaks, then as quickly looks away.

When a last name was called for, all the nigras on McTavish Farm had always used that name. Now she's taken on Allenthorpe.

Each of them in turn introduces himself, giving her a polite nod.

"Reverend Sterling Hunter, recently of Princeton, New Jersey. Nice to meet you, young lady." He is sporting a black wool suit, celluloid collared white shirt and four in hand black tie, top hat—before he removed it with Pearl's arrival—with tufts of gray hair escaping, reminiscent of an etching I saw of the Union President Lincoln in Leslie's Weekly. He is about as thin of face as the Illinois politician and as creviced if not as tall. Hunter may be a reverend, but that doesn't keep him from sporting a stag gripped pocket Derringer which I make out in his waistcoat pocket. He stays seated, but the others rise as they introduce themselves.

I glance over my shoulder to see the man with the skunk striped beard staring at us through the window to our rear. He sees me watching him, and moves away.

The next fellow on the circle is a towhead, white-blond hair and darker blond stubby beard. "I am Lucas Eckland," he says, with a heavy Swedish accent, and wide smile. He, too, is armed, a heavy butt-forward revolver on his side.

"Borg, here, Elton Borg," the next man says. He, too, has an accent and merely nods as he bobs up and down in deference to a lady being seated, and returns to shoveling it in. I catch the glint of a silver handled heavy bladed knife on his side.

Both of them wear heavy shirts and trousers and I'd guess them to be lumberjacks, or such.

The last one is dusky brown, with ebony eyes and long slicked back hair to match, handsome were it not for hollow cheeks and bad teeth. He rises and gives Pearl a slight bow. "Don Enrique Aleandro Sanchez, from Cuba. I am honored to enjoy your acquaintance, Señorita." His weapon of choice, at least all I can see, is a thin bladed dagger, shoved beneath a red sash he wears at his waist.

I remind myself to come heeled the next time I report for a meal aboard the Bold Eagle, and wonder if these fellas know something I don't. I'd hate to face a gun battle with nothing but a dinner roll in hand. I've left the Sharps hidden in the wall and the Colt rolled in my bedroll below.

"And I'm Nolan Byrne," I say, and get an inquisitive look from Pearl, but she doesn't correct me, so I go on, "...and who was the rude jackass who seemed to take offense at...at us joining y'all?"

The reverend answers. "That, sir, is, I believe, one of Bloody Bill Anderson's former lieutenants, if he's who I think he is. As I recall, his name is Silas Jefferson Holland, although he did not introduce himself as such. His nickname, appropriately, is Skunk or so it has been reported, I suppose due to the white stripe in his mangy beard. The rumor is he killed a man for calling him that...a man who wasn't a fellow killer of women and children. He calls himself Wade Jefferson...but I believe that to be a nom-de-plume."

"A what?" I ask.

"A false name, taken on, I imagine, to obscure his dastardly deeds."

As he's bringing up false names, I quickly change the subject. "So, reverend, you're off to make your fortune in the gold fields?"

"No, young man, I'm off to convert the heathen to the true calling, to the one true Lord and his immaculately conceived son, our Lord Jesus Christ."

"And the rest of you fellas?" I ask, slightly interrupting the reverend as it seemed he was about to launch into a sermon.

Each of them, in turn, says, "Gold." So I guess we have something in common.

"Gentlemen," Pearl says as she rises. "I believe I will serve myself."

And the rest of us follow to a buffet table laden with food.

As we re-seat ourselves, the reverend doesn't give us a chance to pick up spoons and forks before he enters into a lengthy blessing and I hear more than one audible sigh as he finally runs out of wind.

The balance of the meal is taken up with rumors of the gold strikes in Dakota Territory, the latest news of the war, and the latest boat to blow itself to smithereens on the river.

When we finish, I offer. "Miss Pearl, would you care to stroll the deck."

"I'd be pleased," she says, and we excuse ourselves and head outside.

As we walk, I ask. "I don't imagine you'd consider sewing me up a contraption to conceal my money around my waist?"

"I'd be happy to do so. I don't imagine you'd consider teaching me how to shoot?"

I laugh. "You going to take up fighting the savages in the territories?"

"No. Madam Allenthorpe has made me the gift of a pocket pistol, and as there're a hundred men to every woman up river, I'd guess a few of them might want to take advantage."

Giving her a sincere smile, I suggest, "Not so long as I'm in shoutin' distance, Pearly."

"I believe I heard you were off to load your mules with gold, and so will not be in shoutin' distance."

I think back on our past, and remember hunting with Ray, but never remember Pearl having a weapon of any kind in hand.

"I'd be pleased to teach you to load and shoot, Miss Pearl, so long as you promise to never put your lessons to use on my hide."

She laughs, and as she does, Ray strides up behind us.

"Pearl, what you doin' walkin' with this rebel?"

I stop and turn and he almost walks into me. I shove him back with a hand, and think he's about to swing a haymaker at me, so I drop back another step out of easy reach. My voice is low, with a bit of a rumble. "Raymond, I always treated you more like a brother than a slave."

"You think that be it? You think I didn't have to done do your biddin', McTavish? I ain't no brother of your'n. I'm a free man, wit a good job, an' Pearl and I don't need the likes of you around, no way, no how, no time. You done understan'?"

"Ray McTavish," Pearl snaps, stepping between us, "this be a new time and we all is starting over. You stay away from Brad, you can't be actin' civil."

I can see the muscles in his jaw and on his neck bulge in anger, and the spittle flies as he yells at his sister. "My name now be Raymond Lincoln Freeman. And you...you done be a no good bitch, that's what you be," and he spins on his heel and stomps away.

Pearl and I take up our walk again, in stony silence for a while, until she puts an arm in mine. "It be three generations—"

"It's been," I correct her, and she smiles.

"It's been three generations of us doing exactly what the McTavish folks say to do, Brad—"

"It's Nolan, at least for a while longer."

"Nolan. You gots to give—"

"You've got to give," I correct again.

"You've got to give Ray some time to get used to how things are now."

"Ain't a lot changed yet, Pearly. At least not until this war is over."

I can see her look harden, then she looks forward over the bow. "It seems Kansas City approaches. Thank you for the walk."

And with that she turns on her heel and heads back toward the aft, where Madam Allenthorpe's stateroom is located. She stops and turns back. "I'll sew you up a belt, and you'll teach me to shoot?"

I nod, and wave, a little sadly as we were getting on fine until I brought up the war, and I suppose she believes I mean to keep the institution of slavery...and maybe I do, hell, I don't really know. It seems our past will always be a mountain between us, and maybe that's the way it has to be.

Then I take note of the fella the reverend has said was called Skunk. He's leaning on the rail just in front of the side wheel, his arms folded, glaring at Pearl as she passes. She keeps eyes forward, and he glances back at me, then leans back and spits a stream of tobacco juice overboard. We both stand and glare at each other until Pearl disappears into Madam Allenthorpe's stateroom, then he turns and leans on the rail and watches the country pass.

L. J. Martin

Chapter Eleven

I decide it's time to make sure Ian is up, so I head below. He should have an easy shift, as the rumor is the Eagle will stay tied up to a Kansas City wharf through the night.

Now if the wire—a message from Marshal County—hasn't alerted the coppers of Kansas City to the fact Ian and I are aboard the Eagle, on the morrow we'll be heading out of reach of even the telegraph.

I shove the Colt into my belt, then awaken Ian and tell him I'll soon be going ashore to get us a change of clothes, he laughs and shrugs.

"Hell, Brad—"

"Nolan for a while longer."

"Hell, Nolan, I been doing with this here shirt and I'm damn proud of these trousers."

"You ain't—" then I remember the Madam's insinuation that I don't know the kings English, and revise, "You are not smelling like a goat yet, and you soon will be."

I have yet to warn him, so I do. "You are the low man on deck, so it's you who cleans out the boiler. You'll come out smelling like the south end of a north bound skunk."

"Into the boiler," his voice is up an octave.

"Yep. Ain't much fun, but not having the dollar and a half for the day is less fun, unless you've taken up not eating."

"You done paid for our eating. Speaking of that, I could eat an ox."

"There is that," I laugh. "Scraping the mud out of that boiler is not so bad, cleans out the pores."

"I ain't surprised."

I can see the lines being thrown ashore.

"I'm off to town. Anything you got to have besides trousers."

"A pretty young lass would be fine."

"You might have to wait til' you've got some of those big paychecks from the railroad." I wave over my shoulder and head for the ladder. Then I turn back. "Keep your eye out for some nosy city law. They got the wire here and they might be hunting Braden McTavish."

He waves back.

As I make my way to the gangplank, I see Pearl and Madam Allenthorpe heading that way. The madam waves me over.

"You're going ashore?"

"Yes, ma'am."

"I will employ you for the rest of the day. Two dollars. You're armed I see. Do you know how to use that horse pistol?"

"Yes, ma'am. A year of gunsmoke behind me."

"You want the position?"

"Yes, ma'am. I've only got one chore ashore, and that's to find some ready made for a change for Ian and me."

"Then you're hired to watch over us, but we must hurry along as the stores will close in an hour or so."

Seems to me two dollars a day strolling the city streets with two beautiful women is somewhat better than one and a half for mucking out the bowel of a one hundred thirty degree boiler, so it may be hard to get the smile off my mug.

Kansas City must have a couple of thousand folks, mostly spread out along the river, but a few houses are atop a bluff that rises above a hundred feet or so. A number of fine establishments line the street nearest the river, wharves and warehouses on the river side, and general stores, saloons, barber shops, and offices of all kinds with their backs to the bluff.

The ladies head straight for a general store which brags on its goods with a large billboard painted on the side of its second story, which rises above Mack's Green Prairie Saloon—which is fine with me as I may be able to find a change of duds for Ian and me.

As we move down the boardwalk, the ladies in front, drays and wagons and a few carriages passing on the muddy street, I get a tingle down my back. Things seem very tense among the folks in Kansas City. The ladies are looked upon with both admiration and scorn, a white and black walking together and chatting as if they were sisters. Both are dressed to the nines, both carrying parasols matching well fitting gowns, both with fine button shoes with heels to add a couple of inches to their height. They pause and look in the window of a tinsmith, admiring his work, and I look across the street to a fine building that appears to have once been a stately hotel. The Union Hotel, or so says a sign above its third floor, however the sign above the front door now announces, Union Prison. And all the windows above the ground floor are boarded up. As I know the city to be the headquarters of Union General Thomas Ewing, commander of the District of the Border, I know this must house many boys from my side of the Mason Dixon. I quell the urge to return to the Eagle and fetch enough powder to blow a hole in the wall big enough to drive the Eagle through and free my fellow rebs, but it's a fool's mission.

I stay several feet behind the ladies as they move on. And keep my attention off the prison. Madam Allenthorpe stops short and Pearl moves forward a couple of feet until the madam calls out to her. "Stay close, Pearl."

Ahead of them, striding our way, is Skunk and the two Swedes, laughing and enjoying the sights. They are ten feet from the ladies before they see them, and Skunk extends an arm, stopping them.

"Damn, if it ain't the lady who sings like a crow and her black ass donkey."

Anger floods my chest. Why wait? I go ahead and pull the Colt from my belt and let it hang loosely at my side, only then does Skunk glance over and see me behind the ladies.

The towheaded Swede, Lucas Eckland, I think his name was, gives Skunk a hard look. "That's no way to talk to a lady," he says, to his credit.

"Them ain't ladies," Skunk growls.

The Swedes both straighten, then glance at each other, before Lucas exclaims, "We'll be going on along to the saloon." He's looking more than a little disgusted. I'm glad to see the two Swedes brush on by and tip their hats to the ladies as they do.

I move up between the full skirts. "Mister, you'd best be apologizing to the ladies then go on about your business."

He glances down to see my Colt, palmed and hanging at my side, but his look only hardens, and his hand is on the sidearm at his side, but still holstered. "I been shot three times, friend, and killed all three of those fellas."

"How about that," I say, and give him a smile I don't truly feel. "I guess those fellas that shot you were lousy marksmen. I, on the other hand, was raised up shooting squirrels out of the treetops with a sidearm," I lie, "and we had tall trees."

"Don't raise that," he says, his voice low and ominous, "as I can draw fast enough to shoot a lightning bolt out of the sky."

Again I smile, this time at Skunk's braggadocio. "Pretty hard to find a hole in a lightning bolt to prove you done it, however it'll be easy for the digger to find one middle of that wide ugly chest of yours."

He seems to weaken, then says, "Let me by, I gotta join my pards."

"Soon as you apologize," I say, my voice matching his low tone.

He tries to pass, pushing Pearl aside, as he mumbles, "I ain't gonna—"

He doesn't get it out before Pearl thrashes him hard upside the head with her parasol with a crack that rings up and down the street.

"You goddamned—," He spins and reaches for her.

And again, he doesn't get it out as I bat him upside the head with the Colt. His hat flies out into the mud, and he sags to his knees. She whacks him again on one side then the other, and I decide he should be on his face and backhand him with the Colt, just over the ear. There's a thump like I've hit a ripe watermelon. And my wish is granted as he pitches forward, without even putting his hands out. He's cold as a banker's heart.

"Are you alright, ladies?" I ask as a crowd is beginning to gather.

"Let's move along," Madam Allenthorpe says, and I can't help but note the smile on her face. As we head on down to the Mercantile, she turns to me. "Two dollars well spent, Mr. Byrne."

"The day is not over, Madam," I say, with some skepticism.

The ladies enter the mercantile and I go straight to a display that announces men's canvas clothing and am surprised at the selection as ready-mades are a fairly new thing here in the west. In no time I've selected a pair of canvas trousers to fit both Ian and me, two pairs of flap-back long johns, and two heavy flannel shirts that I hope will be fitting for Dakota winters. As usual the sleeves are long enough for a knuckle dragger—as all are made to fit anyone—so I buy four garters to hold them to the proper length.

The counterman is wrapping them when I turn to see two fellas with copper badges standing at the entry, scanning the room. Seeing I'm the only man in the place, they walk my way.

"You the fella clubbed that bearded hooligan down outside?" the one in front asks.

"Yes, sir," I say, "he was a scoundrel, an ex-killer from the ranks of Bloody Bill Anderson, and he had a hand on his weapon. That prison across the way would be a fine place for the likes of him." I'm doing my best not to sound like a butternut man.

"And you know that how?" he asks and I see Madam Allenthorpe and Pearl hurrying across the room.

"Hold on there, gentlemen," the madam calls out, and the fellas turn and snatch their hats off as she approaches. "This young man is in my employ just for occasions such as this. That brute outside laid his hands on my lady's maid. I don't imagine that kind of conduct is approved of here in Kansas City?"

"No, ma'am. That fella is at the sawbones getting a few stitches in his noggin, and had to be carried there, but it sounds well deserved."

"What's your name, sir?" she asks.

"Dan Haycox, City Marshal, ma'am."

"Well, Mr. Haycox, we appreciate and thank you for your following up on his attack. I'd suggest you hold him for awhile—"

"He's on the steamboat Bold Eagle. He'll be leaving town with the dawn."

"As are we, so I'd appreciate your holding him."

"We'll fine him a dollar for disturbing the peace, ma'am, but we'll be happy to see him go. Seems like your man here can handle him just fine, should the occasion arise again."

The madam's tone hardens. "He should not have to handle him, should you do your job."

"I'm doing just that, ma'am, seeing he gets out of our town as quickly as possible, and it seems that's aboard the Bold Eagle."

"Humph," she manages. "Thank you, none the less," and spins on her heel and goes back to shopping.

Marshal Haycox turns back to me. "What's your name, for my report?"

"Nolan, Nolan Byrne, come down this way from Cairo, Illinois." I'm beginning to be able to lie a little too easily for my taste. My sweet mama would not approve.

"Well, Mr. Byrne, I presume you're on the Bold Eagle as well."

"Yes, sir."

"Then make sure you're aboard and paddle on up river with her."

"Yes, sir."

I turn back to the counterman and hand him a twenty dollar gold piece. He gives me my twelve dollars and twenty-five cents change, in silver as I've requested, and I head across the room where the ladies are working their way through bolts of cloth. Soon they've carried a pair of them to the counter man who cuts yardage and we're ready to head out.

"Mr. Byrne," the madam says as we exit onto the boardwalk, "I noticed a saddler down the block. I presume he does all sorts of leather work. I'd be happy to purchase a contraption for your firearm so you don't have to carry it stuffed in your belt. Something like that Skunk fella had on."

"Yes, ma'am. A holster I presume you mean."

"Yes, a holster. Then we should find a restaurant and I'll treat us all to something besides boat food."

"As you wish, ma'am," I say. A holster and belt is at least a dollar, and I hope she doesn't mean to take it out of my pay, but either way, I'll be in need of one.

With a fine new brown leather two-belt holster and matching belt with a cap and ball box, I'm following the ladies into O'Hoolihan's Chop House.

I see no more of Skunk nor the Swedes and deposit the ladies back on board and to their rooms just after darkness falls.

She does not take the cost of the belt and holster from my two dollars pay, so I'm richer by far than when I went ashore.

But I've made a very bad enemy. I can only hope he's too injured to find his way back onboard the Bold Eagle.

We don't want her to be known as the Bloody Eagle.

Deciding I could use a bit of Who Hit John to clear my throat, I head for the gentlemen's lounge. And as soon as I lean on the walnut bar, I glance over, and the two owlhoots glaring at me look to be anything but gentlemen.

There are three tables full of men in addition to those at the bar, but they are paying no attention to anything other than their drinks or their card games. The only one I recognize is the gambler, Chance O'Galliger. He's watching me with some interest, I presume, as he thinks me an easy mark for his talents. I give him a nod and he touches his hat brim in return, giving me a smile and flashing that gold tooth.

Then I go back to being glared at from the end of the bar. Wouldn't do to seem anything but at ease, and ready to fight should need be.

L. J. Martin

Chapter Twelve

It's easy to recognize the cockeyed one, Proust I think his name was. The other I remember calling Horse Gas so his name is something like that. And if they aren't trouble enough, while I'm doing my best not to be the first one to break the stare, up walks a big fully bearded man with a newly knotted head, Silas Jefferson Holland, known as Skunk to those brave enough to call him that.

I can't say I'm not surprised to see the drovers as the last I'd heard they were headed out to Dakota, but like me, I presume they decided that skimming across the water beats pounding a dusty trail. I wish they'd found another boat, but as luck would have it...

It seems I've made a half dozen enemies since leaving prison, and half of them are all in one place, ten paces from my current location. I'm at the far end of the bar, and can't hear what they're saying, but the two Dakota drovers are laughing in a derogatory manner, and Skunk looks as if his nose is in the rear end of his namesake. Between them and me is Reverend Sterling Hunter and the two Swedish men, Borg and Eckland, as I recall. I do remember them seeming to be disgusted with Skunk's actions on the boardwalk in town, so I hope they have no dog in what may be a coming fight.

I knock back a couple of fingers of Black Widow whiskey and call for another, watching the three no accounts out of the corner of my eye. As the bartender is pouring, the biggest of the three, Horse Gas, moves away from the bar and rounds the Reverend and the two Swedish fellas and stops just behind my right shoulder. He leans close enough that I can smell his kerosene breath.

"How you doing there, shoat. McMouth, was it."

I turn slowly and give him a tight smile. "Byrne, actually...and you're Horse Gas, right?"

He's a half head taller than me and at least forty, maybe fifty, pounds heavier. "You can call me that until you don't have any teeth to whistle through. Where's your big ugly friend?"

"Ian? Probably just outside with his new scattergun ready to cut you in half."

He laughs. "Probably in the sack snoring away. Don't suppose you'd like to step outside and see how you do when your friend is not behind me like some sneak thief."

I give him a wide grin. "I believe I'll stay right here and scorch my tonsils with a little more of this rotgut."

"A yellow stripe on your back like was on your trousers—"

The reverend has been cocking an ear our way, and turns. "Is there some kind of problem here?"

Gauss laughs. "He ain't much of a problem. Or he will not be when I get through wit him."

And he's not the only one who's been watching what's transpired. Chance O'Galliger rises from his game, his cards folded, and strides over behind Gauss. "Hey, Prussian, you got some problem with my young friend?"

Horst turns and faces the gambler, who's as tall but not nearly so thick. "What business be it of yours?" he asks, and he's not smiling.

O'Galliger shrugs, then says, "It could be the business of Mr. Marston and Mr. Knox."

"Who de hell is dat?" Horst asks, falling back into a fairly thick accent.

I don't know where it came from, but O'Galliger raises his hand and he's palmed a little belly gun, a two barrel affair. "This is both Mr. Marston and Mr. Knox, a Marston-Knox in thirty two caliber, just enough to settle almost any argument. And Mr. Marston and Mr. Knox suggest you retire to your end of the bar."

"Humph," Horst manages, but he backs away, then turns and retreats to his friends.

"Obliged," I say to O'Galliger. "I'd like to buy you a drink."

"It would be my pleasure, Mister...?"

"Nolan Byrne, at your service, Mr. O'Galliger."

"You remembered. A good trait in a young man coming up in the world."

"Whiskey?" I ask, turning to the bartender.

"Gin, if you please," he says, and I order, then remember the reverend and put a hand on his shoulder. "And you, sir?"

"I'm fine, young man. I don't partake in more than one or two and I've had those. I'll bid you goodnight. Watch your back. They seem to be chummy with that redleg."

"I'll do just that, reverend. Thanks for your concern." With that, he excuses himself. Actually I watched him down three, and have no idea what transpired before I arrived.

128

"You ready to try your luck at a little poker or faro?" O'Galliger asks.

I have to laugh and shake my head. "I appreciate your stepping in to my discussion with Gauss, but I'm no gambler." Then I wonder, "I don't suppose you'd be interested in teaching me."

"Sure enough. You can learn as we play."

Again I shake my head. "No sir, I'd be happy to pay you to teach me. What time do you rise in the morning?"

"My nights are long, so mid-morning."

"How about I meet you just after lunch and pay you a half dollar for a couple of hours of lessons?"

He laughs. "A Baton Rouge gambler would be a fool to teach all his tricks."

"Not all, but just enough so I know the game and more so know if I'm being cheated."

He's silent for a moment. "You're a nice enough young fella. Remind me of myself not too many years ago. Join me at lunch, then we'll see if you've got any talent."

We talk about our backgrounds, him being a Southern man from Baton Rouge and all, while sipping our drinks, then he decides he'd better get back to his game. He asks me, "Are you about ready to leave?"

"I am."

"Then do so while I can make sure those soggers don't follow you with evil intent."

"I can take care of myself."

"Against one, maybe even two, but three?"

"See you tomorrow," I say, and accept his offer.

I give Ian a wave as I pass him on the engine deck on my way to my bedroll, as he glances up from feeding four foot lengths into the fire box, and we've got another day behind us.

A few enemies, but another day.

The next three days are uneventful, staying clear of Skunk, Horst, and the other German, who's name I've asked about and who turns out to be Cornel Proust. It seems the German boys loaded a prize bull aboard at Kansas City, a white face bull I'm told is named Brutus. And rightfully so, as he is a brute. I should have seen the Dakota drovers as the bull is stabled right up against my mules, but it seems we were passing like proverbial side wheelers in the night.

Captain Johanson has taken to laying up on shore every night, as there hasn't been much of a moon and the river is particularly full of logs and probably snags. So we're able to graze the stock, whichever of us is not working. We've crossed into Nebraska and tomorrow we lay up at Omaha, the Nebraska territorial capitol, where Ian may be leaving us. I hope not as he's like an older brother to me. He's been spending more and more time following Madam Allenthorpe around like a puppy. She seems amused by him, but I fear for his sake that's the extent of her interest. Pearl has delivered my money belt, made of some cotton material with a tie in the back and two wide, tightly buttoned, pockets in front. And as promised, I've given her shooting lessons off the bow of the boat.

We've dodged a hundred snags, a number of floating obstacles and flanked more than one obstruction, called rafts by the river men, but seem to me to actually be islands covered with timber, trees, and driftwood. Some of them a half mile long. We see fewer and fewer boats as we go farther upriver. Where we were passing other side wheelers, keelboats, mackinaws and lots of smaller flatboats and dugouts, the latter all making way downriver as they're built, floated, then dismantled when reaching their destination. Now it's just a few of the latter smaller vessels.

A notice has been posted on a bulletin board just outside the main salon door. There's to be a concert this evening as a special treat. I'm not surprised to see that Madam Allenthorpe will treat us to several favorites, but am surprised to see she'll be accompanied by her protégé, or so the posting says, Miss Pearl Allenthorpe. Pearly, a songstress? I've heard her sing many an old Southern spiritual, but as a field hand not as an entertainer. The girl seems a long way from the cotton fields of McTavish Farm. Truthfully, I'm pleased for her. I hope she doesn't make a fool of herself. Of course with a hundred or more men in the crowd, they'd probably be pleased if she just stood there and batted her big brown eyes.

It's Ian's night on the fireboxes as Captain Johanson has decided there's enough moonlight, and the river seems less congested, so we can move on upriver to Omaha.

He'll miss the concert. But I won't.

Supper is the last of the oysters, a couple of dozen sage hens killed last evening while we were moored, and a side of pork roasted whole. I'm going to miss this boat and her meals when I'm making my own way somewhere in the Dakota wilds.

After supper the main salon is cleared and tables stacked aside, chairs lined up like a theater, and doors opened to the men's smoking room and bar. The piano forte is carried in and to my great surprise, Pearly takes the seat at the keys. She's only playing cords, but Madam Allenthorpe seems pleased as she takes up the Battle Hymn of the Republic. She laughs as soon as she's finished as she's overwhelmed with requests for Dixie, and complies.

With that out of the way, she goes on to Tarry With Me, Go Down Moses, then Chance O'Galliger takes over the piano forte and Pearl joins in a duet of Maryland My Maryland...and I'm astounded as the crowd stands and gives them a long and exuberant ovation. It seems Pearl's long experience singing while she and her family worked the fields may pay off for her, particularly now that it appears she's getting some training by a true professional. The fact is, she sings like an angel, and nearly as well as Angel Allenthorpe.

By the numbers cheering either Dixie or the Battle Hymn in the raucous crowd, it's plain to me that there are more Southern boys than bluebellys onboard. And I can't help but make note of the fact they are applauding and cheering a black woman. Maybe we are west of the war, and slavery, and it's all rapidly disappearing in our wake.

Listening to her has given me pause to think back on my family and the happy life we had on the river...and on our relationship with Emanuel, Pearl's daddy, and his offspring. That happiness, and the resultant furor of the war, is still confusing to me. I hope it's behind us. I hope I can become friends with Ray, Pearl's brother, who I grew up beside. I truly hope we all prosper, although it seems Ray hopes I rot in hell. I've only seen him across the deck a few times, and he's never acknowledged my existence. I guess I understand that, but it's hard to swallow, but maybe even harder for Ray.

I've been circling the Germans and Skunk every day, avoiding a confrontation with them, but if we make this whole trip without tangling I'll be surprised. They don't seem to be the type to let things drop. After as much lead as whistled around me during the war, I'd hate to bleed out while on my way to make my mark on the world...but I'll run from no man. My daddy oft times told me that a man shot in the back will have a hard time making his way through the pearly gates. Christ faced his fate head on, and Daddy said any real man would follow his great example.

I have, however, made two new friends. The two Swedes are good fellas and I've decided not to hold their prior association with Skunk against them. Sometimes you get taken in by folks and they didn't lay down with that dog long enough to get fleas.

Omaha seems a fine city, at least from the view of the river. On a bluff overlooking all is a three story affair with a fine bell tower that I'm told is the Territory Capitol building.

Ian says his goodbyes to all of us, and I swear I see a tear in the big man's eye. I'm sad to see him walk down the gangway, waving over his shoulder.

Madam Allenthorpe again employs me to be their escort and I'm pleased to do so. This time I'm well heeled with a fine holster for my Colt. It's my night on the boilers and they haven't been mucked for three days, as we continued to run the river with a full moon, so I'm sure I'm in for a hell of an evening. I should be sleeping, but can't turn down the two dollars.

It's mid-morning by the time the ladies are ready to take on the mercantile and general stores of Omaha and noon by the time we've visited two mercantiles, a general store, and an apothecary. My stomach is flapping by the time Madam Allenthorpe suggests we go to the Grand Boston Hotel and enjoy some lunch.

It's a little higher up the bluff and climbing there I suddenly realize that for the last few miles along the river we've seen no trees. There are more trees planted in Omaha than I've seen for miles on the river. And from my vantage point in the restaurant of the Grand Boston, I see no trees on the landscape in any direction. I hope there are some trees in Dakota and Washington Territory.

What I have seen is a few Indians, for the first time. I don't know what tribe these might represent, and it's only been a couple of braves and a handful of women and children, and them on the hillside three hundred yards from the hotel where they have teepees that seem to be wrapped in buffalo hides. Obviously they are not hostiles, as they are ignored by the populace.

We have a fine meal of Sand Hill Crane with all the trimmings and are returning to the boat when I ask to be given a few minutes in the Mercantile. I noticed a second-hand W. J. King of London coach gun there. Its stock and fore grip are scarred and she shows some wear but there are no dents in her metal and she seems to function well—both hammers are tight and she breaks and closes without a waiver. So I fork out the four dollars for it and another dollar for two pounds each of bird shot and buckshot. I have plenty of powder and can use almost anything for wadding. She has short eighteen inch barrels and I imagine she will cut a wide swath at a dozen paces or so. Now, with my Sharps for long work, my Colt for backup, and the King should I have to clear a wide path, I should be trouble on the hoof.

There's nothing like a shotgun, as I learned while in the doorway of my own barn, should you be faced with bad odds. And God only knows what lies before us.

With Indians in front of us and enemies behind, we will be well served to be well armed.

And it seems I'll need to be.

But I won't be without friends, as I'm surprised to see Ian waiting at the top of the gangway upon our return.

"No job?" I ask.

"Good job, but if 'n I gotta be swinging a hammer I might as well be swinging a pick and trying to get rich alongside you."

"Glad you're back, pard." I don't tell him I was dreading a long lonely trail without a friend now as close as a brother.

Again, I swear there's the hint of a tear in the old boy's eye.

L. J. Martin

West of the War

Chapter Thirteen

I've made friends with Alexander Strobridge, a merchant who has crate after crate of goods on board. Some of the powder is his as well as shot and two cases of firearms, flour, salt, sugar, spices, shoes, pie fruit preserved in bottles, wine, brandy, iron hatchets, shovels, picks, and only he knows what else.

Alex is a tall slender fella with good manners and a quiet but determined way. I notice his crates are marked as his, with a return address in St. Louis, but addressed to other merchants in Helena, Great Falls, Deer Lodge, Virginia City, and Bannack. He's a wealth of knowledge and I badger him with questions until his eyes roll back in his head. He's been to all those places and more, and I want to learn all I can.

But he's no gambler.

Chance has been teaching me daily and seems to enjoy doing so even more than the four bits I pay him, and although

I'm no expert, he's pleased with my progress. And he has shown me a few things that he says he wouldn't show the average student. He's taught me how to palm and change a pair of dice from honest to loaded...not that I would, but it pays to know what others can do. He has a pair of dice that will roll a seven four out of five times.

In addition to poker and faro, Chance has taught me Whist and Cribbage...and I've taken eleven dollars from Alex as I've practiced my cards. It's a small fortune for the average working man. Alex laughs it off as if it's nothing.

When and if I get to where he owes me fifteen dollars, I plan to trade him for supplies.

I take an early supper as it's my night to work, and enjoy it with Chance, Alex and the two Swedes, then excuse myself as they head for the Gentlemen's smoking room and a tumbler of brandy.

It's getting dark more and more early, and I'm happy light is coming from more than one stateroom as I head abaft to a midship's ladder.

But I don't quite reach it as Skunk steps from a doorway, blocking my path, close enough his bad breath burns my eyes.

"I hear you done been winning a little money playing cards," he snarls.

I try to brush past him but he puts a hand in the middle of my chest. I start to turn and see the two German boys closing fast behind me.

It seems I'm in a bit of trouble, and my Colt and other weapons are below.

So I turn back to Skunk, who to my great consternation, has filled his hand with a knife that catches the light from a nearby stateroom. It's large enough to chop wood.

"How about you share a little of that new wealth?" Skunk asks, and he and the two now behind me laugh. "In fact, everything you got in your pocket."

"How about you put that pig sticker away before I shove it where the sun don't shine," I bluster, but it's just that.

"I tink we turn him upside down and shake it outta him," Horst says, with a chuckle, now only a pace behind us, "den we drop him overboard and see how he swim."

I turn to the side, and shoot a booted foot to the personals of Horst Gas, who's knocked back, but I spin back to meet the butt of Skunk's knife as it slams into my forehead. I collapse to my knees, my head swimming, then to my hands on all fours as one of the Germans shoves me to my face with a boot in my butt.

I clamor to my knees so I can get up, and am surprised to see Skunk rise in the air as if suspended from the ship's hoist, then realize Ian has come up the ladder and is lifting the big man overhead as if he were a sack of oats. Ian takes two steps, and Skunk flies overboard. I hear him hit the water with a scream.

Gauss is standing holding his personals, bug eyed, looking as if he'd just swallowed a big toad frog. His partner, Proust, is standing, shocked that the big Skunk has flown overboard. I'm still on my knees as Ian squares away with the German with the crooked eye, Horst Gauss. That terrible right hand of Ian's takes Gauss upside the head and the thump of hitting him is only exceeded by the crack of Horst's head hitting the wooden deck.

Proust comes to his senses and leaps forward, suddenly with a blade in hand. When he squares away with Ian he has his back to me, and I kick him behind the knee, which folds under him. He lands on his back and Ian is all over him, stomping away, first on his knife filled hand, crushing his knuckles and then when released he kicks the knife overboard. Proust rolls to his stomach and gets up with his legs under him and his hands still on the deck, and I kick him again, square in the butt propelling him forward. Ian helps him along, and he too flies out into the darkness, screaming then hitting the water.

I'm on my feet and reach down and grab Horst by both ankles as Ian grabs him by the wrists.

"One, two, three," Ian says, as we swing the big German and sling him after his lowlife friends.

"Damn," Ian says, "if we ain't shed of about six hundred pounds or more of useless cargo."

"Damn if we ain't," I say, and we both laugh.

We turn and are staring at Captain Isaac Johanson and his purser Felix Calderon. Johanson looks as serious as a losing Union general and Calderon's mouth is hanging open, even wider than his eyes.

"I don't believe I just saw that," Johanson snaps.

"Damned if you didn't," Ian says. "I'd a throwed them farther had I had my supper. But I'm a tad weak at the moment."

"Them? You mean you threw somebody other than that Gauss…"

"Yes, sir," Ian says, seeming proud as a peacock.

"Who?"

"His pardner and that Skunk fella, the one with the white stripe in his beard."

"You know I can't turn this boat around?" Johanson says, now a little incredulous.

"Hell, Cap'n, you'd just have to turn your salon into a court room and then hang 'em, did you fish 'em out."

"And why would I have to do that?"

"They tried to rob young Bra… Young Nolan here, and two of 'em had knifes long enough to skewer a buffalo for roastin'."

I point to the growing knot on my forehead from the butt of the knife, and rub it a little deciding it'll be about half a hen's egg soon.

The fat purser finally gets his wits about him and speaks up. "The hell you say. You two picked up an unconscious man and flung him overboard...that's what I saw."

"Well, friend," Ian says, bending to look the much shorter man right in the eye, "you didn't see near all of it, now did you?"

"I saw what I saw. I'm placing you both under arrest."

Ian laughs aloud. "Sorry, ol' chum, but you ain't arresting me or nobody for defending themselves from a couple of no account back-stabbin' robbers."

"I'm purser—"

Johanson places a hand on the fat man's shoulder. "Hold on, Felix," he cautions. "These fellas aren't going anywhere. We'll take it up with the law in Sioux City or Yankton."

"Captain, they may have murdered three men..."

"May have. And I'm judge and jury aboard this boat. Right now all we have is their word against three fellas trying to paddle to shore. Maybe drowned, maybe not. I suggest you interview everyone on board and see if you have any testimony to the contrary about what they claim. Until you do, these two are confined to the boat." Johanson turns to us. "You two understand?"

I speak up for the first time. "We've gotta take the stock off to graze when possible."

"So long as we're nowhere near a town, you can take them off...one at a time. One of you stays on board at all times."

Both of us shrug.

"I got to get to work," I say, and with the captain's nod, head for the ladder with Ian close behind.

He laughs again as we descend the ladder, then catches up with me as I head to where Sam is already working.

"Hey, do you suppose them no goods can swim?" Ian asks.

"Hope not," I say.

"What do you think some law dog in Sioux City or Yankton will have to say?"

"I think he'll have to believe what we say, less'n somebody says something different."

"Then we're fine, as anyone aboard who saw the affair will back us up, and them what won't are likely being chomped on by some of them big bottom dwelling muddy Mo catfish as we speak."

"From your lips, friend Ian, to God's ears." I laugh, then get serious. "I have yet to thank you."

"What friends is for, young Brad. What friends is for…"

"I guess it can be Brad again, and I thank you again."

He just laughs and walks back to the ladder. "Don't get cooked in them boilers." And he's gone.

And so are half the enemies I have in the world…or at least I hope they're gone.

In the night I hear the big bull the Germans have aboard starting to bawl. I guess he didn't get his portion of hay, and under the circumstances, I'm not surprised.

I see Ian climb from his bedroll and purloin a couple of forkfuls of hay and throw them to the big monster, and he quiets. I guess the bull, Brutus, has lost his providers and wonders what will happen to him.

Sam, the second engineer, is growing to be a real friend. He's got a quiet and subtle sense of humor and more and more I'm sorry I slighted him when Dag Eriksen, the first engineer, said I was to work for him.

"We got four or five more easy days," Sam says to me as we stoke the firebox.

142

I laugh. "These been easy days?"

"Yep, compared to what comes. After we get past Yankton, then Captain Johanson really gots to watch the river. She gets shallow in places and even as high as she's running, we may have to grasshopper."

"Grasshopper?" I ask.

"Yep, we put out timbers fixed to the hull, drive them in the sand, then winch the upper end forward, lifting de boat a mite and movin' her a few feet at a time. It ain't easy, but it moves us over de low spots."

I've told him about chucking the Germans and Skunk overboard so he's not too shocked when I say, "That is if Ian and I ain't warming the cold iron bench of some jail in Yankton or Sioux City."

This time it's Sam's turn to laugh. "Hell, boy, you and dat Ian is good hands. The Captain won't be turning you over to no law. Good hands is hard to come by, and harder and harder the more we get upstream. Besides, he done come into ownership of a fine bull. He be happy to see them boys go over de rail."

And he's right, as Johanson barely stops at Sioux City, only to take on wood and supplies, then again three days later at Yankton.

Just north of Yankton, in the middle of the day, I'm awakened by a mad ringing of the ships engine room signal bell. I jump up and go amidships to see what's up, and find Dag Eriksen madly directing the day crew to pour the wood to her.

"What's up?" I yell at him.

"The Emilie, she's trying to pass us. Johanson will be like a crazy man if another boat passes, and God forbid, beats us to Benton City."

I walk to the rail and see we have more than a half mile of straight river ahead, and abeam and slightly behind, the larger Emilie, half again as big as the Eagle, is gaining on us and will surely pass.

Moving back to the fire boxes, I again yell to Dag. "Can I help?"

"We can only feed her so much. We got a hundred eighty pounds now…"

"Jesus," I manage, as I know he's thirty pounds into the red.

"Ain't that dangerous as hell?"

"Don't worry, you'll never know what hit you."

"So back off."

"I ain't Captain, Brad. He calls for it, we give it to him."

I've informed all who know me by name that I prefer Brad to Nolan, so most have gone to calling me by my proper name. Deciding it's a good time to be as far from the boilers as I can get, I head for the ladder.

As I'm ascending, I hear cheers ring out from all over the boat, and again move to the rail. The Emilie is at a dead stop, one of her chimneys is pitched forward at an odd angle, and men and passengers are scrambling all over her decks.

"What happened," I yell at a deck hand nearby.

"She grounded. We got her now."

I nod and give him a smile. But what I'm really smiling about is the fact Dag and the boys below can ease up on the fireboxes, and the boilers, so we don't all end up being blown or steamed to death.

We've been in Dakota Territory since we passed Yankton, and after we load wood at Fort Randle it will be four days to the next settlement. The country is still devoid of trees, except in a few deep washes. We did see more than one Indian village during the last week, and yesterday eight buffalo swam the river. I was not too pleased to watch as a couple of passengers shot them just for sport from the rails, and watching two head float down the river and go to waste.

I've heard they are fine eating and will shoot them myself, but only if I can take a knife to them and butcher them out. Waste not, want not, my ma and pa taught me.

It's too more days of easy going, then I'm tossed head over heels on the deck, ending up against the rail, as the boat had shuddered to a sudden stop. I can hear Captain Johanson screaming orders from the wheelhouse high above, and am glad it's not me he's taking his wrath out upon.

We're grounded.

West of the War

Chapter Fourteen

It doesn't take me long to figure out why Johanson didn't complain more about the low fare I paid for my stock, as I'm not requested, but ordered to get them ashore.

We don't have proper harness, but in no time the deck hands have rigged six-inch-wide leather straps to circle the chests of the mares and mules with over-neck straps to hold them in place, and we have eight powerful animals ready to pull. The three saddle horses are offloaded, as is the bull, but just to get their weight off. That, and every able bodied man on board is ashore and on a tow line.

The deck hands have rigged the grasshopper timbers, and soon we're ashore pulling while the deck hands are working both the forward and aft capstans. It takes us until dark to move the boat fifty feet over the sand bar, and it's said we have another hundred feet to go before she floats free.

My stock is now earning their keep.

Everyone is spent, and I'm sure all are ready to head for their bunks as soon as we finish supper, but we're surprised when Captain Johanson announces over dessert that we'll all be pitching in to offload cargo until he says different.

He's not the most popular man on board and continues to snap orders until the boat rings eight bells and it's midnight. Only then are we allowed to seek rest and respite.

And then only until dawn.

With daylight, after a quick breakfast, I'm put to hauling cargo upriver, but on shore, using planks for sleds. I get very familiar with hundreds of crates of all kinds of goods, as my friend Alex and my partner Ian and I load and unload crate after crate. As Alex knows what might be fragile and what is not, he directs the loading and unloading of every box, crate, carton, and barrel.

It's noon when the Captain orders the animals put back in harness.

Even with less weight and more freeboard, the boat is still hard to move.

The capstans, normally used to up-haul the anchors, are operated on both the passenger deck and the lower engine deck with a thru-hull allowing eight men to put their weight into it if necessary. Four men on each deck put their all into it and a smaller donkey steam engine is moved from one rail to the other, and its geared pulleys put tremendous strain on cables, working the grasshopper timbers.

As I'm encouraging my mules and mares to pull, I hear shouting from the deck and see three deckhands running forward to the donkey steam engine. It's putting tremendous strain on a cable on the shore side of the boat, and I watch in wonder as the cable stretches so taut that it doesn't even shiver.

"More, more," a deck hand yells, and I see Ray and another man carrying arm loads of smaller lengths of wood to feed the firebox of the little donkey.

Then a crack as loud as lightening striking rings out, and the cable parts and becomes a whip, and as if in slow motion, I see it pass by, then realize, it's passed thru, Raymond. Not his torso, but his left leg. He pitches backward, but his left leg and trouser, from just below the knee, continues forward with the last two feet of the cable, and flies overboard.

Knocked skidding across the deck, Ray quickly tries to rise, trying to get a leg under himself…a leg that's no longer there.

I run to the shore and yell, "Get a tourniquet on that man. Stop the bleeding." I've seen many a limb shot or cut from a man during the war, and know you can bleed out in short order. But the others merely stand and stare. "Goddamnit," I scream. "Get a belt around that stump."

Finally, another black deck hand jumps forward, pulling his belt as he does, and in seconds more, has it pulled tight around the stump.

I can't get back on board until we clear the sand bar and get the gangplank back in place to reload the cargo. But in moments Johanson is shouting for everyone to go back to work, and I see Pearl working over her brother.

As many as we have on board, I don't remember seeing or meeting one claiming to be a doctor.

I'm sure there are many soldiers heading west, more from the South than the North, and many of them, like me, have had their stomach turned by seeing men have limbs removed.

Still, I may have seen as many or more than most.

I take a deep breath, dive in the water, and swim twenty yards to the Eagle. With almost every stroke I'm yelling at a couple of fellows to help me aboard as there's three feet of freeboard. They do and I run dripping to where Pearl is tending to her brother.

Kneeling beside her, I turn to the growing crowd. "Is there a doctor aboard?" I ask, and get no reply, only passengers or deck hands looking from one to another. "Damn it," I yell out, "a doctor?"

Captain Johanson strides up and glares at Ray, who's on his back and taken to a semi-conscious state due to his injury.

"What the hell happened here?" Johanson demands.

"Your cable parted and took his leg?" I admit my tone is condemning, but I want to blame someone.

His tone's not sympathetic. "Well, get him out of the way. We've got a boat to move."

Had I not been taken with the emergency, had he not intervened when the purser wanted to arrest Ian and me, I would have risen and tried to knock him overboard. But rather I see Madam Allenthorpe approach and beseech her. "Can we use your stateroom for a hospital...until we get him best we can get him?"

She looks down at Ray and I think she's going to be sick. With a hand covering her mouth, I hear, "He's bleeding badly. He'll need to be cauterized. Take him below to the engine deck."

And I realize she's right. There are tools below I'll need if we're to save the leg and to try and close the terrible wound.

Sam, Wheezy, and Alabama, who work with me on the night crew, are among those sightseeing Ray's misfortune, and I yell at Sam, "Y'all give me a hand. We're taking him below."

"Don't hurt him more," Pearl begs as we pick him up.

The men's smoking room bartender is also watching, and I yell to him as we carry Ray past, "Bring me down a bottle of whiskey or rum, a full bottle."

"Who's paying?" he yells back.

I grit my teeth, then snap, "You, you'll pay with your damn teeth you don't beat us to the engine deck."

He pales, turns, and has gone. I yell at Pearl, "Go on ahead and fetch my bedroll and get it rolled out near one of the fireboxes."

And she runs ahead.

The bartender has beaten us below and stands with a full quart of rum in hand.

We get Ray placed on his back, on the deck, near a firebox. I hear him mumbling something and bend to get my ear near. He's saying the Lord's prayer, and I'm glad, as we can use all the help we can muster.

On a nearby wall of the engine shed hang a number of tools. I glance over then ask Sam, "Get me an adze and get it in the fire and hot as you can without burning the handle. Red hot if you can."

A few of the sightseers have followed us down, and as I use my folding knife to cut away another few inches of Rays pants, I again yell. "Anybody find a doctor?"

I get nothing but them looking back and forth between themselves, and shrugs.

Waving the bartender over, I pop the cork on the rum, then turn to Pearl who's nearby, chewing on a knuckle. "Get him propped up, Pearly. We need to get a half bottle of this rotgut down him."

She goes to her knees, as Sam and Alabama raise his upper body, then she slips behind him and holds him upright at a forty-five-degree angle.

"Ray," I yell at him, "get this down." And I feed the bottle to him, it's running out the corners of his mouth, and he goes wide eyed. But he's swallowing, then coughing and spitting, then swallowing again. The bottle is three quarters gone, a good portion spilled, by the time Sam comes my way.

Again I look at the growing crowd. "Still no damn doc?" I ask, and again get no answer.

As I've seen done many times, I take my pocket knife and run it about the stub of remaining bone, which is about six inches below Ray's knee. He screams, and Pearl follows suit.

"Get him something to bite down on," I tell Sam, who is beside Ray with a piece of limb he's broken off a log that's ready to feed the fire.

Ray clamps down on the piece of limb and glares at me, the whites of his eyes showing.

He spits out the limb, and manages to yell at me, "You som'bitch, you rotten..." But Sam jambs the limb back in his mouth.

"I need a saw," I again beseech Sam, who quickly hands me a small crosscut. "Hold him down," I instruct Sam, Alabama and Wheezy, who move Pearl back and put their full weight on Ray, one on each shoulder, one on his legs.

"Bring me a log," I yell at a bystander and in seconds have one to prop the leg up on. "Hold him," I yell and they do. I've got to shorten the bone so flesh will close over it.

It doesn't take too many strokes of the saw to trim the bone back an inch and a half, so I can pull back the remaining meat and skin to cover it.

"Give me that hot adze," I instruct the helper from the crowd, and he does. It's glowing hot and I press it to the bone end. Ray screams again, then goes silent. Thank God, he's passed out.

I fold the meat and skin over the bone, then instruct Sam, who's now able to let go of the unconscious man. "Rip your shirt in strips, Sam. About two inches wide." And he does. Again I bring the iron to the stump and it sears meat. The odor is not pleasant, and half the crowd fades away, but the bleeding is reduced to weeping. I catch a glance of Pearl out of the corner of my eye as she runs for the rail and retches overboard. The smell would gag a maggot, but I've smelled it often and was prepared for the assault on my olfactory.

But I can't let her suffer for long, and yell, "Pearl, get your sewing basket. We need to close this stump."

She looks sick but hurries to the ladder and in moments is back. I've asked Sam to fetch some heavy thread used to close broken bags among the cargo, and tell Pearl to dig out her needle with the largest eye, and soon she's at work. A curved needle as is used on sails on the river boats that utilize them would be better, but there is none, so we make do.

I wrap the stump, running long pieces of Sam's shirt over it and up the sides of his legs, then when I have a half dozen in place, wrap more around and around holding those in place.

To my surprise, Madam Allenthorpe is leaning over my shoulder. "I've arranged a cabin for him...for Pearl's brother...only two down from my stateroom."

I know all the cabins are full of passengers, so I ask, "How did you manage?"

"I paid a couple of young men to double up. Pearl can stay with him until he's well."

Or dead, I think, but don't say. I've seen way too many of these wounds go green and the man die hot, hard, and praying for salvation. "Kind of you, Madam," I say. Then I turn to my helpers. "Let's get him up there." And in five minutes Ray is in a bed wide enough for two and Pearl is in a chair at his side.

I walk out to the deck, suddenly my own stomach roils and I feel like losing my breakfast, but don't. I walk to the rail and take several deep breaths of cold air.

Turning back, I'm face to face with Captain Johanson, who snaps at me. "Get back to those damn critters of yours. We still have to get over this sand bar."

I clamp my jaw and make a promise to beat this man to a pulp as soon as I'm ashore and when he no longer is lord and master.

But now I head to the rail, dive overboard, and swim back to shore and my mules and horses. As the deck crew again begins grasshopping the boat, we whip up the critters and the boat inches forward.

In another few hours we're free of the bar, afloat, and able to get the boat close enough to shore to tie her down and get the gangplank in place.

The horses and mules are stabled just in time for me to have to report for work. Of course, I've missed my supper. So I beseech Ian, "Please go check on Ray and Pearl and see if she needs anything? And bring me a chunk of something to gnaw on."

"You got it," he says, and disappears.

We're two days from Yankton to Fort Randal, where Johanson puts in to load wood. While there, Pearl and Madam Allenthorpe go ashore as the fort has a sutler who has goods for sale. The Madam insists Pearl go, as she has not left Ray's side since the accident.

Ian and I take the opportunity to take the horse and mules up a creek bed until we find a meadow full of grass and spend a few hours there until the Captain blows three shorts on the steam whistle, signaling that he's casting off in a half hour.

Ian and I are stalling the horses when Pearl runs up. "He's gone," she screams.

"Whose gone?" I ask.

"Ray, he done left."

I have to smile. "Ray is a long ways from walking. He's not gone."

The tears begin flowing down her cheeks, and I suddenly wonder if she means Ray died. "What do you mean, gone?"

"The captain, he done put Ray on a keelboat, headed down river. He said he wouldn't be responsible for him. He give Ray eighteen dollars he had coming and paid his fare back to Kansas City on some damn ol' keelboat."

I take a deep breath. "Did Ray want that?" I ask.

"How would I know. This all was while I was at the fort."

"Well, Pearl, maybe the captain is right. Maybe Ray is better off with a real doctor. They've got a hospital in Kansas City—"

"He done had a fever. He'll never make it all that way without me to care for him."

"They'll go down the river five times as fast as they came up." Again I sigh. "Pray he does make it. He's better off in the hos—"

She yells again, only this time at me, not because of her missing brother. "Damn you, Braden McTavish, he be my brother, and I should care for him. That damn captain just wanted to be rid of Ray."

"I'll pay your fare if you want to catch the next boat we come across going down."

"I got my own money now. I don't need nothing from you. You probably kilt my brother with that hot iron and damn saw." She spins on her heel and stomps away, leaving me with my mouth hanging open.

No good deed goes unpunished.

Pearl has regressed back to the farm, in both speech and demeanor.

To hell with her and her damn brother. I hope I'm shed of both of them till eternity rolls around, until hell freezes over, until…hell, I don't know until what.

I don't see Pearl or Madam Allenthorpe for the next four days, except at a distance. We pass Fort Thompson, Fort Pierre—where we again take on wood—and Fort Sully. Now it's a long four-day stretch almost due north to Fort Rice, then another day to Fort Abraham Lincoln which is across the river from Bismarck.

Not far north of Bismarck we'll turn west again and it's westerly, ten or more days, west almost all the way to Fort Benton, or Benton City, whichever you prefer.

And we'll get there, God willing and this damn boat doesn't ground so it becomes an island…

Chapter Fifteen

We're on the river two days before the captain pulls to the east shore and we tie up just as the noon whistle blows. I hear from a deck hand that there's another sand bar just ahead, and we're going to set up to grasshopper; this time before we ground. And it means offloading cargo again, most likely. The gangplanks are soon down and Ian and I offload the animals, including the damn obstinate Brutus. We've not seen so much as a soddy since we left Fort Randle, just wide open grass country with a few cuts full of timber.

We have however, seen more than one Indian village and several bands of mounted redskins, one group of which fired on us indiscriminately from the shore, until a few of us began to return fire. I put my Sharps to work for the first time and know I dropped at least one of the savage's pony out from under him.

The captain has indicated it will take until mid-afternoon to be ready to attack the sand bar and I convince him the stock will need to be well grazed before they set to work. He's indicated he'll try the bar without offloading cargo, which is fine by all of us.

I'm not the only one eager to get some solid ground under foot, and both Sam and my merchant friend, Alex, have offered to lead a pair of horses or mules, and Madam Allenthorpe and Pearl begged to accompany us to get some exercise. Sam seems to get along with the bull, so the huge animal becomes his task. I don't complain about the ladies, as how can one complain about two beautiful woman following along. Pearl, it seems, has somewhat reconsidered my being at fault for her brother's retreat down river.

So, with savages about, and both the stock and women to watch over, I've strapped on my Colt and am carrying my Sharps as we lead the stock up a long ravine until it tops out on a wide grassy plain. Alex has a Colt Root that's been on his side, and Sam has shouldered a .56-56 Spencer that I had no idea he owned. A fine rifle only introduced at the beginning of the war. I'm comforted by their presence.

But our walk to the top of the ravine is uneventful, so we find a spot under the topmost cottonwood and all sit back and relax while the animals graze contentedly. My oldest percheron, Sadie, is sort of the herd matriarch so we keep her on a lead rope and turn the rest of them out to graze on their own. So long as we have Sadie, they won't go far. I have a line long enough to picket them, but see no need.

We're there an hour and a half before we hear three short bursts of the steam whistle and begin to round up the stock to return the quarter mile to the boat, to harness up the horses and mules to help broach the bar. I decide to have Pearl lead Sadie, and let the rest follow along. The bull is an independent cuss—thank God for the ring in his nose—and so long as there's graze and water he seems content to ignore the rest of us.

We only move a hundred yards down the bottom of the ravine, when a roar is heard followed closely by another ten times as loud, and a flaming blast that sends fire and rubble a hundred yards into the sky, then a blast of air that almost takes me off my feet. I scramble upright then up the wall of the ravine so I can see to the river, and am shocked to see planks and timbers and God only knows what descending from the heavens. I move higher and see the remnants of the Eagle, a portion of the forward hull and a portion of the aft, aflame. In less than a half minute, as I watch, steam replaces smoke as the forward hull sinks into the river, and in a minute or only slightly longer, the aft section follows.

Sam, Alex, and Ian have joined me to watch the final throes of the death of a great boat. All of us anxiously watch as debris falls around us, some floating gently, some smashing into the earth. The explosion has spread the boat for a half mile in every direction.

Only one iron chimney is still standing, rising above the surface, and it is canting slightly down stream, until it falls like a great barren pine tree and disappears in another billow of steam.

"Damn dat Johanson," Sam mutters. "He been pushing for more steam, and getting ready to try that bar, I bet he had her at twice de red line. The boilers went, then in seconds that three tons of gunpowder. We're lucky we wasn't kilt way up here."

"Let's get down there and see to survivors," Alex yells, and we run back to see the stock as all disappeared up the ravine, except for the bull, who still grazes as if a volcano erupting nearby is an everyday occurrence. I glance up to see the last of my stock, Sadie, my mare and two mules, as their butts disappear over the ridge.

Pearl is sobbing. "Couldn't hold her, Brad. I jus couldn't."

"There was no holding her, she was crazed," Madam says.

"Let's get down there and see if we can help the others," I say, and start to move at a trot.

We only move another fifty yards before we come upon the first body, then more and more wreckage and several more steamed, blistered, and ripped torsos and limbs. It's as bad as any battlefield I witnessed during my time with Mosby.

We're fifty yards from the shoreline when I see a man moving and run to his side. It's Lucas Eckland, one of the two Swedes I've befriended. He's burned, his left cheek and arm scorched and blackened, but he's alive and moaning. Ten yards more and his friend Elton Borg is sitting upright with legs outstretched, dazed, a cut on his head bleeding badly, but his eyes are open and he seems alert.

"Hello, Brad," he says, as if we'd just met while strolling in the park.

"Lay down, Elton."

"What happened?" he asks.

"The boat blew. Lay down until the ladies can check your injuries."

"I feel fine," he says, and starts to rise, but I gently shove him back.

"Let the ladies check you. I've got to go see about the others."

"I'll just rest here a moment," he says, and lays back down.

Then as I turn, I get a strange rush up my backbone and turn back. He's flat on his back, his eyes open, but his pupils are unmoving. I step up and wave my hand over his eyes and he doesn't flinch, and only then notice the back of his head is caved in.

I poke him. "Elton?"

Nothing. Elton said he felt fine, then died. The Lord works in mysterious ways.

I cannot begin to describe the emptiness that seems a void in the center of my very being. I move on, but don't come across another living soul.

Lucas Eckland is the only among the nearly two hundred passengers and crew we find alive. I ask the women to tend to him.

"What now," Alex asks after we split up and search the shore for two hundred yards in each direction, and have joined back up. I'm happy to see he's carrying a shovel and has an ax slung over his shoulder. Sam, too, has an ax and a crosscut saw, six feet in length.

"What else did you find in your wandering?" I ask.

"Cords of cut wood, scattered everywhere, planks, fittings, lots of lines and cordage, furniture but hardly any in one piece, and bodies. Not a live soul. What now," Alex repeats.

And to add insult to injury, I feel the first few drops of rain we've seen in weeks.

"Shelter, fire, food," I say studying the heavens. "You, Sam and the ladies take on that chore until we get back to help."

"And you and Ian?" he asks.

"We're going after the stock. We may need to ride out of here."

"Well, we got plenty of building materials," Alex says. "Planks and timber all over the damn country."

"Keep a sharp eye. Every savage for ten miles around heard that blast, and I'll be surprised if they don't come at a gallop."

"Let's go," I yell to Ian. "We may not have much time."

The tracks of our stock leads over the top of the ridge. And around a thick forest that dies out onto the plains.

As we top the bluff that borders the east side of the river, we push into that forest, a thick tangle of chokecherry trees. Hard to move thru as their limbs hang to the ground and with the recent cooling weather are devoid of leaves...but still too thick to see through. We're barely into the trees when two fat deer break out ahead of us. Mule deer I'd guess by the size of their ears. The horse and mule tracks had led up the bottom of the ravine and around the forest, but for some reason my hunter's instinct said not to follow. So instead I lead Ian into the tangle of limbs until we have to drop to all fours to get through. Not an easy task as I carry my Sharps and Ian is a big man, not made for tight places.

I suck in a deep breath and hush Ian, who's complaining behind me as he's having to break brush to move forward.

And it's good I'm low to the ground, as two hundred yards beyond the edge of the thicket, a half dozen savages circle the four mules and five big mares. Sadie, my lead mare, is the nearest to an Indian who has dismounted from his paint horse. He's walking slowly toward her, as she's dragging a lead rope and is obviously a domestic animal. As is my habit—from almost two years a military man—I assess their armament. It seems only two of them carry long arms. I have no idea how many might have side arms. The other four have spears. The one on foot has driven his spear into the earth near his horse and merely dropped the reins.

They are bare-chested, hair to mid-back, some braided, some not. A single feather hangs from headbands of some. All wear leggings of elk or buffalo skin, some with moccasins to the knee. None of them are painted up as I understand they do when preparing for battle, and it gives me some consolation.

I have no idea who these men are, they could be friendly. But, odds are, not.

I scan the horizon as best I can from my low position, and see no more sign of life, other than a herd of antelope, maybe forty strong, in the distance. Too far a distance for a shot, even if we weren't facing another band of hunters. Hunters who may think of us as prey.

I know there are Sioux, Cheyenne, Kiowa and Arikara about, as two trappers were among those on board the Eagle and I listened to their conversations every chance I had, and they have claimed to know the tribes of the savages we've seen from the boat. But I have no idea how to tell one savage from the other, or one who wants to take my hair from one who wants to trade and live as neighbors—and hearing the trappers tell it, there are few of those.

"We can't lose the stock," I say in a low voice to Ian.

"Better the stock than our scalps," he says.

"Move back into the trees so you can't be spotted, and run if you wish. I'm going out there."

"You're a damn fool," he says, seemingly slightly astonished, then irritated. "And a bigger damn fool if you think I'd run."

"Probably I am a damn fool from any angle, but I'm not losing my stake." But I get to my feet and move forward, my Sharps at the ready.

I only carry a half dozen balls with me, having left my possibles bag with my other balls and powder behind with Pearl. Damn it.

I stride forward. The Indians are so intent watching the stock, they don't see me coming. Probably the last thing they would expect is a white man on foot, or one approaching six armed warriors as if he's a grizzly bear in search of a meal.

I'm over halfway when the afoot savage nears Sadie, and she begins to edge away. Still grazing, but watching him with the occasional uplifting head, and not trusting his stalking.

As she does, three of the remaining five begin to edge around the small herd. By the time I'm only seventy-five yards distant, and still striding forward, one of those trying to flank the herd glances my way. He lets out the most blood curdling scream I've ever heard, and I'm from a force of men known for rebel yells that freeze the blood of most Yanks.

Which is fine as I'm as close as I care to get without knowing their intent.

I can't help but pull up short and raise the Sharps to my shoulder, panning the little band slowly as if selecting a target.

I hear one yell out so the whole band can hear.

All of them are facing me, but not edging their mounts forward. The man who's afoot trots back to his paint horse and mounts, swinging up into his sparse saddle without a stirrup as easily as I'd flop down into a chair to have my breakfast.

All but one of these men are wild-animal thin, but sturdy with defined muscles, and somewhat red as if cured by the sun, like tough slender trees who've reached for the sun from deep, dark forests. Those with rifles have them shouldered and I'm staring down their muzzles.

But now the mounted man, who seems to be the leader, doesn't spur his animal but rather merely sits and watches me. He seems to put little faith in my ability with the rifle. And the fact is, although I could send him to meet his maker, I'd likely only get reloaded with the single shot enough times to get one or, a slight possibility, two, shots off should they all charge me.

To my astonishment, they are not the only predators after my stock. On the horizon, maybe four hundred yards beyond the herd, four wolves appear. Like the Indians, they put little faith in my ability with the Sharps. They have little fear of any of us.

However, I reason, this may be a fine opportunity to let the savages know that at least one of them is destined to die, should they continue on their quest for new riding stock or to discourage the animals rightful owner, me, from trying to recover them. With luck, my ability with the rifle will dissuade them from any evil intent.

So I drop to one knee, raise the other to prop upon it, take a bead on the wolf who's leading the four, waiting until he sits back pausing to study the animals he's hoping will become his pack's supper. As I've swung the muzzle far to the left of the Indians, they follow the direction and see the pack. I take a deep breath, hold it, release the forward trigger, and ease the back one with no pre-conceived notion of when it will release it's near half ounce of lead to the target. I aim almost three body widths above him.

The Sharps bucks in my hands, racks my shoulder, and the heavy slug from the rifle slams into the big black lead wolf, knocking him head over heels. He rolls at least four times over and over, dust flying from his churning legs. But he's quickly stilled. It's a lucky shot, and a propitious one, as the band of Savages look from me to the wolves, back to me, back to the wolves, giving me plenty of time to reload.

It seems they can hardly believe what they've seen. And I can understand it as I can hardly believe my luck.

I quickly reload then swing the muzzle again from Indian to Indian, and hear the one who was stalking Sadie yell again. A signal, I'd guess, as they quickly spin their horses and, whooping and hollering, ride low in the saddle across the necks of their animals offering as small a target as possible. I'm a little taken aback as the man in the lead reins to a sliding stop, leaps from his horse, and throws the wolf across his animal's rump. The paint takes umbrage and bucks, dumping his load, but the Indian is not to be refused and kicks his mount soundly in the belly until the horse stands quivering. He reloads him, then mounts, and now in the rear of his retreating band, gallops away with one hand behind holding the wolf in place.

The trappers told of the savages keeping bands of dogs, which they eat when food becomes scarce, so I guess wolf could be on the menu as well.

Better the wolf than one of my mules or mares.

The good news is the savages have fled; the bad, so has my stock, but luckily the savages went north the same route as the river while the stock headed east. And they are still in sight, having again stopped a few hundred yards away to graze.

The country beyond the trees is rolling and almost totally without cover excerpt for knee deep grass, other than the occasional brush and tree lined ravine. I turn to see Ian standing at the edge of the chokecherries, shaking his head, and give him a wave and point toward the horses and mules. Then I set out, intent on bringing them home, and fairly sure no savage, at least not one of the six, will ride within five hundred yards of me.

That makes me smile, as I'm not quite ready to make their acquaintance, or to decorate one of their lodges with my long locks of fine Irish hair.

In less than a half hour we have the stock, me leading Sadie, Ian following up with a long switch of chokecherry limb, and are back at the head of the deep ravine leading down to the river and the rubble left of the ride that was to take us in comfort all the way to Benton City, still a thousand miles or more away.

A thousand miles or more, and maybe ten times that many savages between us and our destination. And I'm sure the news of my fine shot, my fine lucky shot, won't travel before us.

Now to see what awaits at the riverside.

Chapter Sixteen

A nd what awaits is a surprise.

Pearl, Madam Allenthorpe, Alex and Sam are busy working on a shelter. The Swede, Lucas Eckland, is laying nearby on a pallet of clothes they must have gathered from the shoreline, some of which are scorched and blackened, but still make a bed of sorts. He's badly burned on one arm and the side of his neck, but is awake and watching the others.

I'm pleased to see Chance O'Galliger, my workmate Willard—also known as Wheezy—Reverend Hunter, and Dag Eriksen working with them. Someone has recovered two bolts, at least six feet wide, of white sailcloth which is being used to encircle partially buried upright planks which Eriksen and the Reverend are nearby sawing more to length. By the bulk of the bolts I'd guess there is at least twenty-five yards on each. A center pole twice the height of the walls has rafters of branches descending to the walls circling the center. It will make a fine shelter, and by the growing cloud cover, and the dark sky in the west, we'll soon need one.

I smile as I see a small structure only four feet on a side nearby, a privy, I'd guess, which I'm sure was the first structure to be built. A large dirt pile nearby testifies to a deep latrine. The women have likely overseen the installation of a smooth seat. The ladies have had their say.

As I tie Sadie to a nearby cottonwood sapling, and the rest of the stock begins to graze near her or moves the thirty yards down to the water's edge to drink, Chance walks over and extends a hand.

"I'm glad to see some more living souls," Chance says, shaking his head.

"You were aboard when she blew?" I ask.

"The four off us were aft, me dealing a little faro using the capstan cover for a table, them playing. We suddenly found ourselves thirty yards from the boat, knocked senseless but trying to stay afloat. Thank God we drifted another thirty before the secondary explosion. Even at that it singed my hair and rolled me in the water, knocking the wind from my chest...nearly doing me in."

"None of you four hurt?"

"Cuts, bruises, splinters, ears may never be right again...Wheezy may have a broken arm. He must have hit the rail on the way over."

"You've seen no one else?"

"As we gathered up on shore a dozen or more bodies floated by, and as we made our way back here...we were a half mile downriver...we saw another half dozen or more that had been blown ashore, some in pieces." He closes his eyes and shakes his head. "A terrible sight to behold."

"Did you see anything of use?"

"Some tools, lots of planks mostly shattered and broken, plenty of firewood, some busted crates and barrels...but some foodstuffs in unbroken bottles. Can you use a case of buttons?" he asks, smiling.

"I heard those trappers onboard talking of trading glass beads for skins. Fact is they may make good trading material."

"Buttons?"

"You bet. We've already had a run in with a band of savages. Where there are men there are bound to be ladies who love their decoration."

He laughs. "You may be right, even buttons may be of value."

"Let's get ourselves some shelter, some supper of some sort, then we need to organize a burial party. We've got lots of work to do."

Chance shrugs. "How about setting them adrift to join the others?"

"No, sir. It's a Christian burial...before the wolves go to work on them."

"Wolves?" Now he looks a little worried.

"Plenty of them, and they looked hungry."

He sighs deeply. "Well, I'm a fair hand with a deck of cards but I'm not much with a shovel, how-some-ever if it's got to be done."

I glance over, and on a ridge across the river, at least three dozen Indians sit on their mounts, quietly watching us work. "Speaking of savages..." I point.

"God help us," he says, shading his eyes with a hand as he counts the Indians. "Let's hope the Emilie is not far behind and we can get aboard."

"Right now it's shelter and supper. I doubt if they'll try and swim the river here as she's shallow, but she's swift, and they'd make fine targets out there fighting the current."

"How about him?" Chance says, pointing up the slope to where the big bull, Brutus, grazes.

"As I understand it, that's a thousand dollar bull. I'm not sure making jerky out of him is the wise thing to do...besides, I saw a few deer and some forty head of antelope up on the plains. We won't lack for meat."

"Then maybe you should hunt while the rest of us build and dig."

I nod, and yell my intention to Ian who's helping with the construction, and turn and start back up the ravine. The sun is nearing the horizon, so an evening hunt it's to be.

I stop and turn back and yell at all of them. "We've got to bury lots of folks. If you get done with the necessaries, then get after it." I get a few nods, but they turn back to the task at hand...shelter. Luckily, firewood is everywhere so that's not a problem...at least for a while.

Bearing north into a fork of the ravine we haven't travelled, I don't go two hundred yards away from the main ravine with its trickle of water, and not more than a half mile from camp, before a white tail doe and her nearly grown yearling fawn move out of the brush ahead of me. They only trot a hundred yards before they stop and look back. A mistake.

At one hundred fifty yards I'm able to neck shoot her so as to not waste much meat, and by the time it's growing dark I'm entering camp with the skinned doe over my shoulder and her liver and heart still warm in the pockets of my coat.

And it's a good thing as the first cold rain drops are beginning to fall. I'll not be surprised if they turn to snow before it's again light.

Madam Allenthorpe seems spent and reclines by a new fire pit in the center of the twenty-five-foot-wide round shelter they've built, both its upright planks wrapped in sail cloth and a fairly decent roof constructed of the same sail material. They've left a hole in the very top for escaping smoke from a fire pit dug near the center pole.

The madam's green gown is soiled and wrinkled, her hair askew, and she's shoeless. She appears plum tuckered out, a bit like a plucked peacock...or I guess peahen would be more proper. But she was a game worker while she lasted.

Pearl, on the other hand, is still going strong. She's cut some willow branches and woven them into a pallet and in short order has the heart and liver sliced in long strips and laid on the pallet which is nearly upright in front of the fire. Next to it she's propped both racks of ribs up to slow cook.

There are ten of us to feed and the little white tail will only last a couple of more meals. In the morning, after we do our burying, I'll go on the hunt again. Should we not become overrun by savages.

After the reverend says grace, blessing the food and the fact ten of us still live, we each find a spot and using willow branches Pearl has sharpened for forks or skewers, and our hands for the ribs, are eating better than should be expected a few hours after a cataclysmic event.

I'd kill for a little salt and a shot of Who Hit John, but even that may be provided as God only knows what's been spread all over the cliff and hillsides rising up and away from the river; if the Indians don't decide they want what little we have, before we have a chance to add to our meager belongings.

It takes all of us digging from dawn to dark and by the end of the fourth day, we have forty-three graves, buried where they were blown, some in pieces, some graves just pieces.

I've seen many a battlefield, and fought over one or more with bodies killed three or four days before, and smelling so of death it makes your mouth wish for a shot of powerful whiskey and your eyes water.

But never anything like this.

And I pray I never will again

Nine of us share a twenty-five-foot, now walled and roofed, circle, while one stands guard up the hill a way.

I heard that the savages do not attack at night, not that I expect an attack, but one can't be too careful. There's enough of us that we can break the night into two hour shifts. We guard borrowing Sam's Spencer for the duty. I take the first, Ian the second, Sam the third, Alex the fourth, and he wakens Chance early for the dawn.

I'm a little surprised when I walk out the flap that serves for our door, and the world is white. A gentle snow still falls, topping the inch on the ground. The good news is we have shelter and lots of firewood, some cut to length but most in six foot lengths blown off the Eagle where it was stacked for her boilers. The bad news is everything we might be able to use that's been blown onto the hillside will soon be covered in snow and very hard to find should this keep up.

More good news, the Indians who seemed interested in our presence from across the river must have returned to the shelter and warmth of their lodges.

If we had a pot we could make a broth for breakfast, but the fact is kitchen implements have yet to be found. So as the men spread out to recover what we might, the ladies go to broiling more meat.

And I head out to see what I might kill to add to the larder. I think about riding, but am without saddle, so I decide to go afoot. The hunting is easier than yesterday as every animal has left tracks in the snow, and it's easy to determine recent tracks from those early on in the fresh snow. I am pleased to find some that are split hoof, like a deer, but much larger. I top out the cut above where the wide river flows and follow track upriver across the plain almost a mile.

The next ravine leading down to the river is covered in evergreen, some pine and some of what I believe to be larch, or tamarack, as the needles are golden and beginning to fall. I move quietly into the pines and soon discover what the trappers have called wapiti, but I've seen drawings of and know to be elk. Twice the size and weight of a mule deer, they'll fill our larder nicely.

Not only do I see them at only two hundred yards, but they lay under some pines. Had it not been for the antlers of a large bull, I'd never have spotted them in the shadows. There's a cow standing so my first shot fells her. As I'm reloading I'm surprised to see more than two dozen appear out of the pines, and due to the ravine and it's echoes, they are confused about where the shot came from and are running down the ravine side and back up my side...directly at me. I quickly reload and stay hidden in the shadows of a pine until I can draw a bead on the bull and my shot knocks him down, but he's up quickly and disappears into the trees, heading down toward the river. I know I hit him solidly and hope he won't go far.

I take the bird-in-hand and drop to the bottom of the ravine, cross a small trickle of water, then up the other side and find the cow stilled in the inch of snow. Two large elk. We could hardly be more fortunate. It's only then that I remember the trappers advice, never shoot twice. The first shot, unexpected by someone in earshot, is impossible to trace. But the second they're listening for.

Hoping no savages are within earshot, I go on about my business, but with an ear cocked for the sound of anyone approaching. I soon have her gutted and skinned and the heart and liver laid out on her hide which I've spread under a nearby pine which has kept the snow from the ground.

She's far more than I can carry, so I roll the heart, liver, and loins in the hide and head out for camp to fetch some help and some animals to pack the rest of the meat home. The bull will keep in this cold, wherever he's fallen. The snow has almost stopped so I'm sure I'll have no trouble tracking him, both blood and prints.

I swing down to where I thought he was when I fired and sure enough, there's a decent blood trail and still clear tracks heading downhill toward the river.

A big smile lights my face as I come back into camp as I see a whole pile of supplies that have been gathered, and in such short order. There are bottles of pie fruit, pickles, sacks of grain, oats, and even a hundred pound sack of flour along with two more broken but partially filled bags. A twenty-five-pound keg of salted cod is a godsend, as even if we don't find salt elsewhere, we can scrape away enough to last a good part of the winter. Ian and I tie a couple of Spanish hackamores so we can ride the saddle horses, bareback, but riding, and lead two of the big mares. I foresee problems ahead, and ask our camp seamstress, Pearl, to fashion two sets of pack bags and two padded saddle blankets from the sailcloth—our best possible substitute for leather saddles. In the future, packing and riding the horses will be much easier should she be successful.

Ian and I set out to retrieve the meat, both of us well armed with both sidearms and long guns, and it's a good thing as we're only a half mile out of camp when we cut the trail of a half dozen unshod horses in the light snow. And, unfortunately, they're headed in the same direction we are.

As we near the remains of the cow, still alongside the tracks of the unshod horses, I wave Ian into a heavy stand of pine and we dismount, scaring off a dozen crows. I caution Ian with a hush, as the crows have given away our movement in the forest. We remain unmoving for several minutes.

Whispering, I wave him to follow. "Let's stay quiet."

As I worried, when we get to the edge of the trees and can see down into the ravine, the same group of savages I saw earlier are butchering the rest of the cow.

"Damn," Ian says quietly, "they got our meat. We could drop two or three and I'd bet the rest would hightail it."

"I don't think it wise to shed the blood of some old boys who are cleaning up after us—"

"It's our damn meat."

I lay a hand on his shoulder. "True, but as you said earlier, it's our damn scalps. Even if we ran 'em off, we don't know they won't come back with two dozen more. Besides, they got the cow, we got the prime cuts already and a bull and lots more meat back aways. Let's slip out of here and not pick a fight."

"It was them picked it," he mumbles.

"Nope, it was them came on some free meat to feed some hungry folks. Damn, if they aren't skinny. In fact, I got a better idea."

"What the hell are you doing?" Ian asks, his mouth hanging open as I walk out onto a rock outcropping in plain view of the working Indians a hundred yards down the slope.

I yell out. "Hey there," and they all look up. Four of them take cover and the other two stand with rifles to their shoulders. I smile and wave, and give them a magnanimous sign by spreading my arms wide, my rifle hanging loose in a hand.

Giving them a bow like I'd just finished a three act play, I turn and move away. I got to tell you, there are some confused savages down the hill. I wave Ian on and we move back, mount up, and head out to find the bull.

We are not pursued, I'm happy to say. I don't know if it is due to my earlier killing of the wolf at over four hundred yards, and they fear being in my sights, or because they think I'm a mad Englishman, too long out in the cold.

Still, after we track the big bull, one of us stands guard while the other skins and butchers the big animal. We trade off, as it's plenty of work. I hang the forequarters over one mare, and one hindquarter between two racks of ribs on another. The heart, lungs, and trim meat from the neck is tied as closely as possible and stuffed wherever we can. I'm sure we can find use for the large antlers, so they are also packed.

I string the two mares together and get another jaw drop from Ian as I hand him the lead rope. "You head back to camp. God willin' and bein' merciful, I'm going to use this hindquarter to make some new friends. I think we already done the preliminaries."

He shakes his head. "You're crazy as a peach orchard boar, boy."

"My daddy always told me it was good business to make friends with your neighbors. You get that meat back to camp. I'll be along, God willin and the creek don't rise...or my scalp don't."

"May you be in heaven an hour before Beelzebub knows you done died of stupidity."

I laugh at that. "You may be right, but better dying face on with weapon in hand than getting an arrow in the back while you got your pants down and your butt hanging over a log."

Now it's his turn to laugh. He reins away and waves over his shoulder. "I'll come back to bury your remains, should there be anything left after the crows and buzzards get done pickin' at ya,...and after I'm sure them ol' boys have done gone."

It only takes me fifteen minutes to be where I can look down to see the savages cooking some trimmings over a low fire. They look up to see me, and stop what they're doing. I wave, smile, and gig my gray down the hill, the hindquarter tied across the back of my saddle.

West of the War

I'm smiling, they're not.

Chapter Seventeen

As I stroll down the ravine slope, leading the gray, I casually lay the Sharps across my shoulder, holding it by the barrel, upside down, as non-threatening as I can make it. The two Indians with rifles lower them but do so carefully. I stop twenty paces from them and lean the Sharps on a rock while I remove the hindquarter from the rump of the gray and move forward, offering it to the man I thought of earlier as leader...the man with the paint horse. I nod my head, encouraging him to take the meat.

His suspicious look softens, and he moves forward, takes the hindquarter, and speaks to the others. He waves me forward to the fire and I take a seat on a rock. One of the men, a stout Indian who unlike the others doesn't look as if he's been missing any meals, takes a limb that's been staked near the fire, a stake that skewers a slab of elk the size of my hand, and hands it to me. I remain seated while I devour the meat. Then I rise, and place a hand on my chest, and inform them. "Brad." They give me a curious look, but the leader seems to get it. I pat my chest again and repeat a couple of times. "Brad. I'm Brad."

He places a hand on his own chest and gives me a guttural word I don't understand, but presume is his name. I repeat it as best I can. I give each man a nod in turn, then move back to my rifle, pick it up, and remount the gray. I hear him say to the others, "Shamus," and wonder if that's not the name of someone, as others shake their head in agreement.

I wave again, and gig the gray and we move up the slope.

I'd give myself a pat on the back if it didn't look so silly.... I'm alive, and hopefully have gained some trust.

When I ride into camp Ian moves away from where he's been stacking firewood gathered from the hillside and stands with hands on hips, shaking his head.

"I still think you're a damn fool," he says as Pearl and Madam Allenthorpe walk over to join him.

"We were about to form up a party to come find you," Madam says.

"You could have joined us for lunch," I say, and laugh.

"I'm glad they didn't have you for lunch," Ian says, his laugh a little sardonic.

I get serious. "I've still got my hair and I'm hoping they'll look on us with more favor."

Pearl walks over and gives me a hug, laying her head on my shoulder. Then she raises her head and gives me a tight smile. "I'm glad you're safe."

"Me too," I say, happy to have a hug from her.

Our relationship has been tenuous from time to time as we both have tried to find our footing in a totally new situation. I was her "masser", even though I most times thought of her as friend, and sometimes wished she were more than that. I hope things settle to at least friendship.

As I watch Ian go back to work, and see some of the others walking back to camp each with a six-foot log over their shoulders, I get an idea. More and more steam driven boats will be heading upriver, and they'll need firewood. Within a mile of this camp are hundreds of acres of pine, much of it standing dead, over a hundred acres dry and ready for the campfire or boiler, where a fire passed through a year or more ago. This spot, where the Eagle easily tied up, can be our gold discovery, at least for a while. There are already five cords of wood stacked and there must be twenty more spread over the hills, already limbed and cut to length.

I'm sure all the rest of our party, including the ladies, will board the first passing riverboat—probably the Emilie— which should be passing anytime. I'll hate to see them go, but then again, it's fewer to share with should my new found project prove fruitful.

It's snowing again and if it keeps up my immediate problem will be making sure the stock has plenty of graze. Until it gets two feet or deeper they'll paw their way to grass, but I'll have to turn them out to roam free and turning them out means risking making a gift of them to any passing savages.

It's a bit of a quandary, as I don't have the tools to harvest meadow grass and get it to camp, even if I could which I can't in snow cover. I'm sure the snow will let up and melt off a time or two before real winter sets in.

We work the day away, gathering wood and whatever we find of use. A jagged sheet of iron blown from a boiler will serve as a fry pan, and an iron sink with a rock driven into its drain hole will make a fine kettle. A bit on the large size, but far better than none at all.

We've earned our elk steaks for supper and a dollop of pie cherries each for desert. Again we leave night guards up the ravine a ways, just in case our neighbors decide they might be in need of scalps.

I'm disappointed to discover with the morning that we now have six inches of snow, and it's still falling. Ian and I drive the stock up to the flats above the river where the wind has blown some hilltops free of snow and they can graze.

It's midday—the snow stopped midmorning—when I spot two riders coming our way. I scan the horizon for more, but the two are all I see. Ian has returned the mile back to camp to fetch us some chow, so I'm alone. I check the loads in my Colt and the Sharps, and move out to meet them. From a distance I can see that one rides the paint, and as they near I am more than a little surprised to see the other has on the fringed coat of a mountain man, and sports a full beard. He yells out when he gets within shouting distance, "Howdy. Mind if we ride in?"

Damn if he's not a white man, wearing a hat of skunk fur over a full head of gray hair that hangs to mid back.

He dismounts, but his riding partner, the Indian who seemed to have led the six, stays mounted.

"Got time to palaver?" the mountain man asks, and I nod and dismount as well.

"Friend," I say, "I got nothing but time."

He extends a hand. "Shamus Carbone."

"Brad McTavish," I say, and we shake.

"You survive that blow up of the smoke boat down on the river?" he asks. The man is not only white, but at one time I'd guess blond. Now he's mostly gray, skin burned brown and as craggy as a walnut, and I'd guess the better part of sixty. He has ice blue eyes, but his accent seems a little French, but long ago.

"I did, if you mean the Eagle. There's most of a dozen of us."

"In one piece?"

L. J. Martin

"Most. A few breaks and bruises, one burned pretty bad but I think he'll mend."

"Don't imagine you got coffee?" he asks.

"Lucky we got our hides. Got a bit of flour, some pie fruit, and other things…but no coffee."

"Damn the luck," he says. "I ain't had a cup of mud in most a year."

"How'd you happen to be way out here, Mr. Carbone?" I ask.

"Shamus, if you would, son. Been here and over the mountain the most part of twenty-five years…best I can recall."

"With the savages?"

"What savages, son. These are fine people. My woman is one of them. This here is Many-Dogs, he's a war chief of the Lakota."

"These are Lakota?"

"That they are, and you're lucky you got your hair. This is Lakota land and they don't take kindly to other's taking their game. You're lucky the lodges hang full of buffalo."

"I shared with them—"

"And a damn good thing you did. Who's that?" Shamus asks, and I look over my shoulder to see Ian riding slowly up. His Spencer's butt resting on a thigh, the barrel pointed at the overcast above.

"That would be Ian Hollihan. He and I will likely be here a while, until we get a mind to head on upriver."

"Everything okay here?" Ian asks.

"You bring some grub?" I ask, and he nods.

"Well, climb on down and let's share it with our neighbors. This is Shamus Carbone and that's Many-Dogs."

Carbone says something in Lakota, and the war chief dismounts. Ian unties a packet of food wrapped in a scrap of sail cloth and breaks a couple of pieces of salted cod in half, handing each of us a chunk. I'm a little amused to watch the Lakota as he bites into it, makes a face, then spits the bite on the ground. He hands it back to Ian, who nods and gives him a smile. It's not returned. However when Ian pours out a palm full of pie cherries and hands them over, he gets a nod, then after a taste, what must pass for a smile.

We plop down on some rocks now surrounded with mud from the melting snow.

"So, the Lakota have a village near?" I ask.

"Yep, quarter day to the north. There's damn nigh fifty in this band, another couple of villages near, a day's ride both east and west. I'll try and spread the word about y'all and ask they fight shy of you. You the one done shot the wolf a couple of days ago?"

"Yes, sir."

"You got their attention. A fine shot as I hear it. But there are plenty of other tribes around, and they won't have heard of Wolf-Long-Shot...which is how you're known in my village."

"Wolf-Long-Shot, eh? I guess that's better than Pile Of Wolf or some damn thing?" I have to smile at that.

I've been called a damn sight worse from time to time.

Old Shamus Carbone stands with hands on hips, seeming happy to be giving the tenderfoot some knowledge. "Yep. You met up with Falls-From-The-Sky, Many-Dogs, Wife-With-No-Nose, Crooked-Finger, Hands-Children—"

"Falls-From-The-Sky?" I ask.

"Yep, the night he was born there was a meteor shower, so that's his handle. They think he's got big magic."

"Many-Dogs I think I get, but Wife-With-No-Nose?"

He laughs. "Yep, his woman likes to sleep around and when a Lakota woman cheats and gets catched, she loses a chunk of her nose. His wife has a couple of chunks gone. She used to be a pretty one...."

"Crooked-Finger is pretty obvious, but Hands-Children?"

"Yep, he done got ten children, as many as fingers on his hands. He's had four wives."

"And if he has another child?"

"Then I guess it'll be Hands-And-A-Toe-Children."

"I guess that makes sense," I say.

"Names is important to these folks, Wolf-Long-Shot."

I laugh again. "I can see that," I say. "There will be more boats passing. You check with me in a few days and I'll get you some coffee, luck has it."

"I'd be obliged more than I can say should you manage a tin of Arbuckle's. I got some furs to trade—"

"It'll be my pleasure to gift you a tin or more can I come by it. You said other tribes?"

"Yep, the Cheyenne, what's left of the Mandan, a band of Snakes once in a while, some Arapahoe wander up to raid us when they get their courage up but don't often come this side of the Big Muddy. They do a dance before they cross. A get ready to die dance, so they don't come often. You want to be careful who you palaver with. The buffalo are moving south and you want to ride shy of them. Should they stampede you don't want to be in the way."

"I saw three dozen Indian riders across the river. Those Arapahoe?"

"Odds are."

"Glad there's a river twixt them and us."

"Won't be for long. That river freezes solid and becomes a road come January or February."

"That's a hell of a note," I say. "Let's hope there's plenty of warm spells to keep the ice thin."

"Let's hope they had a good hunting moon and have lodges full and fat warm women to lay with. The ice will get thick."

"They good eatin'?" I ask. "The buffalo, I mean."

He chuckles. "The hump and the tongue is fine as any Chicago fancy restaurant." He eyes my rifle closely. "I don't imagine you'd like to trade for that Sharps?"

"I don't imagine."

He rises and stretches. "Well, my woman will be worried about me, going to palaver with some crazy white man who kills wolves as far as most can see, so I got to get to breaking brush on the trail home. I'll put the word out to the Lakota to ride shy of Wolf-Long-Shot."

I give him a nod. "I'd be obliged. That said, if I kill anything, I'll share with any man comes calling." I stick my hand out and we shake, then offer a hand to Many-Dogs. He nods, ignoring my hand, but places a hand on his chest, then turns and mounts up.

Then it dawns on me. "How the hell do I tell them apart...tribes I mean."

He laughs. "They shoot at you, they lift your hair, they ain't Lakota. Or at least they ain't any I done spoke with. I'd hate to have you skinned by the tribe's women as I wouldn't get my Arbuckle's."

"Well, I guess that's one way...they shoot at me, they ain't friendly Lakota." I laugh, but a little tightly. "Tell Many-Dogs I'm proud to meet him."

"He likes you, even if he don't like salted cod," Shamus says, and he too mounts.

Many-Dogs says something to Shamus, who nods enthusiastically, then turns to me. "He says next herd of buff he sees coming our way, he'll fetch you and that big gun of your'n. You think you can manage that?"

"I'd be proud to ride with y'all."

He touches the skunk he wears, like he's tipping his top hat then gives me a wave, and they spin their mounts and gig them into a lope.

"So," Ian says as we watch them disappear over the hill, "you gonna give up grubbing for gold and go to buffalo huntin'?"

"No, sir. You and I are going into the wood business."

"The hell you say. We got plenty of wood."

"That's just the point, Ian my friend. We done got us twenty-five or more cords at five bucks each, and there's hundreds more to be felled."

He thinks for a moment and I can see he's counting on his fingers. "Five times twenty-five is enough to get a start in Benton City."

"And five times five hundred is a damn sight more."

"With eight more to split it with it ain't so much."

"That's why you keep this idea to yourself. They'll jump aboard the first boat coming up river…probably the Emilie in short order. You and I can stay behind and build up the wood supply for when the river clears come Spring. Rumor is there will be a half dozen boats making this trip. We can head up river come Summer time with four, maybe five hundred each."

Ian laughs. "Hard cuttin' wood in the snow."

"It cuts the same as it does in the summer, and slides back to camp a damn sight easier. Particularly when we got the stock to pull the weight."

Ian sticks out a big rawboned hand and we shake. "Howdy, pard," he says, and we both laugh.

It's getting dark earlier and earlier, and when we've finished a fine skewer of elk heart and liver, I walk up to our makeshift privy then on up to where we have a picket line set up for the horses. And it's good I do. Two of our mules have pulled free and their tracks lead up the ravine. They must not have gotten their fill during the day.

I've got to get them back before some savages see them wandering the hills above.

West of the War

L. J. Martin

Chapter Eighteen

eturning to the round house I see that Ian has already bedded down, however Pearl is outside, a wool blanket over her legs, stitching away on some pannier bags to make our life easier. I bend low and tell her I'm off to track the animals, afoot.

"I want to come along," she says. "I been elbowing my way between all these men for too long. I got to get some air and stretch some."

"It may be a long hike," I caution her. "And I can't slow down and it'll be damn cold and dead dark before I get back."

"Braden, I done…" she begins, then corrects herself, "I've already ridden you down when you were trying to leave me behind. What makes you think I can't keep up?"

"It's cold."

"I got a fine coat and I'm wrapping myself in this wool blanket."

I have to laugh at that. Not only did she ride me down but she shot down the damn sheriff who had ridden me down.

"Okay, let's go." She sets her work aside.

We set out up the ravine, but I'm a little taken back by the cold and the fact the wind has picked up. This is no weather for a woman. We only go a couple of hundred yards before I turn back to her. "Still time for you to turn back and get curled up beside that fire."

"Let's find those mules, then we can curl up by the fire." She waves me on and I pick up the pace and we go another quarter mile without speaking. I'm hoping the mules are just at the top of the ravine, where the snow's blown thin. The sun is about to touch the mountain tops to the west, so we don't have much time. I want to top a hill just a half mile or so ahead so I can see, but know damn well it will be too dark to see anything by the time we get there.

Then the sleet begins to pepper us.

"Damn it, Pearl," I yell over my shoulder. "You shoulda gone back."

"Shoulda, woulda, coulda, don't get anything done, Braden. Let's find someplace to get out of this until it quits."

I'm madly thinking about "someplace" when I remember a cut in the hillside not a hundred yards from where we now are. Some pines line the top of the cut and roots are exposed below. I remember it's dark behind those roots, and probably dry and out of the wind and rain.

"Come on," I wave. She hooks a hand in my belt and I charge forward, the rain and sleet beating at me as we're going straight into the west, where it's coming from.

It takes me the better part of a half hour in the growing darkness and heavy rain and sleet obscuring what little light is left, but I find the deep depression and have to pry my way between roots as big as my arm to get behind them and into the cut. I'm happy to see that it's dry…dark, but dry, and larger than I'd figured.

Pearl's damn wool blanket is soaked through so I hang it over the root covering, blocking the wind and what little rain and sleet that's managed to get through. And we settle back into the soft earth. Only then do I realize how cold I really am. I'm wondering if we shouldn't run for the camp.

But my teeth are already chattering.

"I'm cold too," she says, and snuggles up to me.

"We got to get a fire going," I manage while shivering.

"How we gonna do that. You got a tinder box?"

"No, but I got a flint and steel. I don't go anywhere without one. And I got my possibles bag and some gunpowder."

"So, wood?"

"Yes, ma'am."

She moves away one way and I the other. This cut has to be thirty or forty paces long and a half dozen steps deep and high enough to stand in most spots, and I find some dry grass in a few steps and manage to break away some roots that seem dry and snap easily. In moments I have an armful and find that she, too, has plenty of dry material. I arrange the grass and even while shivering and chattering manage to get some twigs splintered with my skinning knife. I pour a generous amount of powder onto the grass, then dig out my flint and steel and with the second whack it sparks and the powder flares. We feed it some twigs, then larger twigs as big as my finger, then a few as big as my forearm, and in minutes we're able to get whatever side we have facing the fire warm. But the other side is freezing.

Pearl sighs deeply, then comes to the obvious conclusion. "We got to get these clothes to dry or we're going to freeze solid."

She has on an ankle length dress and some cotton petticoats under that, and as cold as I am I get a shot of warmth to my loins as she begins unbuttoning her dress. In less than a minute she has it and her petticoats spread across the limbs only three feet from the fire. Her breasts are wrapped in a wide band of cloth and her bottom is in pantaloons that stretch to just above the knee. But six inches of her belly and back is exposed between the two garments.

"Well," she says. "You gonna freeze to death or are you gonna get outta them clothes?"

Never admitted to my blessed ma or even my pa, I have visited some pleasure ladies when I went alone to deliver some mares downriver all the way to St. Louie, although I was hardly able to get a glance at them before they scrambled under the covers. The whole affair didn't take long and each of the two ladies I joined in their cribs on that trip were well paid. A dollar was a day's wages for most who labored as I did, and the dollar they earned sure as hell's hot didn't take hardly any part of a day, or an hour for that matter, from howdy to pull back on your trousers.

I do have on long-johns under my linsey woolsey shirt and canvas trousers, but I know if I get shed of them, my appreciation for what I can see of her will show like a tent pole. I don't believe I've ever had such an experience when others were present and watching every move I make. The pleasure ladies I visited in St. Louis, and a couple of times while serving Colonel Mosby, paid little attention to me as I shed my duds and seemed to take little pleasure in the act, although one of them put on a good show of enjoyment.

But Pearl is watching closely.

"Well," she demands again.

"Turn away."

"Braden, that son of a bitch you shot dead done beat me down and showed me what a man carries so you are not going to frighten me."

"Then I'm glad I shot the son of a whore. But that was him and this is me. Turn away."

She does and I peel out of my wet shirt and trousers and hang them on the roots next to her dress.

"Better," she says, over her shoulder.

"Better, but I'm still freezing."

"Lay on down and you turn away. We got to get warm," she says, and says it with authority.

So I do, giving her my bare back. In moments she's spooned up to me. I can feel the hardness of her breasts pushing into my back. She lays a thigh over mine and I catch my breath.

"I got to turn over," I say, and feel her turning, and follow suit, now I'm pressed up against her back, and I know she feels a hardness that I can't hide.

I wrap my arm over her, my wrist sweeps across her breast, and I realize her nipples are as hard as my manhood. I can't help myself, and cup one full breast in my hand. She catches a breath, and I'm hoping it's not merely from my cold hand, then rolls over to face me.

"Lay on your back," she commands, "and close your eyes," and I do.

I can feel her sloughing away what little she still wears and in moments she's astraddle me with a hand between her legs and has fumbled away the buttons of my long johns and clasped my arousal in a soft hand. It's my turn to gasp as my erection is wrapped in wet heat and she moans quietly then begins moving, up and down, her palms pressed into my chest.

It's all I can do not to scream as my body wracks with a shot of heat like I've never felt before. She collapses down on me, her mouth nibbling at my neck.

"My God," I manage to mumble and start to push her away.

"Stop," she commands. "You just stay there and I'll keep you warm."

I do, laying quiet, still inside her. Just about the time my heart stops racing and I'm beginning to feel the cold again, she twitches, then begins to move slowly, but not so much I slip out of her.

Then I feel my interest returning. In moments I'm the one beginning to move, and she rolls over pulling me on top of her.

"Go slow," she commands, and I do, but even moving slowly I'm beginning to feel the heat flood over me again, and again I'm racked.

"That's a fine thing," I manage to mumble, collapsing down on her, and I hear her giggle a little.

"It sure does keep the cold away," she says, and I smile although she can't see it in the dark

"Do we do this all night to stay warm?" I whisper in her ear.

"Long as you can, Braden, you a young bull...long as you can."

"Better I stoke the fire, just in case," I say, and without moving off her, add a few branches to the fire.

And then with my eyes wide open, taking every inch of her bronze body into my wondrous eyes, I return to the business of staying warm her way. And I like it much better than the fire.

We manage to get some sleep and our clothes dry and back on by morning, when I realize the sun is shining through the tangle of roots. Then I hear Ian in the distance, yelling our names. I fight my way through the branches seeing a crimson sky to the east with the sun shining up onto the bottom of the cloud cover, and stumble out into snow that's now knee deep. I yell for him. In moments he appears, riding Sadie. He slips from the pad we now use as a saddle.

"Where's Pearl?" he asks and she sticks her head through the roots.

"I'm fine," she says.

Ian shakes his head. "Damn if I bet you're not. Y'all are only two miles from camp. You couldn't get back last night?"

"We couldn't see two feet in that damn sleet and rain and snow. We holed up to stay dry and not freeze to death."

He's struck silent, merely shaking his head. "Mules came back on their own," he finally manages.

"I'm hungry enough to eat one of them," I say. "Let's get back to camp."

Pearl works her way out of the roots and into the deep snow. As soon as she's even with the big mare, Ian reaches down and wraps his hands around her thin waist, and hoists her up on the horse.

"You ride, we'll walk," he says, and sets out leading the mare.

"Thank you, Ian," she says.

"My goddamn fiddle-fucking pleasure," he says, giving her a wave over his shoulder.

"Ian!" she manages, having never heard him curse.

"Sorry...my pleasure, I should have said."

I follow at a distance, as Ian's given me a heated glance that would bubble the varnish off one of the Eagle's railings, were it not buried in mud.

He's not too happy about Pearl and I getting stuck out in the cold.

But that's not my reaction.

I'm damn pleased about the whole affair.

West of the War

Chapter Nineteen

Had the great Taj Mahal of India been standing on the riverside rather than our round shelter, I couldn't have been more surprised. The Emilie is tied up alongside the shore. Alex and Sam are on either end of a stretcher walking Lucas Eckland aboard. I'm glad to see my former boss and the night engineer of the Eagle, Dag Eriksen, is following. I thank God he survived.

Madam Allenthorpe stands alongside the rail near the head of the gangplank and waves Pearl to join her. Pearly dismounts with a squeal and without looking back, runs up the gangplank to follow the stretcher aboard.

The women hug and we don't get so much as a thank you or go to hell as they turn and walk toward the door to the main salon.

I would be a liar if I didn't admit getting a catch in my throat watching her go.

"Without a goodbye or go to hell," Ian says, echoing my thought. Then he turns to me, "We going aboard?"

"Not me," I say, clearing the catch from my throat, "I got a plan, and it doesn't include landing in Benson City with what little I got left."

"You got the stock, they'll bring a fancy sum."

"They got work to do right here. Don't let me hold you back if you got the gold fever."

He laughs. "My share will wait. It's been laying in that creek bottom or under a ledge long as the stars have been in the sky. Let's sell some wood and get a decent stake so we got more'n a mule and a pan."

I glance up to see a dozen men starting down the gangplank, and with Sharps in hand, I hustle over to block their way, fairly sure of their intent.

"Hold on," I say, blocking the foot of the gangplank. A big burly black headed fellow, bigger than Ian, with a beard to mid-chest and half the width of his wide shoulders is in the lead.

"Move aside there, sonny. We got wood to load."

"All you want is up on the hillsides, lots of standing dead waiting for your ax, but you're not touching that stacked and cut boiler wood."

He stops four feet from me as I've edged the muzzle of the Sharps down where only another foot will bring it to the middle of his ample belly.

"Sonny, I don't suppose you'd be too comfortable with that barrel shoved up your backside."

It's dead silent except for the quiet chugging of the Emilie's steam engine in the background. My cocking of the Sharps is clearly heard by all of those lined up behind old black beard. Then to add even more insult the ratchet of the Spencer's loading lever somewhere behind me makes him cut his eyes.

"I guess you need to talk with the captain," he says, seeming to lose a little steam of his own.

"Get him down here. There's twelve cords of wood there so tell him to bring sixty dollars in gold."

"You'll have to take that up with him." He spins on his heel and all of them head back up the gangplank. As soon as it's clear, Sam and Alex head down, both extend their hands.

"Looks like you're hanging around?" Alex asks.

"Yes, sir. You fellas got some money coming as I'm selling the wood we gathered."

Both of them laugh, but it's Alex who speaks. "Hell, Brad, I lost over two thousand in goods in that explosion, but I've got another two thousand worth right down below on the Emilie that I'll turn into ten if we get safely to Benton City. I'll let you owe me what I'm worth at gathering wood...say a dollar a day so you owe Sam and me two dollars each. He's signed on the Emilie for four dollars a day, so he won't be missing any meals waiting for you to pay up."

Sam yells to Ian. "Hey, Irish, and you owe me ten bucks for the Spencer and four more for the makin's I left you in the round house."

"You're a gentleman," Ian yells back.

A six-foot-tall man with a well-trimmed salt and pepper beard pushes by them and stops with hands on his hips. "I'm Captain Charles Medling and you're in my way."

"Nice to meet you, captain," I say but don't extend my hand. "I'll be happy to sell you all the wood we've got stacked."

"That was the Eagle's wood," he snaps.

"Was is the proper term. We claimed it as salvage. I'm sure you know the law."

His jaw knots and he speaks through his teeth. "Okay, okay, how much?"

"Five dollars a cord."

"River robbery," he says, and spins on his heel and heads back up the gangplank.

"Suit yourself," I say with a shrug. "There'll be more boats along."

He stops and turns slowly and pulls his coat back exposing a revolver on his hip. Giving me an iron hard stare, his voice rings low and equally hard, "And what if I decide to salvage it myself? I got a couple of dozen hands to back me up."

I can't help but smile, then I raise the Sharps and aim at the engine deck of the Emilie. "You know, that old boiler I'm looking at probably doesn't have much pressure at the moment...then again your engineer is likely building up steam for those rapids up ahead. I'm not sure but I'll bet you my dollar to your dime this half ounce of lead will go clean though it."

"And maybe kill all those aboard in the aftermath and make a wanted man out of you...should you live through the doing of it."

I shrug. "That won't bring the Emilie up off the bottom."

"Three dollars a cord," he says, resignation in his voice.

"Sure, three dollars in gold and two dollars a cord in goods from your boat. Coffee, sugar, beans, bacon, potatoes, powder and lead, and some cooking utensils...oh, yeah, you got any leather goods aboard."

"We do, but they belong to merchants in Benton City."

"I'll leave it to you to settle up with them. I need two saddles and bridles and we both need boots."

"You're a damn pirate," he says, and spits over the rail in disgust. "That's a hundred dollars worth of goods."

"Thirty in goods and thirty in gold."

"A bloody pirate," he says, shaking his head in disgust.

"Deal or no deal?"

"Fifty for the goods and ten in gold."

"Forty and twenty and you got a deal."

"Work it out with my purser." He says, ignoring my extended hand, spinning on his heel and heading back up the gangplank. Then he stops and turns. "I'll need at least ten cords on the return trip."

"Count on it," I say. "I'll hold ten cords of good dry in six foot lengths at five dollars the cord.

"I'll be back in thirty days. Don't let me down."

"No, sir," I say, and he gives me his back. I wander back to where Ian is standing with a stupid grin. "I believe you've got a rifle and we've got us a wood yard."

"Damn if we don't," he says, as black beard and his crew brush by us while the Emilie's deckhands swing pallets over the side.

As blackbeard passes, he snaps at me. "I'll be puttin' your face in the mud should I run into you in Benton. You got a name?"

"Yep, Nolan…Nolan Byrne, not that it's any of your business."

"I'll remember that," he says, and moves on toward the wood pile.

Ian laughs. "Now, if he just forgets your ugly mug."

When I awake, I think the weather is getting worse and it's beginning to thunder. I'm not far wrong, but it's thundering hooves.

I don't have to wait for Many-Dogs to invite me to try out the Sharps on the mighty buffalo.

We are awakened in the night, both of us sleeping as we've given up posting a guard as we're now only two, by the pounding of hooves. We are fortunate that the lead cow of the herd decided to go around the round house and not through. We only had seconds to gather what we could and scramble up the hillside. We're now perched a hundred yards up the slope as it's beginning to dawn, and that first single line of buffalo has become hundreds passing down the ravine and fifty feet up both sides. As I watch them thunder past and charge into the Big Mo, I'm deciding there are thousands, not hundreds.

The horses and mules pulled loose with the first of the buff and have headed for the hills, and I don't much blame them. It'll mean a hard hike when the time comes.

For the first time since the Paddle Wheeler pulled away from shore, I notice the bull, Brutus, is missing. I turn to Ian, "where's Brutus?"

"Hell if I know. I ain't seen him since the boat left… You don't suppose."

"That bull was worth a thousand dollars, if the rumor was right."

"He done broke out of jail, or someone broke him out. I was up the mountain when she landed and she was here an hour afore I got down. They could have loaded him up…."

I laugh, if a bit sourly. "I hate someone to steal something I done stole."

Ian joins in the offers, "Particularly if that something is worth a thousand dollars. Odds are the old boy wouldn't have made it through winter, none the less."

"Odds are," I agree. "Of course, we coulda ate him, had he not."

Both of us laugh, but a little disgustedly.

All the hard work that went into the camp is now little more than stomped, torn and ripped canvas and poles and posts pounded into splinters. Our cases of bottled goods are not even wet spots in the soil. About the only thing left of use is the iron sink and the sheet of iron we've been using for a griddle.

"Ain't that the damnedest thing," Ian mutters as we look in amazement.

The sun lights the top of the ravine, almost a mile distant, and we still see buffalo funneling into the narrow descent to the river.

I'm too dumbstruck to answer, so he continues. "We're gonna need the meat."

"I'll drop one or two, but if I kill one in the middle of that mess they'll be nothing but mush in minutes. Wait till the crowd thins out."

"Makes sense. I'm gonna get some more sleep." He lays back in the grass. Damned if he can't sleep through a tornado, or in this case a stampede.

It's a half hour of buffalo pounding past before they begin thinning out. I draw a bead on a big bull and the Sharps bucks. Ian jumps up, startled awake, eyes wide.

"Damn, you coulda gived me a shake."

For a second I think I've missed the big bull as he moves on a dozen steps, but then he goes to his knees as I'm reloading. Blood bubbles out his nose and in seconds he's on his side. I line up on another big trotting bull and this one does half a head-over-heels, then is dead still, while the first is still churning his legs as if he's still moving down to the river.

I start down to where they lay, even though a few more pass, and hear another gun shot. A little confused I glance back but Ian is close behind.

"Who the hell...?" Ian says and we're both looking up the ravine. The sun is still not on its bottom and as it's deep in shadow it's hard to see. Then we make out a half dozen horseback men trailing and working the herd. There are three more buffalo down some distance up the ravine, I presume two of them felled by arrows.

In moments Carbone rides up, throws a leg over his horse's neck and slips from his carved saddle to the ground.

"Couple'a fine bulls you done felled," he says, without bothering with a hello.

I nod. "We'll eat good for a while."

"I'd suggest you offer one to your hosts."

"Hosts?" Ian says, then guffaws.

"Yep," Carbone says, scratching his beard. "Hosts, and if you want to keep being treated like friendly visiting folks, you'll mind what I say."

"Hell, they got three down," Ian presses.

"And another half dozen up on the flats where the women are already working. They be more'n three dozen of us and they take some feedin' and lots of hides to get by till the bird moon."

"Bird moon?" I ask.

"When the birds return from the south."

I decide to help Ian with his manners. "You remember I said how I enjoyed sharing with my neighbors. Y'all pick either bull and we'll have the left over."

Carbone nods, then adds, "Word is the hides is being bought by some traders and are bringing a dollar apiece, just scraped and not cured."

A few stragglers are moving around us, above and over on the other side of the ravine. "Hell, there goes a dollar," I say, and draw another bead on a mature cow. The Sharps bucks and roars and she, too, drops in her tracks.

"Well done," Carbone says, and gives me a pat on the back. Then he glances down at the remnants of our camp. "Guess you fellas could use some lessons in camp placement."

Ian chuckles. "Damn if 'n we couldn't."

"Let's let the ladies give y'all a lesson in hide curing and teepee construction. It don't seem there's a big enough patch of that canvas to blow your nose on."

"We'll take it." I say. "Now, let's get to guttin'."

And we do.

Carbone helps for a while, giving us some lessons on proper buff care, then walks to a spot of snow that hasn't been stomped to brown slush and cleans his hands, and over his shoulder says, "While y'all get to that next bull, I'm headin' back up and gonna fetch the women down to get us some humps and tongue to roastin'. This has been a good hunt and we're due for a jollification."

I bring a smile to him as he passes. "I got you some Arbuckle's, if it can be found."

"Why, son, you are a good neighbor. I'll fetch the ladies."

It takes us until mid afternoon to skin and filet out the two big bulls. I save the cow for the Indians and their ladies, as I'm pretty well spent. While I settle back on a rock I study the women, making bags of buffalo skin and mixing suet and berries, and an occasional sprinkling of hair. It doesn't look to be an appetizing mixture to me, but there must be good reason for it.

We're cleaning up in the ice cold river by the time the Lakota ride into camp, four of them on horses dragging travois behind, piled high with meat and hides.

Carbone gigs his horse on down to the water's edge. "Damn fine job you did of meatin' out them bulls. You decide the cow not worth the trouble? You'll find the cow hides worth more than bull."

"No, sir," I offer, "no decision one way or the other. It's just we done run outta steam."

He laughs. "The women'll get'er done."

While we finish our washing up, I notice the women headed to the two gut piles.

"We got the hearts and livers," I say.

"Yeah, but they use the bladders and gut for lots of things. Them bladders make fine bags and the rest lots of folderol. These folks don't waste nothin'."

"Glad it can be of use," I say, watching the women tear into the offal. They pile pony drags high with meat and hides, and tie it to the mustangs' backs with strips of fresh buffalo hide.

While they do, others are weaving racks from willows and slicing meat into long strips for drying while some skewer the hearts, livers and humps for a feast.

Ian and I have to worry about a place to sleep, so we begin hunting the ravine over for things of use. I do find a few tins of Arbuckle's, some of them damn near stomped flat, but the coffee beans are still there. What I forgot was a way to grind them. I guess it will be smashed beans in lieu of ground, but that should do for a fella who hasn't tasted coffee in a year or more.

All the braves I met before are here, as well as a half dozen more, and six women. The women are in long elk or deer skin dresses, their hair in braids, woven with beads and feathers and paint, but more modestly than some of the men. I'm a little taken aback by the comeliness of some of the woman, particularly one whose glance I've gleaned more than one time while she works.

She's not only comely, but beautiful in a wild untamed sort of way. I'm wondering if my admiring her, even with only a glance, might get me scalped. So I remain silent.

Then Many-Dogs stomps my way. I guess my admiration didn't go unnoticed.

Chapter Twenty

I'm wondering what I'm in for, when he gives me what seems to pass for a smile among these people.

"Bad," he says, and gives me a nod.

I place a hand on my chest and correct him. "Brad."

"Ah, Bad, Wasichu Bad," he says, and waves me to follow. I guess I'm christened. It's the same word I heard the Indians yell when I first came across them. I must remember to ask Carbone if they're calling me a son of a whore or other foul name.

Many-Dogs leads me to where the women are cooking and hands me a chunk of raw liver, which I politely refuse. He dispatches it in three bites then carves me off a chunk of cooked buff tongue as big as my forearm, and hands it to me. It's a bit bloodier than I normally take my beef, but I wouldn't refuse a gift from Many-Dogs if it were raw—so long as it's not raw liver or other innards. I take a big bite, chew, and give him as much of a smile as I can muster with my mouth full.

"Yippee," I hear a yell and turn to see Ian pulling what's left of a bolt of canvas from the mud. It's stomped flat but seems to be intact other than that. That takes a load off my shoulders as I figured we'd be sleeping in a tent made of rotting buffalo hide. I was not looking forward to it.

Ian walks over with the bolt over a shoulder. "I guess we don't want to rebuild down here on buffalo road?"

"There's a flat spot about sixty yards south backed by a little cliff. Let's set up there."

"Now, captain, can we see the enemy from there?"

He never calls me captain, so he's giving me a bad time. "Who's the enemy?"

"No one, everyone, the damned weather, the damned buffalo. Probably half these fine fellas we're breakin' bread with."

"I wish we had some bread and a chug of whisky, even bad whisky."

Many-Dogs walks over and hands Ian an equally large chunk of tongue. He takes a bite and he, too, smiles as he chews, then says with a full mouth, "Damn, that's fine as a St. Louis pleasure house."

"Good, not quite that good," I say, and laugh.

"Let's finish up and study that flat spot."

We do finish and I load up some limbs that will serve as tent poles and we give Carbone and Many-Dogs a wave and move away, toting canvas and poles, to get our camp set up. The flat is backed up by a ten foot high rock wall with an indentation, a wind cave under a sheet of rock, one you could park a farm wagon in. So we only have to build a wall on one side with the poles and canvas. It's forty yards from the river's edge and thirty yards above, so it's a steep slope to water but at least we won't get stomped under. There's a clear field of fire in three directions, but our back is at risk as we can't see up the slope without climbing. I don't like having the high country at my back, but I want to be able to keep a good watch on the river as we need to keep a lookout for customers...and, God forbid, hostiles crossing come ice time. We're half done when Carbone, followed by the young woman I'd admired, leading a pony with a travois full of meat, the iron sink, and the sheet iron, walks up.

"Brought your share," he says, while she unties the travois poles and drops them. "That's a fine cured buff skin twixt them poles and it'll make a good bed for y'all until you get yours cured. This be a larruping good spot, less you get too much snow up above you an a slide buries y'all till spring melt. Should it start to pile up I'd be knocking it down from time to time."

"I'll pay attention."

"Thanks. I don't imagine you'd let the young lady stay on awhile and teach us how to get along."

Carbone gives me a low chuckle, but his eyes don't smile with the effort. "Son, that's my daughter, and I got me enough grandkids from her brothers and sister. I don't need no mongrel pups."

"That wasn't what I had in mind her teaching."

"You two are fine young fellas, but not fine enough for me to leave Pretty Cloud behind. How-some-ever I don't fault ya for askin'. Now should you want to trade that Sharps and half your horses?" This time he gives me a sincere laugh and a slap on the back. I don't know if he's serious or not.

So I change the subject. "We got plenty of meat and I'll bet we can still round up some supplies from the hillsides. We'll do fine. By the way, Many-Dogs calls me Bad Wasichu? What's that mean?"

"Wasichu is the Lakota word for white man. Where'd he get the Bad?"

"His way of saying Brad, I guess."

Carbone chuckles, then stands and stretches. "I got to make sure we all get back safe and my family gets their fair share, then, weather permitting, I'll be back in less than a week to see how you ol' dogs is howlin."

Ian stops hanging the canvas and strides over. "Mr. Carbone, you expectin' bad weather?"

"Worms got a big coat of fuzz on 'em. Geese and ducks left early on. Sure sign of a tough winter. None of 'em winters hereabouts is much good, but this should be extra long and hard."

I laugh. "That would be the one I pick to come this way, whistlin' away like a damn fool."

Carbone gets real fatherly. "Get your wood collected and stacked. Use that flat shale up on the cliff above to get yourself a good stone stack facing into that shallow cave to back a fire against. What you don't stone up, cut some sod and fill the holes. That hole'll make a fine soddy. There's a cairn over here that you can fill with water plus this here little sink. You may not have see'd it yet but there's a little hot spring about a hundred yards up the main ravine off to the north, and it never freezes up. Your carry-water here will freeze soon but you can chip out plenty to keep your whistles wet. Sure as the Big Mo flows there'll be three or four more herds of buff passin'. Remember, them hides will sell. With what you might get for fire boat wood and hides...hells bells, boys, you'll be eatin' high on the ol' hog."

I give him a tight smile. "From your lips to God's ears, old man."

He nods. "We'll be back in a week. I'll bring Pretty Cloud or one of the ladies to teach y'all somethin' about what you can eat that grows hereabout. But they won't be much till spring. Did you see them women breaking up buff bones? They be mixin' the marrow with fat and berries for pemmican. I got a bag for you in that pile. It'll last you all winter. It's woman's work, but since you ain't got no woman...."

With that he and Pretty Cloud head down the slope to where the rest of the Indians are packing up. I can't help but watch her walk away. She's a fine specimen of a woman—not so fine as Pearl, but fine. The thought of Pearl makes me clamp my jaw and determine myself to think on other things.

Now, before we do anything else, I've got to walk down the stock.

"I'm heading out to find the animals," I say to Ian.

"I'm coming with you," he says.

"No, sir. Sure as hell's hot there's wolves following those buffs. We gotta figure out how to protect our meat and get us a fireplace built. You work here, I'll get the critters back. We gotta divide our labor."

"If some of them damn savages ain't got your stock stole or et."

"We've had pretty good luck with them damn savages so far."

"I fear it'll take more'n luck before we head up river."

"Let's make our own luck. My daddy always said the harder you work the luckier you get. You figure a place to stow our meat, lay out more to jerk, and when that's done, get on the fire."

"Yes, sir, cap'n sir," he says, his voice teasing, "and you try and keep your hair and get back here. It'd be a lonely winter just me and them passin' buffalo."

"I'd hate you to be lonely. If I ain't back by spring you come looking."

"Hell, Brad boy, I'll come in a month or so, soon as I run out of meat, should you not show back up."

The weather is decent although the sky lays flat gray and dead without a whisper or streak from wind blown cloud. It's freezing, but as I make my way up the long ravine, stomped with buffalo tracks heading for the river with a dozen or so shoeless mustang tracks—the Lakota's horses—heading the other way. I hope somewhere to find where my horses may have broken away from the churned soil.

I have one advantage. The percheron tracks are damn near twice the size of the mustang's, much larger than the buffalo, and shod. I occasionally catch a piece of a track so know I'm traveling in the right direction. Then, no more partial tracks. So I presume they've turned away from the now quarter mile wide mulched prairie so I double back when the buffalo tracks become scarce and more widely spaced.

I only move a couple of hundred yards backtracking until I come across the large percheron horse tracks and the much smaller mule and saddle horse tracks. They lead off toward the pine forest where I'd killed the elk.

It doesn't take long before I come upon the boned carcass of one of my percherons. Sonofabitch, the Lakota have killed and butchered one of my animals...but then, why would they as they had all the meat they could carry?

I'm a bit heartbroken as I love my mares and the thought of them being on the spit sickens me. I pray it's not Sadie, my lead mare.

The tracks lead away from the direction Carbone had pointed to where the Lakota village lay, a day's ride away. As I follow, more and more mustang tracks join up with the tracks of my horses and mules, and I presume the tracks of whoever has butchered my percheron. The bastards.

I am headed straight north, along the east side of the river. North, following more than two dozen mustang tracks in addition to those of my animals. The farther I follow, across the upper end of ravine after ravine leading down to the river, the dumber I think my quest must be. I'm following more than two dozen tracks of mustangs, unshod, obviously savages, as if there were something I could do to recover my stock. I'm a damn fool...but then it's not the first time.

They are horseback and I'm afoot, but they are driving my stock, so if I move as quickly as I can I'll catch up. So long as there are not any extreme uphill grades, and so far they've stayed up on the plain above the ravines and cuts falling off down to the river. After more than two miles, I come to a steep uphill slope and by the time I top it out, I'm winded. The Sharps I'm carrying, the Colt's on my hip, the possibles bag and the bundle of jerky and bottle of water— empty of pie cherries and corked—I'm carrying on my back must be over thirty pounds...not much but still tiring when you have a quarter mile or more of steep climb. I top out the climb and can see a mile ahead, and across another deep wooded ravine.

And I don't see any riders ahead, nor almost a dozen horses and mules being driven. So they must still be in the forest below.

As it's nearing dark, I presume there's water in the bottom of this deep wooded cut, and that they've found a spot to camp.

I hope so, as I'm at least seven or eight miles from camp, and don't want to stray much farther...particularly when it's one against at least two dozen.

Finding an outcropping where I can see up and down the ravine and across to the far slope, I settle down to chew some jerky, drink some water, and watch.

Just as the sun falls beneath the horizon on my right, I see a tendril of smoke snaking out of the trees in the bottom of the ravine.

They've camped.

There's still the ever-so-slight chance it's Shamus Carbone and the Lakota band, but I don't think so. I'm beginning to think Many-Dogs is an honorable man and that Carbone is a friend, so I'm sure it's not them. So who is it?

Who is it that has butchered one of my Percherons and stolen them and the rest of my stock.?

I'm sure that whoever they are, they will have guards posted, so there's no approaching in daylight. The good news is the sun is below the horizon. So it's wait, stay alert, stay awake, and be patient until any guarding the camp are settled and half asleep. If there's one thing being in Mosby's command taught me, it's how and when to pursue an enemy, and sometimes as important, when to wait.

And it's not pursuing while they're alert and have plenty of light.

So I wait.

The good news is there is not an early moon. Lots of starlight, but no shadow casting moon. When I figure it's at least midnight, I begin to work my way down the ravine side. Entering the tree line I move very slowly, putting each foot down until I'm sure there's not a breakable twig or rock about to give away underfoot.

I'm at least an hour moving the five hundred yards down the side of the ravine, until I can hear the sound of water over rocks, then after a few more yards, the occasional blowing and nickering of stock. And I can smell smoke and horse dung. Now I know there's a guard somewhere in front of me. Unlike the boys in blue, they won't be smoking and lighting up a stogy or chewing and spitting. A hock and spit or the splatter of piss on a flat rock has given away more than one guard's position in my experience.

But singing...singing is another thing altogether. And somewhere, not more than twenty yards in front of me, between me and where I hear horses pawing and nickering, is a man singing a singsong guttural rhythm. Singing low, but singing. Almost like a drum beating, his voice is low and rhythmic.

I drop to my belly and ease forward, my Sharps being picked up and eased forward a quiet foot at a time. Luckily there are at least three small campfires still glowing in the camp forty or fifty yards ahead and below and the guard, who's sitting leaning against a tree trunk, his head laid back against the bark, is backlighted. I'm able to move behind him. It takes me another fifteen minutes to slip up to only three feet from the trunk. I ease to my knees, and his humming stops, as if he's sensed something wrong.

His weight shifts and his head appears around the trunk, making me suck in a breath as his face is painted half black. He looks, just in time to catch the heavy butt of the Sharps as I drive it against his forehead. He goes down, sprawling, and kicks in the pine needles for a second. I'm over him, ready to drive the butt of the rifle against his head again, but it's unnecessary as he's still as the tree trunk against which he was leaning. I rise to my feet, but in a deep crouch, move forward, then freeze as a horse neighs loudly. I wait until they settle, then close the distance. My horses are not among the first few I pass, as the three remaining white Percherons are easy to distinguish, and so much larger than the Indian mustangs or even my mules.

Like the Indian guard, the mustangs wear paint. Yellow, red, and white adorn them.

Dropping to one knee, I bring the muzzle of the Sharps to bear on the camp below as I hear some stirring. It's a man adding a branch to the largest of the three campfires. There are no teepees, only bodies rolled in skins surrounding the fires. I don't think there's a woman among them, and if not it's not the Lakota as they left with woman accompanying them, or at least not Many Dog's people.

217

Finally I come to a mare I know well, who nickers softly in welcome. Sadie, my lead mare, thank the good Lord. I remove her lead rope and set her free, dragging her rope as I mean to lead her as the rest will follow. But they have to be untied. I do so, one by one, and luckily none of them are intent to wander and merely drop their heads to reach the grass they haven't been able to while tied. I've found the sorrel and use his lead rope to tie a Spanish hackamore. Before I move away from the picket line of horses, I untie all the others.

Still without mounting, I lead the sorrel back to where Sadie is quietly grazing. I mount the sorrel with Sadie's lead rope in hand and gig my horse into a slow walk, moving up the hill. The others follow as I was sure they would.

Then when I'm no more than forty yards up the hill, I hear a shout from the camp and turn to see a man moving from body to body, kicking the others awake, and yelling.

I cock the Sharps and put a big chunk of lead into the largest of the camp fires, sending a shower of sparks and scattering the rising men who scramble away, madly seeking the cover of darkness.

But I have no interest in waiting to see them react, and give heels to the sorrel, leading Sadie behind. Running a horse in the dark on a wooded slope is not the smartest thing a fellow could do, but waiting to get your hair lifted may be even more stupid. I'm slapped by a hundred branches, scratched and damn near knocked from the sorrel's back a time or two. But I hang on.

The sorrel is sure footed and leaps more than one time when I can see no obstruction to clear, and Sadie does the same, followed, I hope, by all my other animals.

We don't slow until we clear the crest of the hill and then only to a trot. By the noise behind, I'm sure I'm well accompanied by my stock, and maybe more. I may have gained a few mustangs. I won't know until we get a bright moon, or maybe even the morning sun.

If I live that long.

Chapter Twenty-One

When we break out of the trees onto the flat, I slow to a walk. The moon is over the horizon to the east, and rising, and I can see and hear a number of horses clomping along behind. Far more than I set out to capture. I hope I've left the whole band afoot. Then again, how the hell am I going to feed another two dozen critters even if I could hang on to them, which I'm sure I can't as this whole band will be after me even if only on foot. They will catch up when I slow down.

I'd run the damn Indian mustangs off so my pursuers might be less eager to lift my hair, but that's easier said than done. Odds are they'll follow no matter how many times I push them away, if I know horses. They've taken a shine to old Sadie as the lead mare.

So I decide it's time to pay a visit to Shamus Carbone and Many-Dogs and his people, a day to the northeast if Carbone was pointing in the right direction and not trying to mislead me. Besides, the last thing I want to do is lead this band of angry savages back to Ian and our river camp, which is south a few miles and a bit west.

I can only hope this band are friends of the Lakota and should we all come together, my hide can be saved by Many-Dogs and Shamus.

Pushing hard I keep moving until the sun is directly overhead, as much as can be told through the heavy overcast, then I dismount by a clear running stream and let the stock graze. I'm being followed by thirty-seven horses, by my quick count. They seem content to graze in a deep plush meadow, free of snow, and I move up a low slope, leading then staking the sorrel, where I can see my back trail, hoping to get a couple of hours of shuteye.

I don't.

Three mounted riders are coming our way, a mile away and moving fast at a distance eating but animal saving lope.

There's no way I can stay ahead of them and expect my horses to keep my pace, so I guess it's good ol' southern boy ambush time. I really have no interest in starting out my occupation of this land by killing folks, but I'll be surprised if I have a choice.

So I find a cleft in the rocks where I can see my back trail for three hundred yards across the clearing that's a plush knee deep, if now golden, meadow, and wait for them to pass through a stand of red bark willow between my position and the crest where I spotted them.

I want them to get well out of the trees so they can't turn and find cover before I can reload, but don't want them to get closer than two hundred yards. The first shot should be easy as they'll likely be moving cautiously with their horses in sight, then it will mean dropping a running rider, and I'll likely not get a third shot as I can't reload fast enough. Which means at least one of them will get back to the cover of the willows.

At least that's my logic, but I learned early on in battle that logic is often merely folly.

And there they are. They pause at the edge of the willows and study the lay of the land, then move forward at a slow walk. All three have long guns in hand.

I let them get a hundred yards from the willows, two hundred yards from me, then decide to drop my aim to the chest of the lead horse.

The Sharps bucks and roars, and the pinto horse drops to his knees. I may be a fool, and if so, I could pay with my life.

The now dismounted man runs to the side and dives behind an ant mound that's even taller than the grass, and to my surprise they don't retreat. All of them begin firing in my direction. They are hitting nowhere near me and probably won't determine my location until I fire again. But it looks as if I'll have to change my tactics as the second and third savage do not retreat to the willows, but give heels to their mounts and charge, but into the milling herd of mustangs and my saddle mounts and Percherons and mules. I would guess the savages will try and turn the animals back the way they'd come, but to my surprise they don't. They charge on through and by the time I have a clean target, they are one hundred yards, laying low so as not to offer a target, and coming hard.

All this time the man behind the ant hill is firing what must be a Spencer as the shots are coming too fast for a muzzle loader or single shot breech loader.

I decide to try one more time, and shoot the gray ridden by the nearest savage in the chest, and as he's at a full gallop, he goes head over heels and I can only hope has injured his rider beyond continuing the fight.

But the third man keeps coming, and he's less than forty yards and at a full gallop by the time I'm reloaded. And he knows my location and he's coming hard for the rocks I'm behind.

No choice. I fire for him, laying low across his bay mustang, and cuss myself as I miss.

No time, so I pull the Colt and have to drop to my back and fire up at him as the bay leaps the rocks. I spin and see he's dismounted and bringing his rifle up while he screams a yell that would cause a banshee to take flight...and I fire again and he stumbles back. His weapon discharges into the rocks and kicks gravel over my lower legs, and I fire again, and he's driven back a step or two, blood flowing from his mouth. The fourth shot blows him to his back, and he's unmoving.

I move forward to make sure he's out of the fight and hear a scream behind me. Ducking, dropping to my knee, a man flies over my head, and before he can recover I put a slug into his back and he goes to his face atop the first Indian.

Both men are nearly naked, even in the cold.

Then I remember that the first man whose horse I'd shot was still in the game, and rise to see him running my way, no more than twenty yards from the rocks.

One shot left in the Colt, so I have to make it good.

I wait until he tops the rocks, a hatchet in one hand, a knife in the other. He must have expended all the shells in his Spencer and I'm glad he did.

He leaps and has a foot atop the rocks only ten feet from me when I fire, but his momentum keeps him coming and his ax glances off my head and I'm seeing stars.

I roll to the side and am on my knees trying to clear my vision, when I see all three of my attackers in a tangled pile only a half dozen paces from where I'm trying to catch my breath and clear my eyes. It certainly wasn't planned, but I've stacked them, rather pell mell but stacked.

Reaching up, my hand comes away bloody and I feel a cut in my head and my ear seems half detached. Blood begins dripping off my chin onto my chest.

Better than a split skull, I decide, and drop to my butt on the rocks. I put my face in my hands and realize my heart is beating so hard it might explode from my chest. For some strange reason, I think of Pearl, and hope she's safely arrived at Fort Benton. I think it odd that she comes to mind at this particular time. Then turn my attention to the horses and mules.

After a few deep breaths I walk back to the rocks and recover, and reload my Sharps...and realize I'm down to four slugs.

With any luck at all these three at my feet, unmoving, are the only savages to have found mounts for my pursuit. With any luck at all.

The hell of it is, the stock seems to have been considerably disturbed by the gunfire and have scattered in every direction.

As my head and ear continue to bleed, I tear the tail off my shirt and bind my head.

I'm bleeding, seeing a little bit double and head still swimming, but I'm alive.

And the good news, these savages are seemingly different than the Lakota. Their markings are different, their hair worn unlike, even the breechcloth is not the same. Let's hope they're enemies of whom I hope are my new friends—Many-Dogs and his band.

If not, I may have double trouble. Generally, folks don't appreciate one who kills their friends.

There's a trickle of water in the middle of the meadow so I lead the sorrel down and let him water while I wash the blood away from my face and neck and regain my senses. Spotting Sadie in the distance I mount up and move slowly over and gather up her lead rope, which she's been dragging but I'm happy to find still intact. My other Percherons, saddle horse, and four mules are nearby and as I head out wander along behind. As we move to the top of a low rise, a number of mustangs join up as well.

Other than a dozen mule deer and a large herd of antelope, moving south, a few circling hawks and flushing some sage hens, we don't see a sign of life for over two miles. Then I rein up short.

On a ridge not more than a half mile to the northeast a half dozen savages appear on the horizon. It's mid-afternoon and the cover of darkness is hours away, even though it's getting darker and darker earlier and earlier.

I'm undecided what to do. If I spin and gig the sorrel away, even leading Sadie, I'm not sure the others will follow at even a trot, much less a gallop.

Then I shade my eyes and study the group more closely. I swear one of them is wearing a fur hat, and he's mounted and next to a man on a paint horse.

Could it be Carbone and Many-Dogs?

I drop Sadie's lead rope, she drops her head to graze, and I gig the sorrel forward. If I can get within a quarter of a mile I can have some confidence I recognize friend or possibly foe.

Rather than move directly toward them, I move down toward the river and into a stand of pine and find a well worn game trail. Like me, the game wants to stay just inside the cover of the trees.

After moving north what I figure to be four hundred yards, I move back to the edge of the trees, but my high-lined riders are no longer on the horizon. I'm forced to move on to the top of a low ridge, but rather than top it mounted, I ground tie the well trained sorrel, letting him stand over his reins, and move forward on foot.

I can't contain the smile when I see the group of riders no more than three hundred yards to the east, moving south toward where they last sighted me.

Recovering my mount, I give him the heels and in moments am reining up beside Shamus Carbone. I give Many-Dogs a nod and a tight smile, and he gives me his usual stoic look in return.

"Mr. Carbone. I'm glad to see you…I think?"

"Proud to see you son, but why the 'I think'?"

"I had a run in with some Indians a couple of hours ago and they tried to ventilate my hide. I had to put the Sharps to work on them."

"Our people are all with us or in camp, if that's what worries you?"

"Those fellas came from a camp I had to raid last night to retrieve my stock which was driven off when that buff herd came stompin' through. I'd hoped I'd left them fellas all afoot, but it seems they had three mounts hid out somewhere. They are not dressed like Many-Dogs and his people. Fact is, they're painted up looking like they rode straight out of hades."

"God damn Crow, I'd wager. It would seem they came near to winning that confrontation." He nods to my chest which is covered with dried blood and my blood soaked head-tie.

"Too close for my taste. It was a dying swipe, but he damn near took my head off and may have got an ear."

"We got a medicine man," he offers.

"If need be…but I don't think it'll send me to a box. I'm doing better already."

"We heard the Crow done crossed the river and we're doing a little ride about to see if we can prove the rumor. We heard shots fired and figured it was the Crow stealing some of our buffs or some damn thing as they was too many shots for a simple hunt. Odds are they was coming to raid our camp how-some-ever...but it seems you done got in the way. Damn Crow always seem to get hungry for horses and women to warm their lodges, come the moon of the falling leaves. Can you take us to whatever you left of 'em."

"Moon-of-the-falling-leaves?"

"Yep, November to you. Then the moon-when-the-deer-lose-their-horns...December."

"I can take you, but there's a whole lot more of them back behind somewhere and they may be catchin' up by now. I was bringing a herd of their ponies to y'all as I figured you could use them."

He gives me a broad smile, then laughs aloud. "Damn, you want'n to trade for Pretty Cloud?"

"That is a pleasurable thought, sir. But the truth is, I want to make a gift of them. No strings attached."

"How many horses?" he asks curiously.

"Two dozen or so, if they're still gathered up. I left them when I saw y'all in the distance."

This time he guffaws loudly and slaps a thigh. "Damn if you ain't in fine fettle, son. Let's go fetch 'em, and hope them are Crows you shot full of big ol' Sharps holes."

I lead them away.

We move at a lope as I'd like to get there before a mad-as-hell group of savages on foot arrive. And I'd like to deliver my new won herd of horses and get back to Ian, who must be about to come hunting me. I'd hate for him to be ambushed by two dozen Crow, even if afoot. Afoot doesn't mean you can't lay in wait.

We top a rise and see three dozen horses and mules grazing in the distance and I spot the scattered rocks and pile that offered me cover. I rein that way with Carbone and Many-Dogs and his warriors close behind.

To be truthful, I'm holding my breath as we dismount. The warriors are suddenly very animated and loud, although I cannot understand a word of what they're saying. I'm watching my back, thinking it might be a target for a lance or arrow, when in fact it's the target of a healthy slap from Shamus Carbone.

"Damn good work, Wasichu Bad. You killed Walks-With-A-Hawk, a war chief of the Crow. He's taken many a Lakota scalp and stole more than one woman from the people. Dang if you ain't a hero."

Now it's my turn to laugh. "Well sir, that and a half dollar will get me steak and eggs in Benton City...were we in Benton City. There's your horses over yonder...after I cut mine out. By the way, am I Wolf-Long-Shot or Wasichu Bad?"

"Don't be worrying about what you're called, so long as the Great Spirit don't call you home. I'd say we'd have us a jollification right here and now, but these young bucks are eager to find a gaggle of Crow without mounts."

While I'm listening to him, three of the Lakota warriors have dismounted and are lifting the hair of the three dead Crows. Shamus notices me watching, and likely the revolted look on my face.

"You coulda counted coup on them, but the one kills them can't."

"All I want is to head back to my camp and make sure Ian still has a fine head of hair."

"We will send a couple of young bucks with you to help you drive. Another group of us, less experienced at killing Crows, is a half mile behind." Shamus turns and yells to a brave, who spins his mount and disappears over the rise at a gallop.

We no more than get my stock separated from the others when another half dozen Lakota come over the rise at a gallop and join up with Many-Dogs. He barks orders and two young men, two of those I originally met when I shot the wolf, come over and give me a nod.

I give Many-Dogs and Shamus a wave, and start off back to my camp, leading Sadie. The Indians have to continue to nudge the mustangs away to keep them from following, as do the two young men who come along to help me drive. The fact is, with Sadie in tow, my remaining two Percherons, two saddle horses, and four mules need no driving...but I'm happy to have the company and the additional four eyes who'll watch out for the Crow. And maybe join in a fight, if need be. Although I note that only one of them has an old cap and ball revolver, while both have bows and knifes.

My head hurts, my head wound is still weeping, and I've had my fill of fighting and killing. I hope I can get peacefully back to camp.

I just want to head for home...such as it is.

Chapter Twenty-Two

A s we amble along at a leisurely walk, I remember the young man's name. Falls-From-Sky as I recall, and speak to him pointing. "You are Falls-From-Sky." And am surprised when he replies.

"You Wasichu Bad."

"You speak English?"

"I have words English. Little Belly learn me."

"Little Belly?"

"Shamus to Wasichu."

"Ah, Shamus...Little Belly." I have to laugh at that as I have noticed that Shamus has a pronounced bulge over his beaded belt.

As we move along, I sigh deeply as it's beginning to snow.

"Snow early." He says.

"Moon-of-the-falling-leaves normally."

He shrugs. A universal expression, I guess. "Snow come moon-of-the-deer-lose-horns. Early now."

"What do I feed these horses when the snow is deep."

Again, he shrugs. "Horse feed horse until snow..." And he indicates snow over eighteen inches or so, then he imitates the pawing of a horse. "Moon-of-the-popping-trees or moon-of-the-sore-eyes, maybe too deep."

"That's January and February?" He half shrugs and half nods.

"Wasichu names."

"So, what then?"

"Bark of waga chun...tree of knocking leaves."

"You'll show me?" I ask, and he nods.

I presume it's a cottonwood as I've seen horses fed the bark of narrow leaf cottonwood trees, and they do have leaves that rattle in the breeze.

As we get a mile or so from the mile long ravine leading down to the camp, I see a rider coming our way. Ian, I guess he figures I'm crow bait, which now has a double meaning as the Indians trying to raise my hair were Crow.

He reins up when a little over a hundred yards from us with the butt of his Spencer on a thigh, at the ready.

As we near he calls out. "I guess them are friends?"

"Yes, sir. Drovers giving me a hand."

"I got a gallon of stew on the fire, should y'all have an appetite."

"Damn sure could eat," I call back. He lets us pass and falls in behind to help move the stock along.

When we rein up near camp he comes up alongside to dismount. "Missing a Perch mare," he says.

"Yep, damn Crow Indians et her. I hope they choked."

"I'm surprised you didn't choke them yourself."

"They were three dozen. I did put three of them under, thanks to Mr. Sharps and Colonel Colt, and I'll be surprised if

Shamus and Many-Dogs don't send lots more somewhere up in the clouds or down below, or whatever they believe."

"The Lakota showed back up?"

"They did, come on like Mosby and the Cavalry. Damned if they didn't."

"And loaned you a couple of troopers to get you home safe."

"That they did, and are happy with us as I left them two dozen mustangs that wandered out of the Crow camp. I guess they took a shine to me. I believe we got friends for the duration."

"Seems like we may need them."

It's my turn to shrug.

"You got a letter," he says, a crooked grin on his ugly Irish mug.

I look at him like he might be as crazy as what he's said.

"There's a post office hereabout?" I say, and laugh.

"Special delivery from a keel boat headed downriver. Seems they was happy to help out a pretty girl with chocolate skin and a smile as big as a fingernail moon."

He reaches in a shirt pocket and hands me a folded paper. I take it and walk away until I find a rock to perch on.

> Dear Braden:
> I am sorry I could not say goodbye but we were so busy getting our things together. I hope that when you catch up you'll come visit me in Benton City. Madam Allenthorpe is going to purchase or build a saloon and Opera house and I'm to help. Be careful. Stay in one piece.
> Your friend, Miss Pearl Allenthorpe.

Well, it's a nice letter...I guess. I'd hoped for a little more as our keeping each other from freezing to death obviously meant quite a bit more to me than it did to her.

Your friend, Miss Pearl Allenthorpe. I would have hoped for something as personal as we'd been to each other. But then I guess she learned to be personal from others, maybe more than one other? Maybe that is what she'll be doing, working for Madam Allenthorpe in what she calls a saloon. Maybe saloon is a polite way of saying pleasure house?

The thought of that brings the heat up my spine and flushes my cheeks.

It's time I forgot about Miss Pearl Allenthorpe. In fact it's time I forget about my past and think only of my future. To hell with the past. To hell with Pearly.

I wad the paper up, walk over to our soddy, and throw it into a pile of kindling. It'll help start a fire someday soon.

I do see our iron sink tilted up at a forty-five-degree angle and resting in a bed of hot coals. There's at least a gallon of stew bubbling there.

"Looks good, eh?" Ian says from over my shoulder. He's followed closely by Falls-From-Sky.

"Name?" I ask Falls-From-Sky, pointing to the other young Indian who looks to be no more than sixteen.

"Sheo...in Wasichu, Prairie Chicken."

"Sheo, Falls-From-Sky, we eat now."

The stew is delicious. As we have only three spoons we've gathered from the hillside and four peach cans for bowls, the Indian boys have to share a spoon. Sheo refuses the loan of one and uses his knife to spear the meat and drinks the liquid.

We'll get along just fine without Pearl. I'll get along just fine without Pearly.

I turn to Ian who's chewing away. "I don't see our stockpile of meat?"

"No, and you won't see it unless you pull apart that stone wall over there." He points to another wind cave that's been completely walled up with flat shale.

"Damn, you been busy."

"Dried a few pounds as well. But I ain't been as busy as someone killing Crows, and hope I don't have to get that busy."

It's nearing dusk by the time we've finished our stew, still snowing lightly, and I think there's a real storm coming as I'm hearing thunder...then realize it's far to steady.

Another herd of buffalo is coming, and me with only four loads ready to go.

What the hell, four dollars is four dollars, and maybe more with the Indian bows and Ian's Spencer. With the weather like it is, we can freeze a lot of meat and if my thinking is right can use the offal and whatnot for bait. Wolf hides are worth even more than buff.

I guess it's time to go to work.

I am surprised at the proficiency of the young Indians, and their bravery, as they bring down three bulls. They ride in very close and let fly with an arrow, then again and again, while many other buffalo are at a dead run nearby. If their horse stumbles, they would be very lucky to survive. They impress me with both their skill and their bravado.

One of their bulls dies, slowly, after making the river and in the very cold water but we're able to recover the body a quarter mile downriver.

Four bulls fall to my Sharps and three to Ian's Spencer. Unfortunately two bulls are totally ruined, stomped and kicked, by the oncoming herd, which doesn't stop for over two hours. I have no idea how many animals passed during that time, and I rue the work that we four will have to apply over the next two days. We have ten bulls down but two of which will only be good for wolf bait.

We are two full days skinning and scraping hides—a task that disgusts the young braves as they say it's women's work—and boning out the meat. They do teach us a trick by beheading a bull and staking his forequarters to the ground, starting the skinning from the shoulders down, then using two of my big strong mares to strip, dragging the hide away. Peeling, not carefully cutting, saving a quarter day's work on each carcass.

I've convinced the young braves to stay on with us for as long as we can hunt, and promise them a Spencer each, should it be as long as a month, but they insist they will have to return to their camp and obtain Many-Dogs permission. I also have to make them understand the Spencer will have to come from trading with a passing boat.

Leaving Ian with the task of drying what meat he can and stowing the rest in his walled up cold-box of solid rock, I decide to leave with the boys and ride to the Lakota camp. I should know its location if we have an emergency or if I need to warn them of impending danger—so I can find it as quickly as possible.

Besides, I'd like to see Pretty Cloud again. I had foolishly felt some obligation to Pearl, but with her rather off-hand letter, I no longer have any illusions in her direction. She's moving on. So shall I.

We'll leave with the morning light.

As we stop work for the day and Ian takes some prime cuts from a bull to cook for our supper, Falls-From-Sky waves me up the hillside. We climb, him carrying two four foot long pointed sticks, to a hundred yards from the top of the ridge with him only telling me it's a "lesson." When he stops he plunges his stick into the earth next to a half-inch thick stem. The earth is now covered with an inch of snow and he digs until he comes up with a spindle shaped tuber about five inches long.

"Timpsula," he says, and scrapes away the soil and takes a bite, then hands it to me.

I follow suit and chew, and find it to be rather pleasant. A little astringent or bitter, but palatable enough.

"Good," I say.

"You call wild turnip. We eat. We dry, grind, use for bread."

"Can we dig more?" I check the ground and see lots of dead and dying plants with hairy stalks and pointed leaves the size of my hand.

"All turnips…timpsula," he says, and we go to work. We return to camp with as much as we can carry in a bag made of my coat.

When we were first stranded I had visions of us going hungry, now I have visions of growing out of my clothes. I've never eaten so much heart, liver, and rich red loin.

I have one more chore before I can lay my head down, and that's to reload some brass for the Sharps, and I do. I'm low on caps and lead, but have plenty of powder and hopefully can trade for my necessaries from the next passing boat.

There's room for Falls-From-Sky and Sheo in our little soddy cave and now they have plenty of buff hides to sleep on, but tomorrow it'll be us working on them to get them cured—a job I'll leave for Ian as I'm off to contract for the help of the young braves. As instructed earlier, we've saved the brains of the buff to mix with ashes, which are used in an Indian method of preserving hides.

I'm the first to awake, and even before adding a log or two to our fire, peek out between skins we've draped to help enclose our shelter entrance, and note the sun just beginning to lighten the sky to the east.

Of course I've foolishly left my Sharps and the makings of more loads alongside the skin I'm sleeping on, as I'm surprised by more than a dozen wolves snapping and snarling as they attack the piles of offal we've dragged down to the riverside with the plan of throwing what we don't save for wolf bait to the catfish or setting it adrift on logs. It obviously will work fine for bait, if we have any left.

The trappers aboard the Eagle told of the poisoning of wolves using strychnine infused buffalo carcasses. It seems a dreadful business to me and were I to take their skins I'd prefer a gunshot...however one would have to be accurate as I'm told hides with holes in them quickly lose their value.

The wolves are not to be surprised and one yaps when he sees me, and they all are scattering as I scramble back for my rifle.

And all are out of sight by the time I get back to my place.

We have a breakfast of cold buffalo and a tea made of some bark Falls-From-Sky has brought in. And it's not bad. Already the lads have taught us two foods provided by God and their knowledge of his works...foods that will warm us and may just keep us alive.

When done we pack as much meat as we can on the rumps of the boy's ponies, using wet strips of buff hide to secure the loads.

Now, it's off to the Lakota village, hopefully not stumbling across any hornet mad Crows on the way. With my head still bound with my shirttail, and a still shooting pain from ear to ear upon occasion, I'm not much in the mood to trade blows or even gunshots with another group of savages.

Before we top out the ravine, Falls-From-Sky reins up and drops off his horse, waving me to follow. We move forty feet up a small side ravine and he bends at a cluster of bushes with tiny but very sharp thorns on their branches and begins plucking what appears to be dried berries, but when I follow his lead, realize they are wild rose hips. The dried blossoms are barely withered strings, but still recognizable as former flowers. He pops one in his mouth and nods at me as he chews. So I mimic him, and wrinkle up my nose. Where the turnips were a little bitter, these are sour enough to keep the smile off my face for an hour. But if they're edible, maybe they work to flavor a stew, or more importantly to keep us alive at some time.

We're back to only a half mile from where I had my run in with the three Crow warriors, when Sheo reins up and points to the west, toward the river.

At first I see nothing, then realize it's a column of smoke, so dissipated that it's barely recognizable as such, but it's smoke, and it's moving down river. I'm sure it's one of the river boats returning from Fort Benton, but even if I wanted to I couldn't get to the river in time to wave her down. And we've yet to re-stack enough wood to be of interest to a passing side wheeler. But come Spring....

"Wasichu Bad," Sheo calls to me as I'm looking, admittedly a little longingly, at the distant smoke.

"Wasichu Bad, hoh-host," he repeats, and I realize his voice is more than a little insistent.

I turn back and see him pointing and have to adjust my gaze, then shade my eyes from the rising morning sun to the east.

There, at little more than two hundred yards, digging what must be the same turnips I'd learned to dig, is the biggest damn bear I've ever seen. He's dark brown on the back down to honey colored legs. He's a beautiful animal, and ferocious appearing as he rips and pulls at the ground, throwing up more soil than I could with the best shovel. At first glance you might think him fat as his belly fur swings beneath his massive body, then you seen the muscles ripple in his back on and legs.

"Should I shoot him?" I ask, rather hoping my Indian friends suggest not.

"No," Falls-From-Sky snaps, emphatically. "Is hoh-host."

"Grizzly?" I ask, and he nods.

The monster either heard or sensed our presence and turns his massive head our way. He lifts his snout and sniffs the air, but I realize the slight breeze is from him to us toward the river, not the other way.

We don't move and he rotates his head back and forth, testing the air some more. We remain dead-still, however I can feel the Sorrel shivering between my knees. The bear goes back to his task, giving us his back, and Falls-From-Sky waves us forward. The animals need no encouragement, and stride out with new vigor.

Topping a ridge, the bear is out of sight, and to be truthful, I'm glad it's so. I've heard stories of these grizzly bears taking a half dozen shots from a weapon as formidable as my Sharps, and still eviscerating a hunter before they give up the ghost.

I wonder if this image will haunt me in my sleep. There's no doubt in my mind that I'll be watchful when hunting turnips...or anything else. The monster might not enjoy sharing.

Chapter Twenty-Three

The sun now low at our backs, the light snow abated, the two young braves pick up the pace as we get within a mile of their camp, which crouches in a hollow surrounded with pines and cut by a small stream, below a twenty foot water fall from the meadow above. There are two dozen lodges, seemingly of elk or buffalo hide, each a half dozen large paces across and over twice as high.

A dozen dogs run out to greet us and a half dozen women follow. I note that there are few horses nearby and wonder if the main remuda is not hidden in the trees, but then realize that there are few men among those in camp.

I wonder if they are out hunting, and hope they were not hunted down by the Crow warriors?

Falls-From-Sky dismounts and takes the reins of my horse as I slide to the ground. Then he gives me the first smile I've seen from him, and points to a woman in a long white elk skin dress who's approaching. "Mother," he says, and I return the smile and nod.

He introduces me to Swallow and I wonder if I'm to smile or what, but as she smiles at me I feel comfortable returning one.

"Many-Dogs? Shamus?" I ask Falls-From-Sky, and he turns to his mother and they chatter back and forth, then turns back to me.

"All men out again...looking for Crow dogs."

"But they returned after we last saw them?"

He chatters again and she nods and speaks, and again he turns to me. "Yes, then leave with sun." He points to the east and I presume he means sunrise. "We wait," he says.

I nod. I'm not willing to stay away from the river camp for long, so if they're not back by morning, I'm heading back to join up with Ian and hope these two young men will get permission to follow. Then my worry is resolved as Swallow points over my shoulder and I turn to see nearly two dozen men in the distance, coming our way at a lope. At the latest, I'll head back in the morning, with or without Falls-From-Sky and Sheo.

As they near I'm happy to see Many-Dogs is in the lead with Shamus close behind.

Shamus slips from the saddle as I ask, "Did you get back here with the mustangs?"

"Sure did, son. They're up in the meadow above. We still ain't found them Crow dogs, other than the three you did under. You done left a couple of fine war clubs scattered about. You musta been born with the silver spoon.... Found they camp but them dogs slinked into the trees like the skunks they be. Maybe you discouraged them and they be takin' shank's mare home...but I doubt it."

"I can't stay long. Back to my camp with the morning sun. I need to talk with you and Many-Dogs."

"That's permissible. Let us shake out the kinks, sop some vittles, then we'll smoke and palaver."

"I'd like to say hello to Pretty Cloud as well, with your permission?"

He chuckles. "Should she want to jaw with you, you got my blessing, son. She's up in the meadow watchin' the herd, but she'll be here to sup right soon. She don't have much English…but Fall's-From-Sky can help you young folks with the how-you-be and what not."

I give him a smile and nod and then suggest, "I'm going to see to my horse, rub him down and make sure he's got good graze and water. When's supper?"

"You'll hear the women give that yodel they do…Lakota dinner bell…then you come running."

"I'm obliged."

"Hell, boy, you done earned five seasons worth of grub."

I wave over my shoulder then move to where the sorrel is ground tied and grazing, and lead him to the little stream, fifty yards or so from the edge of the lodges.

As the sorrel begins to drink, I decide to strip away his tack and let the ol' boy breath free. I reach for the cinch, when the sound of a scream sends a chill down my back.

I jerk my head around toward the sound and an arrow passes so closely by my face I feel the wind, and buries in the pommel of the sorrel's saddle.

Not even bothering to look where it's come from, I jerk the Sharps from the rifle boot and grab my possibles back from where it hangs from the horn and spin, dropping to one knee and cocking the rifle as I do. I expect the next arrow to bury in my chest, and my first thought is the Lakota have turned on me, then I see hand to hand fighting among the lodges behind me.

Crow!

And plenty of them. I start picking my targets, the first one being a mounted Indian with half his face painted red who's only thirty yards from me and closing fast, screaming a war cry, swinging a war club in one hand and yielding a knife in the other.

The big slug from the Sharps knocks him flying off the back of his painted horse.

I reload quickly and then have to be careful picking another target as all are Indians, and I'm having trouble picking Crow from Lakota, but then see a barrel chested man locked up with Shamus, each of them with a knife in hand and each with their wrists held by the other. Old Shamus is badly mismatched and the big warrior drives him to this back, but makes the mistake of being high over the man below. Another shot to mid-chest and he does most of a back flip off old man Carbone.

Before I can reload I've caught the attention of two Crow warriors and they charge my way, one notching an arrow in his bow, one cocking a lance to throw as soon as he's in range. Whipping the Colt from my holster, my first shot takes the lancer in the hip and he spins around, going to the ground. Firing too fast I hit the man with the bow in the belly and he let's his arrow fly into the sky as he goes to his back. Before I can bring my muzzle back to the lancer, who's trying to rise, Shamus falls on him from the rear, driving his knife into the man's chest, then again, then again.

The man I belly shot is crawling my way. So rather than expend another load, I re-holster the Colt and use the heavy barrel of the Sharps to smash the man's skull and he goes to his face.

As suddenly as it began, the Crow have fled the village, leaving four behind. To my shock, the women are hacking them to pieces. It's a scene almost as gruesome as the wreck of the Eagle.

Shamus is at my side, looking victorious, then his face falls and he yells as he spins on his heel. "Pretty Cloud," and he begins to run to a trail that I'd noticed that leads up the steep cut near the waterfall.

Rather than follow on foot, I quickly reload the Sharps and swing into the saddle. I pass Shamus before he makes the foot of the steep trail and the sorrel is atop the cut in five strong leaps, me having to hang onto the horn to keep from being dumped on the steep incline.

The wide meadow above is empty. Not a soul, not a horse. I presume the attack on the village was a feint to keep us from knowing the main force were retrieving their horses.

But where's Pretty Cloud?

Shamus said the Crow had taken many Lakota scalps…and many women.

I'd be a damn fool to try and run down two dozen or more warriors by myself, but then again, I'll never see Pretty Cloud again if they get away with her. And she is the daughter of the first friend I've made in the country I've chosen as my new home.

Damned if I have a choice.

One thing I'm sure of…they can't be far ahead and my sorrel is fast and sure footed, and more importantly, unless there were two dozen in the raiding party they're having to drive some horses as well as try and stay ahead of me and what's likely to be a couple of dozen Lakota and a very determined and angry Shamus.

Their trail is wide and well marked, but the sun was on the horizon when they attacked, and it'll be dark as a bat cave in a few minutes. And the moon is late rising…damn it. I know where they were camped when I went to recover my mares and mules and wonder, as I move through the thick pines if that's not where they're headed? I won't be able to track them for more than a few more minutes, besides, I hate following a deadly enemy with my head down trying to make tracks out of a needle covered forest floor. I'd ride right up on a bushwhacker.

So I break away to the right, toward the river. I'll take my chances losing the trail rather than taking my chances getting an arrow or slug in the brisket. In a half mile, pine boughs slapping me in the face all the way, I ride out into the grass covered, now snow-free, slopes above the tree covered ravines leading down to the river. The damn cloud cover is occluding whatever starlight there might be. I rein the sorrel toward the river and give him his head. It's more or less the same direction as our river camp and the home of the horses and mules he's been running with, so I have little trouble keeping him moving.

Those big eyes of a horse can see so much better than we frail humans that I trust his sure footedness. The pines are to my right, open country to my left, and the river a couple of miles ahead, west, of me. If the Crow are heading back to the camp they formerly occupied, and some of them may still, they'll have to cross my path somewhere between here and the river. The camp is at least eight, maybe as many as twelve, miles south and only a half to three quarters of a mile from the river.

So I push the sorrel hard and when I come to a rock ridge, follow it until the slope begins dropping away steeply. I find a deep hollow and stake the sorrel where he's belly deep in grass, then work my way on foot until I find a perch where I hope, but can't be sure, that I have a view of a wide swatch of country between me and the river, a place I hope the Crow will have to pass if, and only if, they're heading back to their former camp.

Now it's wait, listen, and hope against hope that I've guessed right.

It's less than an hour when I think, sense, there's movement a quarter a mile or so down the slope. Unshod horses on grass or pine covered trails move quietly, so I don't hear anything, at least don't think I do. I've often thought, believed, that we have senses that work in ways we don't understand, and maybe that's what's happening now. I wish it were an hour later as the moon would be up and maybe I could see what's down below...but I can't see, and can't risk riding down into a line of savages.

Finally, I hear the neighing of a horse, a shrill neigh of a horse that's stepped in a gopher hole or slipped on a rock and barked his shin bone. Then silence, but it's enough to encourage me. I wait a half hour, letting them pass, then return to the gelding and tighten his chinch and mount up. Very slowly, I move down the slope until I come upon a wide game trail just inside the tree line. I dismount and find a muddy spot and more by feel than sight, find dozens of hoof impressions. I watch for a moment and realize some of the deep ones are still filling slowly with water. They can't be more than a few moments ahead of me.

So I wait a while before I follow again.

I want them to camp so I can reconnoiter and see if there's any chance to slip Pretty Cloud away from them...if she's there.

Moving quietly along the well beaten path, I'm pleased to see the moon begin to silver the horizon in the distance. In a short time I'll be able to see much better.

Having hunted as much as I have down in the Missouri bottoms, I've learned to pay attention to my mount. It's disconcerting to have your animal stop in his tracks and look back, turning that long neck so he can see beyond your leg. But I gig him forward, hoping it's a raccoon or coyote that's moved in the brush behind us. Then his ears shoot forward and he hesitates in mid stride. I don't like it worth a damn, but I'm on the trail and the pines and underbrush are thick on my flanks so it's move forward. I keep a palm resting on the butt of the holstered Colt, should it need pulling...then snap my head back as a scream curdles my blood and before I can pull the weapon, a body drops on me from above and I'm knocked from the saddle.

I hit the ground hard, a painted savage beside me, then sense more surrounding me.

A blow rattles my head as I try and pull my weapon, then another, and another, and suddenly I'm blessed by quiet darkness and silence.

I awaken, my arms stretched out like I'm Holy Jesus on the cross, only I'm trussed between two trees, hanging spread-eagle from thongs tied to my wrists, facing a small bonfire circled by sitting Crow Indians. My head feels as if a sweating swearing blacksmith is pounding hot horseshoes between my ears—a ringing and shooting pain from ear to ear as his hammer glances off the inside of my skull.

And I'm cold, cold to the bone, and shivering...I hope the Indians I can hear chanting know my goosebumps and shivering are from the cold and not from fear. I've been told that a captive should never show fear. Easier to say than do.

Managing to get my feet under me, realizing my ankles are bound together, I can just stand. My hands have no feeling but as I get my weight off my wrists they begin to tingle and pain as if a thousand needles are pricking me. My mouth, already dry, becomes even more so as I look at the menagerie of savages, painted as colorfully as pictures I've seen of South American McCaws, begin to stand from where they circle a small bonfire and walk my way. I should have feigned being unconscious.

Glancing down, I realize I'm stripped naked, my chest, belly, and hips, which haven't seen the sun since I last swam near our farm, shine white as the belly of a beached catfish in the firelight, even though I'm hairy on chest, legs, arms and back.

My only covering is my head wrap, which they've left in place, strangely. Maybe they were amused by it.

These Indians seem as gleeful as I'm afraid. And one of them, the upper half of his face painted yellow, the lower red, carries a branch from the fire, it's end a glowing ember.

I don't think he plans to light me up a cigar.

Trying to appear as if I'm about to yawn my indifference, I glance at the overcast sky, then at the slight round light that's the moon behind the overcast. It's now a quarter way in its path, so I've been unconscious a couple of hours.

He pokes at me with the hot tipped ember, near enough to my personal parts that I feel the heat and give him a hip instead, which he touches and I jerk back and spin the other way, knocking his ember aside. He's laughing as are his cohorts, a dozen of them. With me backed against my restraints as much as possible, he pokes the hot branch against the base of my throat and draws a line down my chest, which I discourage by plunging forward. And thank God it knocks the ember off the branch, but not before I get the stench of burning hair and scorched flesh.

But I don't scream, although my eyes tear up and my cries are choked down and buried deep in my chest. I cough them away and grind my teeth.

Which seems to impress them. And they give each other a nod. And a laugh.

The braves return to the fire and what they've been eating, roasted meat that would look good to me if I wasn't smelling my own burnt flesh.

At first I'm happy to see the men go back to the fire, then my mouth goes dry again as a half dozen women appear and are walking my way, each with a pointed stick in hand.

Where the hell did they come from? I didn't see them in the camp when I raided it to recover my horses.

They are laughing and giggling, looking as if they're about to have a real good time...at my expense.

Chapter Twenty-Four

Even more than the men, the women are laughing and making what I presume are lewd remarks, as they laugh after each guttural comment.

I'm surprised by a poke in the buttock from behind, then find myself dodging and cursing as the women surround me. I work hard to keep from taking a sharp stick in the eye, then ducking my head, gaining a stab to the forehead, those efforts are impaired by my bleeding forehead and blood occluding the vision from the very eyes I'm trying to protect. All I can do is drop my chin to my chest and take blows on the top and back of my head as I wiggle and thrust to throw off their aim at my lower parts.

I can't help but get the mental picture of the Lakota women dismembering the dead crow braves, and a chill racks my back as I wonder if that fate awaits me.

A pair of the women are particularly vindictive and torturous and after their sticks are dulled and bloodied turn them and use them as clubs, beating me on the head and shoulders, then my torso. They try to bring them up between my legs, but I manage to shift from side to side until one of the men rises and moves over and snaps at the women, and they nod in compliance to whatever he's told them, and retreat.

I must be bleeding from two or three dozen stabs and more than one split in my scalp and forehead, but manage a deep breath and sigh of relief as the women move away.

I'm still alive...embarrassed, beaten, bloody, head still pounding from the blows I've taken...but alive.

Just as I'm feeling a little better about my condition, I see the women returning, but not with pointed sticks, with larger branches and some broken logs as thick as my calves.

What the hell?

They begin stacking them around me and I realize....

They're building a fire.

I'm about to be roasted alive.

I don't pray often. I'm sure I don't pray enough. And when I do, I'm sure it's not seriously enough. I try to change all that as I close my eyes and entreat the good Lord to save me from this horrid end. I almost jerk my arms from their sockets trying to break free of the leather tethers...to no avail.

And it seems the Lord is busy at the moment as the women retreat and sit just beyond the circle of men, ducks in a row as if they're at the theater and preparing to see a stage act of monkeys and court jesters. One of the men rises...I guess he's finished his supper and ready for some entertainment...and grabs a flaming bough and moves my way.

Stopping in front of me, he begins a litany I don't understand, but fear I know the meaning...and he means to start the fire and sear the flesh from my bones.

I scream, not in fear but in anger, spittle flinging, curses I don't believe I've ever used, flying at him like lead shot from a scattergun. At first he's a bit taken aback, but then he begins to laugh, and steps forward with the bough extended, looking for the best place in the pile to get the inferno started.

Seemingly he's found it, and looks up at me and gives me a snarl, then his face explodes and his blood mingles with mine. I feel goop dripping off my cheeks, and know it's come from the open hole in his face.

As quickly he pitches forward, instead of the bough going into the pyre at my feet, his upper torso does.

There's a shocked silence for a long second, then the Indians, both men and women, scatter, and the camp is suddenly filled with mounted milling Lakota. They're firing their rifles, swinging war clubs, and riding fleeing Crow down with their mustangs and lances.

It's all I can do not to cry out in joy, but it's too soon as one of the Crow women, one who must outweigh me by half, is charging at me with a gleaming trade knife in hand. Her overly large breasts, untethered beneath an elk skin dress, swing back and forth as she comes and I can only hope they'll throw her off balance and she'll fall on her face. But it's not to be. Just as she's a step from striking distance, an arrowhead appears out of her chest. Her eyes go wide and she stops in her tracks...then sags.

Many-Dogs leaps from his horse and is on her before she, face first, hits the ground with a feathered shaft protruding between her shoulders. Flinging aside his bow, he drives his own flint knife between her shoulder blades next to the arrow, as if it weren't enough. While he jerks the knife from her back, he glances over his shoulder to make sure he's not about to meet the same fate, then leaps to my side and saws away the leather thongs tying my left hand...then goes back to the fight, leaving me to free my right and my ankles.

As soon as I do, Shamus appears in front of me with his cheek badly sliced. "Pretty Cloud?" he mumbles as blood leaks from the side of his mouth.

"Never saw her," I say. Swinging my gaze around I still don't, but do see a dead Crow brave wearing my trousers.

The fight, what's left of it, has moved into the pines. I get my trousers off the Indian and back where they belong and move around the camp looking for more of my duds, but don't find them so I come back to the man who'd purloined my pants and strip away his elk skin shirt and moccasins, and am soon again fully clothed. And I'm warm again for the first time since I regained consciousness.

Shamus yells at me. "Come on, younger, they got a bunch of our stock. Let's get some horseflesh under us."

As I set out to follow him, Many-Dogs again appears at my side and hands me my Sharps and my possibles bag. I was sure I'd never see the rifle again and don't have time to thank him before he disappears into the pines.

A hundred yards from the Crow camp the pines open into a meadow, and although it's too dark to count them I know there must be three dozen horses scattered about, and I spot at least two of my remaining three Percherons. In a few steps I find my sorrel, tethered to a lodgepole pine, the saddle, bridle and blanket on the ground at the base of the tree.

Shamus rides up beside me as I'm saddling up and I can see he's still bleeding from the slice on his cheek. "Mr. Carbone, we need to get a wrap on that face or you'll bleed out and we'll have to plant you here."

As I talk, he's unwrapping a neckerchief from his neck.

I wave him off his mustang as I continue, "Dismount so I can help you with that." He does and I start to tie him a bandage, when a young Indian runs from the pines, a wad of green and brown leaves in hand. Shamus takes them and packs the cut, removes his skunk-fur cap, then gives me a high sign. I have to tie the handkerchief over his head and under chin to get it to cover and he won't be flapping his jaw for a while, which I'm sure will hurt him more than the cut. But he quickly remounts and waves me to follow. I can see the contingent of Lakota forming up to follow tracks into the pines, but Shamus doesn't follow and instead waves me to fall in behind him.

Now we're a pair, both of us with head wraps. Me for my sliced ear, him for his opened cheek.

I fall in behind, and it's all I can do to keep up with the old man as he pounds away through the slapping pine boughs, until we break out onto a grassy slope. Over the pines I can see the river a half mile below. He rides hard for most of three miles with the wooded slopes below us, then reins up near a rock outcropping only a couple of hundred yards from the edge of the Big Mo, and fifty yards above. Our horses are blowing hard, winded from the ride, and I'm not doing much better. Blood still weeps from so many spots on my body I worry that I'll run out, and my head still pounds and the pain has been shooting from ear to ear with every footfall of the animals.

It would be harder to find a spot on my body that's pain or cut free than one that's not. A bloody mess would be an understatement for my condition, but at least none of my wounds impair my ability to move, or more importantly, to aim and fire.

Shamus dismounts and points me to the furthest point of the rocks. The pines below go right up to the side of the river below and I quickly realize I won't be able to see anyone until they're likely fifty yards out into the water, and likely two hundred fifty yards from my perch. I scramble out to the point and he soon joins me. He can only mumble, but makes enough sense that I can understand.

"River's near a mile wide here and shallow. Only good crossin' for ten miles either way. But she's movin' fast and you got to be of a mind or she'll sweep you away. If them Crow got Pretty Cloud, or even if not, it'll be here they try and cross to get to their stinkin' territory. That is, should Many-Dogs and the boys not catch up with them in the woods."

"We got to have more light," I say, even with the moon now high in the sky, I can't imagine shooting into a group where I'd have to worry about hitting Pretty Cloud. "They wouldn't have killed her, would they?" I ask, suddenly wondering if we're not on a fool's mission.

He looks at me as if I'm daft. "Their women would, but you musta forgot how comely the girl is. No man in his right mind, unless he walks backward, would waste a woman like that 'til she done dried up."

"Walks backward?" I ask, not remembering ever hearing the term.

"A man what favors men over women."

That one makes me shrug, so I remain silent.

"By my reckonin'," Shamus mumbles, "it'll be light in a couple of hours. Let's hope they be fightin' shy of Many-Dogs and the boys and don't come afore light."

"Let's hope," I say, and again it's sit and wait.

As luck would have it, the wind rises which will make a long shot even more difficult. But then we're blessed as the clouds begin to thin just as the moon nears the western horizon.

Still, no Crow. But Shamus looks confident and is reclining back on a rock. I'm wondering if he's going to doze off, when he snaps his head up and cups a hand near his ear. "You hear that?" he asks.

Not wanting to compete with any sound coming from the distance, I merely shake my head. Then I do hear what sounds like a hoof clipping a rock, then in a second, a rock bouncing down a slope.

"They be here," Shamus whispers.

As if the good Lord was listening, the sky is growing silver to the east. It's another fifteen or more minutes before a few head of riderless horses, then the first of a column of riders appears heading out into the river.

"There," Shamus says. "Eighth rider back, leading a horse with Pretty Cloud...her hands is tied behind her back."

I count back from the lead rider, then realize the eighth has an arm extended behind him, dragging a reluctant horse. A horse mounted by a woman wearing a skirt. Then a half dozen more riders each with a woman afoot behind, holding onto the tail of the horse leading.

"Can you make that shot?" Shamus asks.

"Man or horse, either one," I say with confidence.

"Your choice, just don't hit my little girl."

Using a rock in front of me to steady my aim, I lay down on the rider, then he changes direction a few degrees and Pretty Cloud is almost directly behind him, in my line of fire.

"Damn," I mumble.

"Stay on him. He'll change again."

And he does, reining his mustang back downstream a little...just enough.

I take a deep breath and hold it, steadying my aim, release the forward trigger then apply pressure to the rear, tracking him, leading two feet and aiming most of three feet high at the three hundred yards he's now distant.

The Sharps bucks in my hands and I pray it hasn't been knocked around since it's been out of my grasp...if the sights are off, I might not be able to live with myself with the result.

At first I think I've missed, then the Indian's mount rears high on his back legs, twists, and goes over backwards taking his rider with him. By the time the man recovers he's twenty feet downstream and being swept away by a current moving faster than his mustang could run...but he'll never run again. He's rolled to his back and his four feet extend up out of the water. I think I must have broken his neck. He's being swept downstream but not nearly so fast as his rider.

The Indian released his lead rope while trying to hang onto his mount and I can see Pretty Cloud madly giving her heels to the flanks of the mustang. With her hands tied behind her, it's a wonder she can stay mounted as her paint horse spins and water flies as he pounds back toward the tree line, knee deep in water. In seconds, with horses and Indians fleeing in every direction, she's out of sight but coming back our way.

"Let's go fetch her," Shamus yells, and springs off a rock and into the saddle. Before I can sheath the Sharps, he's a hundred feet down the hillside riding as if a griz is on his tail. By the time I'm following, he's out of sight into the trees.

Knowing there may be a half a hundred hostiles in the trees ahead, I palm my Colt and let the sorrel pick his way, but have only gone fifty yards into the pines when I hear a couple of gunshots, then a horse...no, two horses, coming my way at a gallop. Forty yards away I see Shamus, leading the pinto with Pretty Cloud still in the saddle with her hands tied behind her, as they pound by at a gallop.

I spin the sorrel and he kicks clods and grass out behind as I give him my heels.

Riding as far back as the rock pile, I leap from the saddle with the Sharps in hand and set up, sure that Shamus will be pursued.

And I'm not wrong.

Three Crow braves burst from the tree line only a hundred and fifty yards from me. I lay down on the man in the lead and blow him from the back of his horse. The two following spin their horses, lay low across the necks of their animals, and ride back for the cover of the tree line.

As I've given up my position, and as Shamus and Pretty Cloud are disappearing over the ridge three hundred yards above, I don't tarry. Mounting, I let the sorrel show his speed and endurance as he puts the rock pile and pines behind us.

By the time I top the ridge line, Shamus has reined up, dismounted, and is cutting the leather thongs binding Pretty Cloud's wrists. Then he goes to work cutting thongs binding her thighs to the cinch. No wonder she was able to hang on as she was tied on the horse.

"Did you knock one of those dogs off his horse? I heard that Sharps roar," he asks me as he works. Then we hear more shooting from down in the pines.

"I did and the rest turned tail."

"Sounds like Many-Dogs done catched up with them. I'm taking my girl back to the village," he says, mounting up.

"And I'm heading back to my river camp to check on my pard."

"Keep the wind at your back, younger," Shamus says, giving me a wave.

"Send Falls-From-Sky and Sheo my way with the rest of my stock. I'll do right by them," I yell after him, as he spurs away and gives me a wave over his shoulder.

I watch them disappear into the rising sun, then realize how badly I feel, as if I've fallen off a hundred-foot-high cliff and bounced my way to the bottom.

Sighing deeply, I head the sorrel downriver, still hearing sporadic gunfire coming from the pines.

I hope I can make it the ten or so miles back to camp.

And hope Ian hasn't had his hair lifted while I've been gallivanting around over the Dakota plains.

As if I didn't need more trouble, before I've gone a mile, the sky darkens and it begins to snow. Soon I can only hope the sorrel knows his way home as I can't see far past his ears. At least it might discourage any pursuers, but I imagine the Lakota have already discouraged the Crow sufficiently.

Damn the Crow, damn the weather, and God bless my horse as he plods on as if he knows exactly where he's going.

I hunker down in the saddle, take a turn around the horn with his reins, and shove my hands up under the elk skin shirt I've stolen from the Crow who stole my trousers.

I wish I had my coat and my hat. My sliced ear is aching, my head still feels like the pistons of a steam engine are banging around inside, with every shift in the saddle and plodding step of the sorrel my poked and prodded limbs pain me…and to add to the mess I feel like I could easily freeze to death before I find our soddy.

Chapter Twenty-Five

I have no idea how I cling to the saddle, but realize I'm being pulled to the ground and almost panic thinking I'm back in the hands of the Crow…when I recognize it's Ian.

"Let's get you inside," he says, and half carries, half drags me to the skins covering the opening to our soddy. It's strange as there's a fire in what passes for a hearth for us, yet I'm still cold to the bone. Then my hands and feet begin to pain me even more than the poke and bat wounds as he pushes me down onto a bed of buff skins.

"I hope you ain't frost bit," Ian manages, then adds, "I got a stew going."

"Sleep," I manage.

"Hell, you was sleepin' in the saddle," he says. "What the hell happened to you? You get catched up in a buffalo stampede?"

"Crows happened to me."

"They get away with the stock?"

"No, sir. God willin' the Lakota have the stock and should they be as honest as they done proved to be, Falls-From-Sky and Sheo will be along with our critters, first break in the weather. I do believe I'll have a peach can full of that stew, then a little nap for two or three days."

He laughs. "Stew coming up." Then he flashes me a worried glance. "Them Crow didn't track you here, I don't suppose."

"I don't suppose. They were hotfootin' it across the Big Mo with Many-Dogs and his boys close behind, last I saw of them."

"Let's hope they keep a'goin'. Anything I can do for all them holes in you?"

"Keep the critters from eatin' me while I sleep, and heal."

"You're too damn ugly to eat."

"No argument. Stew?"

And I do sleep until after dawn. I awake wondering if the mountain hasn't fallen down on me, but realize as I shove off the buff skins Ian has covered me with that it is just the weight on all those cuts and bruises I am feeling…that, and my head still beats like an Indian drum.

I can see daylight coming through the break in the door skins and a bit of snow on the ground outside, but Ian is nowhere to be found.

What is left of the stew is still in the iron sink, and near enough to the embers that it's still warm. I crawl over and dish up another peach can full, down it, then move about trying to stretch the kinks out, but to little avail. I finally just decide it is my lot to ache in every joint and muscle, and fight my way to my feet.

I slip my head out of the break in the skins to see Ian plopped on a rock near a fire he's built outside, and he has a buff pelt in his lap, working on something.

Pushing my way on out I wander over and ease myself down on another rock near the fire. "You taking up sewing?" I ask, as he's working a leather thong back and forth through holes in the pelts, binding two together.

"Not a'purpose. I'm buildin' you a buff skin coat as it's the only material about other than that thin canvas and as you won't be worth a damn stacking wood or shooting more buff should you freeze to death. Speaking of that, how's them fingers and toes?"

"Still aching a mite, but I don't believe they're gonna rot off."

"Good, we got lots of work to do. The Emilie should be coming back this way in a week or two...the last trip before the ice starts to keep the boats all downriver. We should have a couple of dozen cords lined up down by the water by then."

"How about I heal up a bit more before you set me to working that cross cut saw."

"Be my pleasure," he says, with a wide grin, "so long as we're at it in a couple of days."

"And I thought my old man was a son of a bitch."

"Why, Braden McTavish, that's the first hard word I've heard you say about your dear old daddy."

"He didn't build that farm being a mealy mouth. He was a son of a bitch, but he was my son of a bitch and I'm the only one can call him that, God rest his soul."

Ian laughs at that. "Well, sir, I didn't know the gentleman so you'll not hear me calling him anything but the father of a son of a bitch." With that, he laughs and slaps his thighs.

"You get back to your woman's work. I'm getting cold just setting here and your blabber ain't warming me a bit."

"You won't be setting long, soon as we get you healed up."

"Humph," I manage, and get to my feet to stumble back to the pallet of hides and the warmth of the soddy.

I heal enough to get back to work and we do have fifteen cords of wood stacked when the Emilie shows up ten days later. As she's on a downhill run that takes less than a fifth the time going against the current, she only takes on ten cords but that puts thirty dollars in our poke. And more.

We add twenty dollars worth of trade coffee, whiskey, salt, and some sow belly and beans to our stores. Not to speak of more lead and powder, a new axe, a crosscut saw, and some tin utensils as well as an Iron frying pan for the kitchen. To keep my word, I trade pelts for two Spencers and the two young braves who've been helping us will be the envy of their tribe.

To my surprise I meet up with Sam, the big strong black who was second engineer on the Eagle and my former boss. I'm truly happy to see him and to learn he's now employed on the Emilie. As we chat, I can't help but ask about Pearl and Madam Allenthorpe, and he informs me that a saloon and opera house is under construction in Fort Benton, begun the day after the Emilie arrived. It seems the Madam and her new partner, who's to run the saloon, don't waste any time. And her new partner is not Pearl, but the gambler with the gold tooth, Chance O'Galliger. I feel some heat in my backbone as I remember how O'Galliger's gaze swept up and down Pearl's willowy frame more than one time. I turn my thoughts elsewhere as the Emilie steams away downriver.

We've only seen a few buffalo since I've returned from the Crow fight and the Lakota camp, and even though the weather's been decent and there's still no snow holding onto the land, Falls-From-Sky and Sheo have not returned with our stock, or ready to go to work as I'd hoped.

I hope even more that they've not ridden off to somewhere over the distant mountains, and taken my stock with them. As it is we've only my sorrel and Ian's gray in camp.

But I don't have long to worry on it as before the sun's fully up on the fifteenth morning of my return, the ground begins to rumble again.

By the time the dust settles, the last buffalo has past, and the sun is low in the western sky we have twenty-two buffalo cows on the ground. We've learned that cow hides are easier to harvest and less damaged by fighting. And are easily stripped away using the percherons to pull.

Shamus, Falls-From-Sky, Sheo and Pretty Cloud rest at our campfire, the Lakota having followed the buff herd. And my stock—three percherons, four mules, and a buckskin saddle horse—are grazing the hillside up above the soddy with nearly a dozen Lakota mustangs. Another half dozen Lakota are camped up above the little hot spring.

We have enough meat in our cache to last a long winter, a pile of hides beginning to rise high, enough bones and waste to bait wolves for a month or more, and Many-Dogs has taught me the art of hunting beaver. Not trapping, but hunting. With Shamus adding to the conversation and interpreting, I learn that the beaver must leave their dens late in the winter as they run low of the branches and twigs they feed upon, and can be shot then while working among the trees in the deep snow. And even later, when the moving ice of the thaw in both the river and nearby creeks destroys their dens. Shamus tells me they are not shy of gunfire and at times a half dozen can be shot before they retreat into an ice clogged river or stream.

We've seen no more sign of hostile savages, but with the river frozen over, it's easily crossed.

The Lakota pack up and leave well before what I think must be December. I hate to see Pretty Cloud go, not to speak of my many friends, but even though invited by Shamus I'm not ready to take on a woman and start a wilderness family.

I still have the itch of gold niggling at me. And Pearl. I'm strangely haunted by a woman I should hate, but can't. And my thoughts of her are not a bit hateful.

By the time hard winter keeps us deep in our soddy on most days, with only a snow tunnel to the outside, we have over forty wolf hides, seventy-seven buff hides, and a half dozen beaver skins in our cache. The Lakota have retreated to a winter camp somewhere in the distant mountains. Ian and I have managed to tolerate each other in the close quarters, although it's a true test of friendship.

Spring is upon us and the snow is dripping from the pines and refreezing in long icicles during the night.

I know Spring has truly begun when I bolt upright with a sound so thunderous it shakes our soddy. For seconds I think I'm back in the war, and a brace of cannons is raining grape shot and explosive shells down on me, then realize it's coming from the river. At dawn we push our way out to see an amazing vista. Chunks of ice, many seemingly as big as our McTavish farmhouse, are grinding and heaving their way down river. We watch in wonder as these mammoth sharp-shouldered icebergs fight each other for position. I fear for our stores of wood, only twenty feet above what I thought was the high water mark of the river. But I am wrong as it swells to just within ten feet while mounds of ice scour the banks. A few more feet and we'll have to race to move them higher…but then it begins to recede. In a week, the giant mountains of ice are reduced to floating barges interspersed with paths of water. Much as I've seen many times near our farm.

When the thaw begins in earnest we go back to cutting and stacking wood—and soon to hunting beaver, mostly afoot. The stock have all survived the winter— making their own way by pawing deeply to graze, except for the cottonwood bark we bring in after each wood cutting expedition. They've survived, but I can count their ribs. We keep two of the percheron mares with us and have built a large skid, a sled, that will carry a cord of wood as well as bark feed piled high. In this way, leaving my faithful lead mare, Sadie, with the wandering horses, they return nightly to the hot spring near the river camp where they can water and partake of the cottonwood.

I'm surprised the wolves haven't taken any of the horses as, like the stock, the wolves ribs are clearly outlined on bodies with not an observable ounce of fat. It's been a long hard winter for every living thing.

Shamus gave me some valuable advice before leaving, and that was to watch a nest in a large cottonwood down near the river's edge. He said when the fish eagle returns, then you can expect the river to be clear enough for the side wheelers to start up, and we should be ready to sell wood as they labor upstream. And to sell some wood but more hides as they return in two to five week's time, depending upon their upstream destination.

And today, an eagle and his mate have returned proving to be excellent fishermen as they hit the river and most always come up with a fish which they adjust in their grip so that it is easily carried against the wind.

That night, after observing the eagle, which Ian calls an Osprey, he breaks out a line and some bone fishhooks traded from the Lakota, and we enjoy a change of diet, trout fried crisp in sowbelly grease.

Upriver, between our location and the end of the navigable river at Benton City, a thousand miles from us, are a half dozen forts and the growing trading post and village of Bismarck across from Fort McKeen…and thousands of square miles of wilderness, savages, grizzlies, and God knows what.

But we're ready for visitors, with over fifty cords of wood, mostly in four foot lengths for the larger boats, seventy-seven buff hides, now over one hundred wolf hides and nearly that many beaver. By summer we should be ready to head upriver with our saddlebags heavy with gold coin.

The first boat we wave over is the side wheeler Andrew Jackson, smaller than either the Eagle or the Emilie, but able to take on twenty cords and leave us resupplied with powder and lead, coffee, sowbelly, flour, cornmeal, sugar, salt, and eighty dollars in gold. We gift them a side of buffalo, and make fine friends of the crew. We won't be able to hold our meat for long anyway as it's warming up.

We can see that we're rapidly going to run out of wood supply, and the next side wheeler, the Anna Mae, takes all but ten cords of our remaining. But she leaves us with a way to quickly restock. Anna Mae's captain is not happy as during the loading I've come across Lukas Eckland, the Swedish lad who survived the sinking of the Eagle and was in camp with us—but badly burned—until he went upriver on the Emilie where I guess he hired on until he joined the Anna Mae. He's not too pretty, with bad scars on his neck and arm, but he seems to not be impaired when it comes to hard physical work.

With the offer of two dollars a day guarantee against two dollars for every cord of wood he cuts and stacks, I manage to hire him away. That, and I tell him he can hunt beaver, buff, and wolf in his off time and we'll split the take with him. And he convinces a friend and fellow deck hand, Lars Ostland, who's worked as a lumberjack in the past, to join us as well. Lars is an ax handle wide with legs to match the percherons, and an accent so thick I can seldom understand him, but I have no question he's up to any task. Both have muzzle loaders and we can use the extra firepower, in case the hostiles return...and I'm sure they will.

Shamus assured me the Crow have long memories.

Within two days the two enterprising blond boys have built themselves a respectable soddy up against the rock wall, and are ready for hard but profitable labor.

Soon our wood yard grows by as many as six cords a day. Still leaving me time to hunt wolves and beaver, and I'm sure very soon, buffalo, as they begin to return and cross the river to the rich fields of soon-to-be belly deep meadow grass now greening the low hills at our backs.

We supplied more than a dozen boats as the weather continues to warm, and the buff have returned with the wolves dogging their tracks. We continue to add to our pelt bundles.

Every day now, Ian harangues me with our leaving the wood yard to Lucas and Lars and heading for the gold fields. I keep waiting for the return of Shamus and the Lakota, but there's no sign of them even though the rising and setting sun continues to march northward and the days become sweat hot.

Finally, I decide our poke is full enough, as we have nearly two thousand dollars apiece, thanks mostly to the sale of wolf hides and beaver pelts that bring us four dollars each, and bargain away the remaining wood and our soddy to our employees. And we gain another hundred each at two dollars a cord, plus fifty dollars each for the gray and the sorrel and two mules. We take the wood money from the pay due them, and agree to leave them our supplies of meat and foodstuffs. They agree to send payment for the horses and mules up river to Benton City to what we've learned is Miner's Bank, newly formed there.   Payment is to be made by the end of the season.

As I watch the approach of a side wheeler, name yet to be determined, I'm a little sad to leave the river camp and our soddy, particularly since I've not seen the return of the Lakota, Shamus and Pretty Cloud—but as my mother often told me with her limited Latin, carpe diem, seize the day.

If I can wave this boat down, and we light a large bonfire as has been our method to do so, and she swings toward our shore, I can see…we're soon off to the gold fields.

L. J. Martin

Chapter Twenty-Six

She's the Glasgow, a double boiler side wheeler of one hundred thirty feet, carrying seventy-seven passengers if you consider only cabin space, with all her cabins occupied, plus another forty or so taking up residence on the various decks. Again it's the engine deck for Ian and me, and my remaining stock. We still have one saddle horse, a buckskin; two mules; and my three percheron mares. Each of us has nearly two thousand dollars in gold and I'm owed another two hundred for the stock, which I've sold too cheaply but Lars and Lucas have become good friends, and my daddy taught me long ago to cut a fair deal, particularly with someone who's to owe you for the transaction. A fellow who feels cheated is likely to forget his debt. Speaking of daddy, he had years on the several thousand acres of McTavish Farm, years when he, working the family and all our nigras, didn't clear as much as I've made in one winter.

Not only are we relegated to the engine deck, but we have to re-arrange freight to make room for the stock, and have to build stalls to contain them. We're able to arrange crates so they are walled in by wooden boxes on three sides and I only have to construct simple gates to finalize the enclosure. Luckily we had two days worth of graze stowed up at the river camp we could haul aboard. With Bismarck only two or three days upriver in the fast Glasgow, I'm sure I'll be able to buy grain and meadow grass hay there.

As soon as we're underway I climb to the wheelhouse and try to convince Captain Elias Easton to hire us, but it seems we're to be gentlemen of leisure on this trip. Which, to be truthful, is some relief.

Particularly when I stop at the door to the main salon and see the menu posted there:

Soups
Chicken Giblet and Consommé, with Egg

Fish
Salmon, au Beurre Noir

Relieves
Filet a Boeuf, a la Financier
Leg of Lamb, Sauce, Oysters

Cold Meats
Loin of Beef, Loin of Ham, Loin of Pork, Westphalia
Ham, Corned Beef

Boiled Meats
Leg of Mutton, Ribs of Beef, Corned Beef and Cabbage,
Russian River Bacon

Entrees
Pinons a Poulett, aux Champignons
Cream Fricasse of Chicken, Asparagus Points
Lapine Domestique, a la Matire d'Hote
Casserole d'Ritz aux Oeufs, a la Chinoise
Ducks of Mutton, Braze, with Chipoluta Ragout
California Fresh Peach, a la Conde

Roasts
Loin of Beef, Loin of Mutton, Leg of Pork
Apple Sauce, Suckling Pig, with Jelly, Chicken Stuffed
Veal

Pastry
Peach, Apple, Plum, and Custard Pies
English Plum Pudding, Hard Sauce, Lemon Flavor

This dinner will be served for 50 cents.

Was the cook not a little gnome of a man, rather than a woman, with a bulbous nose and an arrogant manner, I'd ask ol' cook to wed me.

I'm sure the menu at Delmonico's in far away New York City is no better. Again our fare was one hundred dollars, as much as our original fare from Brunswick. But the fact is, we have little negotiating power. I make up my mind to eat my way all the way to Benton City and make the captain sorry he let us onboard.

Captain Easton is kind enough to direct me to a cabin where a barber is working with razor and scissors, and renting out a tub of hot water, and to another cabin he says houses a haberdasher who's hauling goods all the way to Benton City. My first visit, with Ian in tow, is to have my shaggy mane cut, a tangle that Ian has been sawing with a sharp knife as

I've been doing for him, and my beard trimmed. Then to the man who's said to have ready-made clothes for sale…and I'm only slightly shocked to have Alex Strobridge open the door to my rap.

"Damn if it isn't Braden McTavish," he says with a grin, before I can recover my dropped chin, and pumps my hand.

"You, sir, are a man of great determination," I manage, as I enter.

"Head down, tail up, charge forward, lad. It looks as if you've had a rough row to hoe? You've got a few more scars and gone Indian on us?" He's surveying my neck and face, where the scars of the Crow women's efforts still shine, particularly now that my hair and beard are trimmed short—and me wearing my elk skin shirt and moccasins.

"Yes, sir, I have a few more beauty marks, but I have not gone Indian, which is the reason for my calling on what the captain has said was a haberdasher. Might I trouble you to break out some duds that might fit me? I'm sure they can smell these all the way back to St. Louis."

"I sure do, you got that two dollars you owe me for stacking wood." He laughs.

"Yes, sir. I wish you'd have waited for me to mention it."

"I'll flip you for it, and the cost of whatever you need. Double or nothing?"

"No, sir. I'll pay up for both. When did you leave Benton City?"

"On the first boat out more than two months ago. I gave a wave to your camp as we passed. How'd you winter?"

"We did fine. Just fine," I say, and can't keep the smile off my face. "Ian is fat and sassy, we killed buff until they quit passing then wolf and beaver when we weren't putting up wood, or when the weather didn't keep us boxed in. Then it all started again as the buff returned." I pause a moment, then ask what I really want to know. "So, how's the rest of the folks?" I hedge, not wanting to be obvious.

"Folks?"

"The rest of those of us survived the Eagle?"

"Fine, just fine. Lucas Eckland healed up and went back to work—"

"He and a friend are now running the wood yard."

"The hell you say. Lucas was a fine fellow."

"And the rest...Madam Allenthorpe and Chance?"

"Funny you should lump them together. It seems they took up together. In fact by the time we get there they should be ready to open a saloon and opera house."

"Really. Ian won't fancy that as he talked of her long, and longingly, all the long, long winter?"

"He may be better off. Fine feathers don't always make a good eatin' bird."

"And the others," I continue to press.

"Pearl?"

"You bet, Pearl?"

"Pearl is still working with Miss Allenthorpe...Madam Allenthorpe. She looked fine last time I saw her, fat as a toad, as I guess all that fine food sets well with her...but fit as a fiddle."

"Fat?"

"Seemed to me. Done lost that girlish figure. I was working hard trying to get a mercantile built and didn't pay attention to much else. Benton City has become a bit of a rough and tumble town. You got to look out for yourself if you want to stay in one piece. We got a sheriff and a deputy and I'm not sure that's enough."

"A good lawman, I hope?" I say, wanting to ask more about Pearl, but not wanting to seem the panting cur. Fat, I can't imagine Pearly letting herself get fat. Neither her mama nor her daddy carried any extra weight.

"A good lawman? I don't know. Seems tough enough. Come to think of it, you might remember him. Wade Jefferson, fellow with a white streak in his black beard...rumor was he rode with Bloody Bill, but that's just a rumor."

"Skunk?"

Alex shakes his head. "I wouldn't be calling him that. He beat a young fella half to death in the middle of the road for doing so. You know him?"

I can feel the heat in my cheeks. "Know the son of a bitch? Silas something is his real name...it'll come to me. I guess you could say I know him. He was trying to rob me when Ian picked him up like a sack of cow shit and flung him over the rail of the Eagle. We were sure he had drowned, and hoped he had."

Alex raises his eyebrows, then shakes his head thoughtfully. "You two might not be too welcome in Benton City," Alex says, his brow furrows.

"We don't plan to stay long. We'll be off to the goldfields soon enough."

"Don't tarry. He's a mean one and the town fathers, such as they are, seem to be all behind him."

"We'll only hang around long enough for me to sell my percherons and to buy another good saddle horse and some prospecting gear. I've got two of my pack mules."

"I'll stake you and Ian for a third cut?" Alex offers.

"I appreciate the offer and will pass it along to Ian, but we've got a good stake and all we need is a good fast saddle horse and tack, a couple of good pack saddles, and shovels and picks and pans...plus grub, of course."

"I've got all that on board, except the saddle horse. I'll give you as good a price as anyone in Benton City, so you won't have to hang around town long."

I shrug. "I'm not afraid of Skunk."

275

"I'm not saying you are, but he's the law in Benton City and you don't want trouble with the law, right or wrong."

He's right, of course. A picture of my daddy rotting at the end of a rope flashes through my mind's eye and I get a bad taste in my mouth. One McTavish at the end of a rope is enough for a dozen lifetimes. I shake my head slowly in agreement, then slap him on the back. "Let's go find Ian and we'll stand you to a few shots of hooch, then figure out what you can sell us."

"Let's get you some duds first, those smell like you've been living in a wolf den…or worse. It may be you gets shucked overboard."

"Worse. More like a pigsty I'd guess."

He chuckles. "I'd hate to see you buried way up in Benton City smelling like a goat and looking like a savage. They already got a boot hill going and you'd have lots of company."

While we enjoy good company and decent whisky, I catch up on the war, and the date. It is July 25, 1864 when we wave goodbye to our river camp.

My old friends in the 43rd Battalion have been busy. Sorry to learn my old commander Colonel Mosby has been wounded, shot through the thigh, but is expected to be back in the thick of things soon. Hell, had I stayed in the fight, I might be in line to take over the battalion…unless someone was smart enough to figure out it was my damned uncontrollable mount that made me look the hero and got me promoted time and time again. Or I'd likely be dead, as many of my fellows surely are.

However, it's not going well for the South. A series of battles called The Overland Campaign is costing General Lee and the Army of Northern Virginia heavy casualties and he's retreating closer to the Confederate capitol of Richmond. Another Union general, Nathaniel Banks, is moving upriver from Louisiana, and if the north gets their hands on cotton, thousands and thousands of bales of cotton, it will cost the South dearly and benefit the north equally.

To be truthful, I'm happy to be off to a new life in what I now learn has just become its own territory, capitol being a place called Bannack. And there are three or four new gold discoveries in the new Montana Territory. Names like Bannack, Alder Gulch, and others are pouring gold into many pokes, and Ian and I plan to reap our share.

If we can get to Benton City without another damn boat blowing itself all to hell, with us aboard.

Alex, Ian, and I shut the boat's saloon down, along with a dozen others, then Ian and I stumble our way back to the engine deck. Alex has offered us his floor, but his room is full of crates and bags of goods so there's little room. We quickly determine it's too damn hot to sleep on a warm night so near the boilers, so we take our bedrolls and saddle bags up to the hurricane deck high above the water where we can catch as much breeze as possible, and roll up. Since all our worldly wealth is in those saddle bags it's our habit to sleep with the bag's back strap under our necks and our sidearms in hand. I decide to split mine up and divide it between my bags and the money belt Pearl sewed up for me. When wearing it I look like I've gained a few pounds but better safety than vanity.

I'm not so soaked with demon rum—actually, Who Hit John, corn whiskey—that I don't take extra precautions. I have an eight-foot leather thong, a fine dark strand, and tie it a few feet from our spot at the end of the deck, so any who approach will likely stumble and upset a couple of rope spools I've stacked so they'll easily fall.

I didn't work all winter and nearly freeze my fingers and toes off only to lose my poke to a thief in the night. And I have seen the folly of stowing your wealth in the purser's safe, only to have it rest on the bottom of the Big Mo.

I guess it's terrible to thank the good Lord for someone's horrid luck, but a fight at breakfast had folks diving for the floor as gunfire broke out. It seems some German hooligan did not favor his breakfast and upon entering the cook's holy sanctum, the small kitchen, threatened the cook with bodily harm, and reached for his sixgun. A mistake. Particularly when the cook is a stout Mexican lad used to moving quickly to serve over a hundred diners plus crew three meals a day. His well sharpened chopping knife found the German's backbone before his six gun cleared its holster, and found it by first passing through the German's generous beer belly.

That German squealed like a Hampshire hog until his squealing diminished to a final loud sigh.

Having his food in great favor, there was little complaint from the other travelers, twelve of whom also sit, between breakfast and lunch, on the jury quickly impaneled by the captain. The German is prepared for burial at the next stop, wrapped in a sheet, and the Mexican doesn't miss a beat and has lunch on the tables on time. Of course he is assisted by three helpers…who were not impaneled as jurors as it would have interfered with the preparation of lunch.

Such is life…and death…on the riverboats.

Which is why I'm not too heartbroken over the German's bad luck, but the fact was, I disliked him from what little exposure I had to him in the saloon.

And there certainly is no complaint from Ian and I as we outbid others, offering forty dollars, for the German's cabin, and now find ourselves traveling in style as well as having our worldly wealth in a much safer place. The small bed is barely room for two so we make a pallet on the floor with the single buff skin we've kept and flip for who'll spend the first night there…as we'll trade off from here on out.

With a stop in Bismarck we treat ourselves to some decent coats and more new duds. I now have a fine pair of boots and have replaced the coach gun I lost when the Eagle went to the bottom. More than once I wished for it when we were in the middle of a dog fight with the Crow. Nothing like a sawed down scatter gun for close work as the Union boys discovered when they came to rob our farm and hang my daddy. However, even a half dozen more double barrels couldn't have prevented that outrage.

As there was on the Eagle, the Glasgow has an interesting mix of folks—gold seekers, merchants, trappers, and even a couple of professional men—and I'm happy to join in some games of chance. Particularly since I've had several lessons from Chance O'Galliger and was fortunate in my play as a result.

And I win steadily, except from a gentleman with a high top hat, not as tall as Mr. Lincoln's custom, but high. Mr. Johnathan Gilbert, with a nicely trimmed van dyke under his high hat and pince-nez spectacles, says he's a man of the law, and another fair player is a physician, Albert Whittle—both gentlemen originated their trip in far off Philadelphia. And both truly are gentlemen and I spend a great deal of time with each, sipping good brandy, questioning them about their chosen profession. And both are tolerant of a young man trying to gain an education.

As the river becomes more and more shallow and in spots narrower, as tight as a couple of hundred yards in spots, the captain is now putting into shore every night, and every night either Ian or I, not both as one of us stays close to the cabin to protect our pokes, goes ashore to graze the stock.

After Bismarck the river, which has been almost due north and south, begins to bend to the west. As we travel, with little to do, an old trapper I've befriended, Nester Peabody, gives me an education on the country, critters, and savages. He's been as far west as the Blackfeet country, and seems to know of what he speaks. He points out Mandan, Gros Ventre, and Arikara Indians we see from the boat. Having to hit the deck more than once as they fire at what they call the smoke-boat. We return fire a time or two, but I do so with little enthusiasm as I've grown to understand why one would take umbrage at others riding roughshod over their land. As the Union did over McTavish Farm, and as Sheriff Oscar Scroggins tried to do and paid for with his life. Thanks to Pearl. Pearl, about who I have such mixed emotions.

We put in at the old fur trading post of Fort Berthold, once a stronghold area of the Sioux, the eastern Sioux known as the Dakota who arrived from Minnesota. Only two years ago was the conclusion of what was called the Dakota Conflict which ended with thirty-eight Dakota men being executed, hanged by the neck. The bulk of the conflict was east of here in southwest Minnesota. There was never an official report on the number of settlers killed, although it was estimated not less than eight hundred men, women, and children had died. So it seems the thirty-eight deserved the rope. And it seems a small price for that tribe to pay...of course no one knows how many they lost in the war. Come to think of it, they lost all—their way of life.

Battles between the Dakota and settlers and later, the United States Army, ended with the surrender of most of the Dakota bands. By late December 1862, soldiers had taken captive more than a thousand Dakota, who were interned in jails in Minnesota. It's said the hanging of the thirty-eight was the largest one-day execution in American history. In April of only last year, the rest of the Dakota, more than a thousand of them, were expelled from northern Dakota and Minnesota to Nebraska and farther south in Dakota Territory.

I can't help but wonder what Many Dogs thinks of this, and am surprised he didn't take my hair when he often had the chance. But it seems one band of natives is not overly concerned—and at times are even jubilant—when something bad happens to another tribe.

As we near Fort Buford and Fort Union, I'm elated. In a very few miles we'll be at the mouth of the Yellowstone River, where it dumps into and widens the Big Mo, and then into the new Territory of Montana.

Then there's nothing but wild country until we reach Benton City. Fort Benton, where Madam Allenthorpe is constructing a saloon and opera house. I'm eager to see both of the ladies, and smile at the thought Pearl has gotten fat. I'll bet Chance O'Galliger is not sweeping his gaze up and down her as he once did.

I've continued my games of poker, whist, cribbage, and occasionally chess, with only two others faithfully taking part. Albert Whittle, the physician, and Johnathan Gilbert, the law dog. I'm about twenty-five dollars ahead, and happy to be as most who've been in games with Mr. Gilbert, esquire, have left with nothing but lint in their pockets. He's been kind teaching me chess and not taking any winnings as he explained to me it would be unfair from a neophyte. I'll have to look that word up if and when I'm in the company of a copy of Mr. Webster's fine book. I presume it's not something too terrible to be called.

I've truly enjoyed meeting Whittle and Gilbert, and will hate to lose their company.

I'm not, however, looking forward to meeting up with Silas Jefferson Holland, now going by Wade Jefferson, known as Skunk to those brave enough to call him that.

Wade Jefferson, the law in Benton City.

Chapter Twenty-Seven

From the mouth of the Yellowstone over the hundreds of miles of river to where the captain informs us we're only a day out of Fort Benton, we see Indians at a distance, and more and more buffalo—a thing I thought impossible—as well as herds of deer, elk, and antelope too many to count. The occasional black bear feeds along the shore and less often, but more impressive, is the sighting of a grizzly—we're careful when grazing the stock, keeping the Sharps at hand, and have them back aboard before it's full dark. The country is low along the river and slightly rolling, the banks almost continually lined with cottonwood. The low hills are ravine-cut and sage covered with little in the way of evergreens but lots and lots of grass. The soil looks rich to me and were I still a farmer...

Finally, we're told we'll see Fort Benton on the morrow.

As it's our last night on the Glasgow we have what old Shamus would call a jollification, and see if we can drink the boat's saloon dry. I'm not one to be reckless with my money, but do buy the house a drink, which gains me a sore back from the slaps. I don't know how late it is when Ian and I stumble back to our cabin, but it's dead dark with hardly a star to light the deck…but when we near it's light enough to see our door is standing open.

Ian gasps, as I have a good share of my poke in the money belt Pearl sewed up for me, but other than what he has in his pockets, all of Ian's share is hidden on the underside of a small wash stand. A clever spot and I'd congratulated him on finding it, but not a spot that would take an earnest thief long to find. Ian beats me to the doorway, and is almost bowled over by a man trying to burst out.

As Ian goes to his back, he catches the ankles of the man and he, too, crashes to the deck.

The thief's on his feet almost as quickly and tries to run past me, but I have my revolver in hand and crack him one alongside the head, knocking him staggering backward, and into the grasp of a very angry Ian Hollihan.

The man tries to shove Ian aside and pass, but this time Ian sees him coming and manages to get an arm around the man's neck.

But the thief pulls a knife from his belt and slashes at Ian's arm before I can get to him. A moment too late I bring the barrel of the Colt down and smash his forearm and the knife skitters away across the deck.

Now Ian has the man's neck between his bleeding forearm—on the big fellow's throat—and his other forearm across the back of it with an eye-bulging choke hold. The thief is not easy to handle as he's lunging back and forth until they crash against the rail and the man flings himself over, but Ian still has a death grip on the neck.

The thief is hanging over the rail, kicking, and Ian is bringing all the pressure he can. The man's eyes are bulging and he's slapping at Ian's forearm. Ian's jaw is clamped tightly and I can see he's not going to release the man until he stops kicking. In seconds, he does, and Ian drags him back over the rail and flings him to the deck.

Others have seen the scuffle from a distance and come running. I'm thinking of turning the man to his back and binding his wrists with my belt, but then realize his eyes are open…but he's not seeing.

"You hung the bastard," I mumble to Ian, who's trying to get the bleeding in his forearm stopped.

"I heard his neck go. Don't think I hung him, think I broke his bloody neck."

The first mate, a fellow named Quincy runs up and kneels by the man. "This is O'Shea, one of our deck hands." Then he raises up and eyes the two of us. "What happened here."

I start to speak but Ian steps forward only a couple of feet from Quincy and snaps, "We caught the bastard in our cabin." Ian walks over and sees that all our things are in disarray. "Son of a bitch ransacked the place, looking to see what he could steal."

"Hummm," Quincy says, his hands on his hips. "You sure that's what happened?"

A short stocky man steps forward from the growing crowd. "I was up on the hurricane deck rail having a smoke. I saw it all. These fellas was coming to their cabin and this old boy burst out and knocked the big fella here down and run right over him. McTavish," he points at me, "gave him a whack as he ran by and knocked him back into the big fella who got a neck squeeze on him but this guy down here pulled a knife and went to whackin' at this'n, and the knife went flying and he got his'sef' hoisted over the rail where he kicked until he didn't."

Quincy had a laugh at that, smiling for the first time. "So, O'Shea was in their cabin?"

"Sure as there's water under this here boat."

"Okay, okay. A couple of you fellas give me a hand. Let's haul O'Shea down to the engine deck and get him ready for the sod. Then I'll get the captain and we'll schedule a hearing to clear McTavish and…" He turns to Ian, "What did you say your handle was?"

"Hollihan, Ian Hollihan."

"So it's McTavish and Hollihan. We got to get something done first thing as we'll be at Benton City before noon tomorrow."

But Ian doesn't wait for Quincy to finish and strides into the cabin, kicking his way through the mess. He reaches under the wash stand and comes out with the leather pouch he's bought in Bismarck to serve as his poke. Easier to hide than his saddle bags, he said, and he's proven to be right.

He gives me a wide grin, holding it out as if it's a fat trout he's just caught. And as if he hadn't just broken a man's neck and sent him to hell.

I sigh deeply. "Let's clean up this mess. It's your night on the pallet."

"Damn if it ain't, but you need to take a needle and some cat gut to this arm first." He unties the kerchief and shows me the cut and damned if it doesn't look like it will take more than a dozen stitches to close the gash. I re-tie the bandage and give him a nod.

"I'll go wake the purser and see what he's got in the way of medical supplies. And I'll grab a bottle of whiskey as you'll need to douse that gash."

He guffaws, "And douse my gullet with a few more if you're gonna be taking a needle to me."

"I'd sew your damn mouth shut, should I get the needle. I understand the purser is a fine hand with needle and splint, should it be called for. Use your good hand to clean up this mess while I'm gone."

"Humph," he says, as I head for the crew's cabin.

I'm a bit surprised, and dismayed, that the captain decides to leave the matter of O'Shea to the law in Fort Benton, as we're so close.

Damn it.

That means Skunk will be deciding our fate.

We can't let that happen.

We only sleep in spurts, and rise early, taking only coffee and some bread and jam as nothing is ready yet. Our problem is the stock. We're normally expected to let everyone who wants to disembark do so before we unload the critters, and in Fort Benton all will be leaving the boat. Our only chance to avoid Skunk, the city marshal, is to get off the boat well before anyone else, and well before the captain can send word to get him back to the Glasgow to investigate.

A twenty dollar gold piece is a fairly princely sum to a man making three dollars a day, so I try that number on the purser, as soon as we have our goods all packed and the stock in headstalls with lead ropes, and our one saddle horse ready to ride. He settles for twenty-five in gold, agreeing to put the aft gangplank down to the quay first which is not normal procedure. The aft gangplank is normally to load and unload freight and supplies, not passengers.

We plan to be gathered aft, ready to disembark as soon as the deckhands get the lines secured and the gangplank touches down. It's Captain Easton's habit to stay in the wheelhouse for most of a half hour and complete his log after each mooring, and we pray he'll do the same—or possibly longer—as this upstream leg of the voyage is complete, for he'll surely force us to stay aboard. As we'd be up against a crew of at least twenty-five, we've got to escape.

We've got to ride…

Ride where, I'm not sure, but west. I am sure we have to leave Fort Benton far behind.

Two other side wheelers are tied up along the long quay, and on each end of the side wheelers section a keel boat is under construction, being built to float down with the current. It's a busy river port, and folks bustle about as if there's a purpose in their walk. At least two dozen drays, beer wagons, and a stage move about on Front Street, as well as that many, or more, horse backers. Men toting various goods and boxes, and more than one man pushing a hand truck, weave their way from here to there and back.

We have the stock tied to the rails as the gangplank is swung in place. I lead the saddle horse down first and have to walk him thirty yards to a rail, and when I return to the boat, find a big burly deck hand poking Ian in the chest with a corncob size index finger.

And his voice rings all the way down the gangplank to where I hesitate re-boarding. "Capt'n says you two are staying aboard till he gets the law here."

Knowing that Ian will likely knock the big man on his butt—his look says so—I double time it up the gangway. "Hey there, pardner, no problem. We've just got to get this stock unloaded or they can't move the freight. Ask that big redheaded fella down below. He told us to get the hell out of the way with these animals." It's a plausible argument. "We want to get this cleared up more than Captain Easton does."

He looks a bit confused, then shrugs. "Okay, but don't get out of sight. I'll be watching."

"We wouldn't think of it," I lie, with a big grin.

He moves twenty feet down the rail and leans there, rolling himself a smoke.

Ian leads the pair of mules down, the latter tail-tied to the leader, and I fetch Sadie and have a big surprise when I again make the bottom. I glance up at a broad-shouldered black man with one peg leg, and have to grin broadly.

Damned if it's not Raymond, Pearl's brother, my old friend and youthful playmate, my former slave…which now seems a century ago. He has a wide brimmed straw hat shading his face, but it's definitely Ray.

"Ray," I yell. He looks over and does not return the smile. Damned if he doesn't give me a look that might kill this big percheron I'm leading. He makes no effort to come my way, so I set my jaw and continue leading Sadie to the rail to tie her with the buckskin and the mules.

Ian approaches with the other two percherons as I finish and stand just staring at Ray, only thirty yards from me, arms folded, hip canted favoring his peg leg, totally ignoring me.

"Ain't that…" Ian says.

"It is. Raymond, Pearl's brother."

"He ain't exactly happy to see you, looks as if…"

"No, sir, appears he's not."

"Want me to stuff that peg leg up his backside."

"Nope, we got more important business. I can just ignore him at least as well as he can ignore me."

"Okay, what now?" Ian asks.

"Let's get back onboard and coax that big ugly deck hand down below and get him out of the mix so we can get our satchels and weapons and light a shuck out of here."

"A fine plan. String these critters up so they'll lead. I'll head down and you find an excuse to get him to follow you after I find a place he won't see me a'comin'."

"Let's do it," I say, and spend a few minutes stringing the two mules together. One of us will ride the buckskin, one Sadie, and we'll get out of the way of Skunk and his deputy should they appear. I follow Ian back onboard, and see he's disappeared down to the engine deck.

I take a moment to head for our cabin and make sure that our satchels and weapons are ready to join us on a fast trip out of town, and they are nicely lined up on the bed.

I take a small risk, as passengers are moving about the deck, and leave the door unlocked so we don't have to take the extra time to mess with it. Quickly, I return to where the big deck hand still leans on the rail, smoking, watching us and the other gangway being placed on the quay.

I pass him and make the stairway down to the engine deck and descend, then immediately return to the passenger deck, and wave him over.

"That redhead...the straw boss down below. He wants your help."

"Humph," he says. "I'm a deck hand, not a damn firebox stoker."

"Don't look at me. I'm just passin' the message along. He says we all got to help move something."

"Lazy louts. We'd do all the damn work they had their way."

I lead the way, and am pleased he follows. We hit the deck and there are a half dozen other deck hands and engine hands scurrying about. I look one way then the other, and don't see Ian, then he appears on the far side and waves at me. Then he steps back behind some freight near the far side, where there's an opening and the river a few feet below.

"This way," I say, and wave the man to follow, and he does. I walk all the way across the engine deck to the riverside rail, and lean over. "What the hell..." I say, as if I see something untoward.

"What?" he questions as he joins me on the rail.

But he's only there a second before Ian's at his back and he's flying out into the river. He disappears for a moment and I'm afraid he can't swim. But he surfaces in the fairly fast flowing current and by the time he starts stroking, he's past the aft end of the boat. But unless he's a strong swimmer he won't make the space between riverboats and doesn't. He's swept on down the river.

The quay beyond the boats is a vertical wall six feet above the water, so he won't be in our hair for a while.

Another deck hand, who's seen the man go overboard, runs over to join Ian and I at the rail. "What the hell?" he says, repeating my last statement.

I turn and give him a shrug. "Damned if he didn't say he was too hot and wanted to cool off."

"Bullshit," he says, eying the two of us. But we don't wait to parlay with him, and head for the ladder.

With our satchels and saddlebags over our shoulders, and weapons in hand, we trot to the aft gangway, now having to tread our way through departing passengers. I'm able to give my friend, Alex Strobridge, a head's up as I pass. I've bought some goods from him that I'm not able to gather, under the circumstances.

I pause just long enough. "Alex, hold on to my goods. It seems the Capt'n wants us to have a chat with the good City Marshal or Sheriff or whatever the hell Skunk is, and we can't wait for that conversation."

"A wise move," he agrees.

"Are you at the hotel?"

"Got a room at Mrs. Ole's, ground floor, northwest corner."

"I'll find you, a dark night soon as I can…maybe tonight."

He nods, and we're off.

He yells after me. "If not there, try Angel's or Tennessee Slim's."

I wave over my shoulder. As we mount up, I see Skunk striding toward the Glasgow, a deputy following closely behind.

Raymond is standing as stiff as a statue, watching all this transpire. By his look I'm sure he'll put them on our trail if he discovers the reason Skunk has arrived and boarded the Glasgow.

I have no problem killing a thief, but when the thief is a lawman, that could be a bad decision. But it's a damn sight better than rotting in a cell or swinging from a rope. The McTavish family has seen enough of that.

Or fill him full of cut up square nails, I will, if it comes to that.

Chapter Twenty-Eight

At a brisk walk, as fast as we dare move without attracting attention, we're out onto the street fronting the river and heading for what I hope is a road up the bluff and out of town. I'm riding bareback and we have no pack saddles, as all our new tack is still with Alex.

It's the Mullan Road I seek, built by the military from this terminus of the riverboat trade all the way over the Rockies to Walla Walla, Washington and the Columbia River. The road ties the two great river systems together and weds one side of the country to the other. It's a tenuous fine thread, but the country has finally been sewed together.

I've paid close attention to my new friend, the old trapper, Nester Peabody. In fact, I've taken notes as he spun tales of hunting and trapping the country all the way into Idaho Territory.

But we're not quite ready yet for the Mullan Road; we have to go back and find Alex and get our gear or it's many miles before we can get supplies and equipment. You can't hunt gold without picks and shovels and pans.

Only three or so years ago, Fort Benton, named for Senator Thomas Hart Benton, was nothing more than a ramshackle group of run down log buildings—established long ago as an American Fur Company trading post—now, with the gold discoveries, it's a growing town with a Miner's Bank, the only stone building in town; Mrs. Ole's, a small hotel and boarding house which I make note of as we pass; two mercantile establishments, one of which is still under construction and I presume the Strobridge store; a tonsorial parlor; Angel's, a brand new saloon and opera house whose owners I know well; McFadden's Land Office; Polkinghorn's Assay & Shipping; a blacksmith and leather works; and three saloons, Fanny's, Bucket of Suds, and Tennessee Slim's. Mr. Peabody has informed me of two pleasure houses on the edge of town; Garden of Aiden belonging to a woman name Alice Aiden, and The Louisiana French Palace belonging to a mulatto woman from New Orleans.

A handful of other businesses are on the street inland a block.

It's a thriving town. However, I notice no church.

All but two of the buildings I can see are built below a long bluff rising well over a hundred feet above the river, but a cut, with a road I presume is Mullan Road, comes down from atop. Only two structures are high overlooking the rest. One seems to be a saloon, and another the other side of the cut appears to be a house…rather stately and two story.

As soon as we clear the edge of town and its drays and wagons, and get on top of the slope, we give heels to the animals and lope for a mile until we come to a rocky, dry, stream bed. A path where hoof tracks off the well-marked two-track road will not be easily followed. I swing off the road and clatter along west for a mile, then turn south again back to the river's edge.

We have to work our way down a steep cliff side to the cottonwoods on a narrow game trail, but when it flattens it's belly deep in grass and a small side channel of the river makes easy water. The stock will have no reason to wander.

It's mid-afternoon when we settle in. Ian is still healing so I encourage him to find a shady spot and settle down with a bit of fishing line and hook I now carry in my possibles bag, while I gather firewood. There's an infestation of fat grasshoppers for bait, and as soon as I have a pile of wood, he has a mess of small trout he's caught from the side channel and a pair of sharpened roasting sticks he's cut from river willow lining the bank.

We're in hog heaven.

The quarter mile wide cottonwood flat will conceal us and we'll be able to easily graze and water the stock. It's my plan to return to town, alone, and fetch our gear.

When the sun falls and it begins to cool down, I brace Ian, knowing he'll not favor my plan. "Mr. Hollihan, I want you to stay here and watch over the stock while I slip back into town and get our gear. I'll ride the buckskin and lead the mules."

"And why the hell do you get to have all the fun?" he snaps.

"Who's gonna break me out of jail should I get caught?"

That stumps him for a minute, then he drops his head and gives me a questioning look. "And what makes you think you'll be an easy catch were I backing you up?"

"They are looking for two of us. One man dragging two mules won't be out of the ordinary. They'll be looking for these white percherons that stand out like a wart on a whore's nose."

That makes him laugh. "So how long do you want me to wait a'fore I come and tear the damn jail down? Not that I know where the hell the damn jail is."

"I'm going in when it's dead dark and not leaving town in the light. I may have to lay low through the next light if we can't get supplied up with grub, so go to worrying about ten o'clock tomorrow night."

"That's real patient for me."

"You can handle it. Catch a mess of fish and dry them in case we have to get out of here without any grub. In fact come morning slip on upstream aways and drop one of those many whitetail we've been seeing and jerk some meat...you can keep busy."

"Okay, Cap'n, but come ten o'clock tomorrow night, you're not back, I'm getting my steam up and coming to town."

"I'll be back." I hope.

The sun is only down an hour before we get a bright three quarter moon. This time of year it's right overhead, and so bright it's casting shadows. But I have no choice. I'm sure Skunk is hunting us. I hope he's twenty miles down the Mullan Road thinking we'll be easy to run down as we're dragging stock, but then again he looks to be a lazy lout to me. Which is bad news as he may have said good riddance and be leaning on a bar in Benton City.

As there's a chance of running into him, or worse him and his deputy. I've brought along my coach gun, sawed to seventeen inches, shells loaded with cut up square nails as well as a couple of thirty-six caliber balls in each, and have a half dozen extra shells in my pocket.

I have to take the risk, we've got to have supplies, so I saddle the buckskin and let him pick his way through the cottonwoods heading downstream the two miles or so to town. And the town is pretty well lit up. There are a half dozen coal oil street lights along Front Street not to speak of the moon and light flooding from the establishments on the inland side and from well lit riverboats along the quay. So I avoid Front Street and stay a block inland until I think I'm even with where I'd spotted Mrs. Ole's boarding house, and turn that way, toward the river.

And as luck would have it, I'm a block short, but there's an alley, so, leading the mules, we clomp slowly down it until I see the two story clapboard building. At the front of the building there's lots of laughing and hooraying as men, and a lady or two, wander up and down Front Street. A buckboard or two passes, as well as more than one pair of horse backers. The wafting odor of a pie cooling on a window sill makes my mouth water. I'm sure it will be a good long while before the wonder of a woman's cooking blesses my pallet.

I tie the animals to a hitching rail on the side street and with little hope of finding Alex in his room, make my way to the window of the room on the southwest corner, where no light burns. I can't imagine on his first night in town that, after being on board a riverboat for over two months since heading back upriver from St. Louis, that he doesn't have an itch that only a pleasure lady can scratch.

I decide the alley is a fine way to move through town, however a man dragging two mules with no loads is much more noticeable than a man on foot.

So I ease the cinch off the buckskin and leave the critters tied near what must be Alex's room, and light out on foot down the alley. I only go a block before I hear a pianoforte and singing, and I recognize that voice. Few sing as beautifully as Madam Allenthorpe. On the next corner stands a partially completed building, with only framed walls but the roof is on. And under the roof is a makeshift stage, lined with a dozen reflecting oil lamps and in front of it are at least forty men, silent and raptured, on boxes and benches made of boards on boxes.

I slip between to thick lilac bushes, heavy with blossoms. The sweet odor reminds me of Pearl and I'm not to be disappointed.

Madam Allenthorpe has them mesmerized with her rendition of Beautiful Dreamer, but I'm more mesmerized by the woman on the pianoforte. Pearl. At first I wonder what Alex meant by her getting fat, then as I move farther along the alley and get even with the back of the building and have a better side-view of her, I realize what early on Alex mistook for fat, is now a very pregnant young lady. In fact, so pregnant I'm surprised she can maintain her seat or reach the keys of the instrument.

It seems she must have quickly put her talents to work on some no account Benton City hooligan or…and the heat floods my cheeks and backbone, Chance O'Galliger, the gold-toothed gambler. I can still remember him looking at her like she was a fine sugared and cured ham hanging in the smokehouse, and he was a week since eating.

I look at every face in the crowd and decide Alex is not among them, so I reluctantly move on, as Pearl and Madam Allenthorpe launch into Now We Gather At the River. And now I'm more determined than ever to get my mission accomplished and to get the hell out of Benton City and as far from this part of the river as I can.

In the next block I hear the raucous noise of a saloon, and risk moving out onto Front Street. All three saloons are side by side, and the one Alex mentioned to me, Tennessee Slim's, is in the center. I have to elbow my way through some fellows to get to the bat wing doors of Slim's. It's a false front affair with small-paned large six foot square windows flanking the swinging doors and with a tent over fifty feet long and twenty-five wide taking up the rear. I imagine there's a privy, and maybe cribs if Slim has some soiled doves working.

The bar runs half the length of the place and there's a small stage in a back corner where a fellow who's likely all thumbs is making some noise from a banjo. The stench of cigar smoke, so thick you can taste it, and sweaty men permeates the place. Maybe three dozen drovers, miners, and river men crowd the place. Some at round poker tables, some at a wheel of chance, some playing Faro. Alex is standing at the bar...talking to Raymond.

Damn the flies. I don't need to attract attention by having a ruckus, and Raymond looks to be ruckus on the hoof...at least on one hoof.

I search the place making sure I don't see a big ugly lawman with a black stripe in his beard, and when satisfied, move down the bar.

If I had a brain I'd wait for Alex to get shed of Raymond, but to be truthful, I can't help myself.

L. J. Martin

Chapter Twenty-Nine

S o I elbow my way down the bar and sidle up between them just as if I belonged there. My scattergun hangs in my hand, but no one much notices as a good portion of the men in the saloon have long arms on the floor by their chairs, leaning up against the bar between their legs, or against the stair rail along the tent wall.

This time Raymond gives me a nod and Alex offers his hand, and speaks in low tones, "You want to get out of here?"

"No, sir, I want a beer," and I turn to Raymond. "How's the leg?"

He shrugs. "What leg, you mean how's the stub. The stub is sore. Folks tell me it will be sore for a while more. I done get by."

"I guess you can't expect it not to be sore." His tone is surly and causes my jaw to knot.

Alex has ordered me a beer and it arrives and tastes like something from heaven. The foam lines my lips and I use the towel hanging under the bar to sop it away, before I respond.

"No, sur, I guess I can't."

Ray's sour look suddenly goes a little sheepish, and he stutters. "Pearly done tolt me you did me right when it happened. Said I'd be flappin' my wings with the angels had you not…"

I laugh, if a little tightly. "Or shoveling coal stokin' the fire down below."

For the first time since we were on the farm together, I get a whisper of a smile from him. "My daddy would agree wit dat down below part."

"Ray, I saw your daddy, he stood me to a fine meal. I was sorry…my heart still aches at the thought…to hear of your mama's passing."

"De done tolt me. I miss 'em some terrible."

"As I miss mine. Are you going back to find your folks?"

"I'm going to the gold fields. Don't matter you a slave, a son of a bitch from the south, or the king of England out der in the fields…at least that's what I done be tolt."

"Go easy on the south, old friend." I give him a hard look, but it softens. "You got an outfit…a stake? Maybe you'd like to go along…" I say, but let it trail off.

"Ain't got nothing but a need. Pearl say she can stake me, soon as she has your baby—"

"What?" I say, stunned. Then stutter. "When…when is she due?"

"Any ol' day now," Raymond says, slightly cocking his head like a hound that doesn't understand a command.

But it's me who hardly understands. "I didn't know…I never thought…I can't hardly believe…" I manage to spit out, my head swimming a little. But I do a quick calculation, and it sure as hell could be.

"She done wrote you a letter."

"I never got it," I manage.

"I tolt her," he said, his demeanor a little defensive, "dat you wouldn't have nothin' to do with no baby that was half her. But she said you done outta know, no matter."

"I had no idea…," I manage, still in shock.

Alex speaks up. "He would have told me something like that, Ray. Look at him, you might as well have broke one of those beer barrels over his head."

"I got to go to her," I say, and spin on my heel, but I'm going nowhere as I'm face to face with Wade Jefferson, Skunk, or Silas Jefferson Holland…all of his names suddenly come to me.

And he's wearing a copper badge and holding a revolver, aimed dead center at my gut.

"If it ain't McTavish. I got a warrant for your worthless ass." He grins like a wolf eying a helpless fawn. "I don't suppose your running mate, Hollihan is about?"

"He went to Oregon," I lie, my eyes narrowing. And Skunk's not alone, he's got two fellows backing him up. Fellas he took a swim down the river with a few months ago. Cornel Proust and Horst Gauss, the German boys we chucked over the rail of the Eagle alongside Skunk. Both of them wear copper badges as well. And Proust has a revolver hanging loose at his side, not as well armed as Gauss who has a coach gun, much like mine, cradled in the crook of his arm.

I look from man to man, and laugh, although I see little funny about the situation. Without taking my eyes off them, I say to my drinking chums, "I'd suggest you two find another spot to lean on the bar."

With that, I cock both barrels of my scattergun, even though it's still aimed at the rough board floor.

Skunk glances down then back to glare at me. "What the hell do you think you're doing?"

Rather than answer him, I speak to Proust. "You raise that scattergun a half inch and you'll be the first to get a belly full from mine." Then I turn to Skunk. "And that's a single action Colt, you gotta cock. You cock it and I'm giving you both barrels right in your fat gut."

Skunk laughs low, but unsure. "There's three of us, and I'm two feet with this .44 that'll blow your backbone out. I suggest you drop that bird gun."

"A sane fella would," I say, and laugh again. "However, I never been accused of being sane. This coach gun ain't loaded for birds, it's loaded for skunks and other vermin. If you don't blow my backbone out, maybe even if you do, I'll get you for sure and this cannon will blow you in half. Hell, there won't be enough left to feed the hogs—not that the hogs would eat your rotten ass."

Alex and Raymond have moved away, but the bartender, a tall slender fella who I presume is Tennessee Slim, leans over and snaps at Skunk. "Marshal, you take it outside. Won't be no shooting in my place."

"This man is wanted—"

Sometimes you just have to take the initiative, and I make sure I'm loud enough they can hear me in both adjoining saloons. They can surely hear me in this one, as it's so deadly quiet you could hear a mouse burp. "And you're a goddamned thief and a murderin' coward of women and children who rode with Bloody Bill Anderson. Did all these fine Union boys in Benton City know that when they hired you on?"

I can hear the men in the saloon begin to buzz with that revelation.

"The hell I did," Skunk says, but his face reddens.

"Your name is not Wade Jefferson, it's Silas Jefferson Holland, Captain Holland as I recall. I think I heard it was Hack 'em up Holland and some said you liked Take Their Hair Holland." I'm lying through my teeth as I'd never heard of him before we met on the Eagle, but you got to make do at times.

"None of that matters," he stammers. "You're under arrest."

"Matters to a lot of these fellas…hell, some of them may have had relatives in Centralia or God knows where else you did your dirty work. I'll bet you still got that string of ears you showed me aboard the Eagle. Ears cut off of folks you bushwhacked…innocent folks."

Spittle flies as he yells. "You son of a bitch, you rode with the south, with Mosby, and—"

"Damn right I did and proud of it. And I didn't kill women and children."

The bartender has rounded the bar, carrying a scatter gun as well, and he steps between us, facing Skunk, his accent is soft as a southern maiden's, so I'm sure I know his sympathies. "Marshal, y'all get your ass out of here and take these two Hessians of yours. Take this out in the street. These three shotguns go off and half my customers will be leaking beer outta holes in their bellies. Get out, now."

"Bullshit," Skunk manages, but the bartender has no back up in him.

The bartender stands his ground, and pokes with his double barrel. "You fellas go out the front, Jefferson. I'm sending this fella out the back. You can take it to the street, but it ain't gonna happen in my place."

I guess the fact the bartender has the double barrels pushed up against the side of Skunk's generous belly is fairly convincing. The bearded city marshal begins to back up.

"Get on out," Skunk instructs the Germans, and they turn and head for the batwings. Skunk keeps his eyes on me, but he's backing toward the door.

The bartender says over his shoulder, my way. "I suggest you get out the back…now."

And I do, but as I head that way, I note that Alex and Raymond are slipping out the framed opening that serves as a back entrance.

When I push through the canvas hanging under the frame, they're both waiting.

"This is my fight," I snap as I pass them and head for the alley.

I hear Raymond clomping along behind me. "Mr. Strobridge may not owe you, but I do, and I'm in it."

I stop and turn. "Ray, you and your family paid for all your lives on McTavish Farm, you don't owe me nothing'."

Alex yells at me. "I'm going to get your goods together. I'm no gunman but I can at least get you ready to get on the trail."

"Please do, my mules are tied near your room," I yell back, and he heads back into the saloon, I guess to go out the front and down Front Street to fetch the mules.

Ray palms an Army Remington he's had stuffed in his belt under his shirt. "You gonna flap your jaw or are we gonna get set up and ready for these murderin' bastards? They hung a friend a mine, so this ain't all on you."

"Good, Pearl would never forgive me I got you killed for my own reasons. Let's hope they split up," I say, and turn down the alley back toward where I've tied the buckskin and mules.

Before we reach the end of the alley and the cross street, I'm not surprised when Skunk and his two deputies fan out forty yards in front of us.

Only this time there are five of them. It's too dark to see if the other two wear badges, but I'd guess not. It's likely he gathered up a couple of townsmen who want to be in on the action.

"Stay back," I say over my shoulder to Ray, who's clomping along behind me.

"Why?" he asks.

"That Army your carrying is good at a distance. I need to get closer with this scattergun. Get some cover."

Ray stops at thirty yards and moves to the side next to some crates and empty beer barrels, but I want to close another ten at least.

I think they're surprised I keep coming.

"Who's that with you?" Skunk shouts out.

"Some bum out in the alley. Nothing to do with me," I lie, which I'm getting pretty good at. I stop thirty yards from the five of them. "Who's that with you?"

"All deputized," he yells back.

"All ready to die for some redleg son of a bitch?" I ask.

"What," one of the two I've never seen before snaps.

"You didn't know. This ugly bastard you think is Wade Jefferson is actually Captain Silas Holland, recently a cohort of Bloody Bill Anderson."

"This ain't our fight," the man says, and grabs his friend by the arm and they ease away.

We're back to three of them.

I'm using the scattergun in my left hand, and have palmed the Colt in my right, all three hammers are cocked.

"Skunk," I say, my voice a bit lower, "you got thrown over the rail for being a thief and those two German jerks followed for the same reason. You can turn around and walk away and leave me be, so I can ride out of here and not see you again, or you can die in the street."

"Big talk for one man against three, lay down your weapons," he says, his revolver is leveled at me, as is Gauss's, but it's Proust who concerns me most as he has a scattergun much like mine.

"All right, all right," I say, my voice sounding resigned, and I start to bend as if I'm going to set the shotgun on the ground, but instead drop to one knee, a barrel roars and lights the night, as I give one barrel full of cut up square nails to Proust, who's blown back flat on his back, both his barrels lighting up the night as they discharge into the air.

At the same time I fire with the Colt but it goes astray, and both Skunk and Gauss fire.

It's dark as hell in the alley except for the lightning-like muzzle flashes, and now our vision is further occluded by gun smoke and we're firing at those muzzle flashes.

And I take one in the side and I'm sure through a rib, and spin. The pain rips through me and it seems a lightning bolt has gone off in my face and burned its way to my toes...but I land facing forward flat on the ground, an even more difficult target, and I can hear the roar and see the flashes from Ray's Remington firing behind me and those of my enemies through the smoke.

I manage to get the other barrel discharged in their direction before a slug takes the shotgun out of my hand and a piece of my forearm with it.

Still, I'm able to empty the Colt before a cloud passes over my eyes, and all goes black and deathly silent.

Someone is holding my hand. I believe I'm conscious but fear opening my eyes. I hope the hand-holder is not a demon leading me into the molten rock and sulfur stench of hell. But I don't smell sulfur. In fact, I smell lilacs. I doubt if there're lilacs in hell, so maybe it's an angel leading me to the pearly gates. My tongue is so dry I fear it'll break if I try

307

and give it a wiggle, and my mouth tastes as if someone has been spooning me jackass corral leavings, and dry ones at that.

I try and pry my eyes open but there's such a bright light I have to shut them tightly.

"Oh, he's awakening," a voice says, and my hand is dropped and I hear curtains being drawn. Now when I try and pry my lids apart, the burning light is gone. The sun, pouring through a window into a room smelling of lilacs, and onto the now again seated woman who is not an angel leading me to the pearly gates, but Pearly—who looks like an angel to me.

"You're awake," she says, and gives me a smile.

"Water," I manage.

"Ray!" she calls, then turns back to me. "You don't try and move. I've got to go."

"Go, you just got here," I croak.

"No, sir, you just got here. You been out for more'n two days."

"Why do you have to go?" I ask, as Ray sidles up to the bed and lifts my head enough so I can sip from the water glass he's pressing up to my lips.

Pearl lays a soft hand on my shoulder, and gives me a smile that turns to a wince and she almost doubles over.

"What's the matter?" I ask, alarmed.

"My water done broke and Dr. Whittle is waiting."

"Your water…the baby?" I ask.

"Yes, sir. You get back to sleep and Ray will bring you some soup. I'm going to be busy a while."

"That's an understatement," another voice calls out. "Let's go Pearl. You don't want to birth that baby in front of these men." I realize it's Madam Allenthorpe's voice.

And Pearl's gone, and Ray replaces her in the chair, and Chance O'Galliger moves up behind him.

308

"You're gonna be fine," Chance says. "I've got most of a hundred dollars riding on it. There's a pool set up over at Angels…that's our saloon…and I took the longest time."

"The longest time?" I mumble.

"Yep, the longest time as to when you would die. Looks like you're going to live, so I'm going to win."

"Well, congratulations. I'm real proud you won. How long have I been here?"

"You've been unconscious two days. You lost lots of blood, taking one through the side like you did and breaking two rib bones. Not to speak of your broke wing."

I try to move my left arm and realize it's strapped down to a body well wrapped in bandages.

"I can see Ray is okay."

He gives me a grin. "Fine as Sunday morn'n. Thought they was gonna hang me for a while, but Judge Gilbert—"

"Johnathan Gilbert?"

"Yep, he's the new territorial judge. Appointed by Lincoln, came out from Philadelphia. Surprised you didn't meet up with him on the Glasgow.

I have to chuckle, even though it pains my ribs. "Hell, I played cards with him for a thousand miles."

"That's what Doc Whittle said," Chance adds. "He saved your ugly hide."

"And Skunk and the Hessians?"

"You kilt Proust and you or I kilt Hauss…and one of us shot Skunk through the leg. They had to hold him up to get the noose on him."

"Noose? Hell, I thought he was the law."

"He was, but Judge Gilbert swore in a new Territorial Marshal while Skunk was laid up and the new boy, name of Sam Sullivan, arrested Skunk right there in his bed and they tried him the next day and done strung him up yesterday."

"For what?"

"Seems like he and the land man, McFadden, were trying to buy out an old boy, Horace Bartelsville, who started farming on some fine bottom land down river a ways. He wouldn't sell and they shot him down like a dog. Seems they wanted to start another town as his farm fronts the river and has a natural quay for nearly a mile. They didn't know his woman was watching from a hideout up under the meadow hay in the loft, where she'd taken the kids. I guess McFadden had caused the folks concern a time or two before. His woman and her kids got away and hid out up at The Louisiana Palace with that mulatto woman until she heard there was a new judge come to town. She and her five kids all testified…youngest only five you couldn't understand for her wailing, but she did. McFadden will be tried tomorrow."

Chance interrupts Ray. "You want some soup?" he asks. "Good chicken soup. Pearl made it just for you. Said it used to be your favorite."

"I could take a cup, maybe. Right now I want to go back to sleep…but a cup first. And, Ray, wake me when Pearl…when Pearl…so I know how Pearly is doing."

And I do manage to get a cup down and get back to sleep.

When I awake, Doc Whittle is standing over me.

"Howdy Doc. Sorry to cause you all this trouble."

"Trouble? That son of yours was a lot more trouble than you."

"Son?"

"Yep. Miss Pearl said he was Braden Allenthorpe McTavish. A fine looking young man."

"Damn. He got all his toes and fingers and such?"

"He does."

Ray is right behind him, and adds, "Yeah, he's damn near as ugly as you, but don't have all the scars yet."

I can't seem to keep the grin off my face as Chance enters the room. "I got another cup of this fine chicken soup. You better get some down before Ray and I lick the pot clean."

I'm getting concerned as it seems all I can do is sleep, and more so as Pearl has yet to come to see me. So, sleep I do.

It's two more days before I can sit up, and do to see Pearl holding a bundle. "Mr. McTavish, this is Mr. McTavish," and places the baby on my chest. I wince, and she grabs him back up.

"Oh, we didn't mean to hurt you."

"Set him back down there. I want to see if he's as ugly as Ray says."

"I'll slap that Ray silly," she says, but she's grinning.

"How come you didn't come right away?" I ask.

"You ever birthed an eleven pound boy? I was down awhile."

"I'm glad you're here," I say, admiring the lad. He has a straight McTavish nose and small Irish ears...and except for his caramel color, I don't believe I could deny him. Not that I'd want to.

"Fact is, we're glad you're here," she says, "a boy needs a daddy," and bends down and gives me a peck on the cheek. "I got to get this baby on his mama's tit. You get back to sleep."

"Yes, ma'am."

But I can't as Ian stomps into the room. "You left me outta all the fun. How some ever, I just got to watch that highbinder, McFadden swing in the breeze."

"Him too, this town seems to like to hang 'em high. I didn't know the gentlemen."

"Well, I know the young man who worked for him and done took the land office over. He's seems an honest lad. I put a deposit down on the Bartlesville place. The widow made me a fair deal, and we got it bought. And I filed a homestead on the forty next to it and you and Pearl can file on eighty it up. That'll give us a section of fine land, almost three twenty of bottom land and that much grazing. Kinda reminds me of Kerry County, Ireland."

"What about the gold fields?" I ask, a little amazed as all he's been able to talk about for a year is grubbin' for gold. He seems even more excited now.

"Braden McTavish," he says, looking down his nose at me, "you're a family man, or you will be officially as soon as you hitch up with Pearl, and you can't go running off. Besides, I always wanted to be an uncle and I think farming's a lot better than losing your hair. The Blackfeet are raising hell west of here. I hear the Arapaho are hunting scalps on farther south."

I have to shake my head, as I guess my future is planned out for me. At least I think so, until Judge Johnathan Gilbert comes to call.

It's been two weeks and I'm just now able to take a chair at the table, and we talk about our trip, and our card games, and chess for a while, before he asks me, "Braden, you're a smart young man, you picked up chess quickly, you're articulate in a country sort of way and seem to be a hard worker. You've proven yourself to be brave...and to tell the truth, open-minded. It's not many men who'd honor fatherhood when the mother was a woman of color. Don't get me wrong. You know that folks who'll laugh and stomp when she sings will not share a supper table with her. I think Pearl is a wonderful, talented girl...but you both have a hard row of stumps to dig as many folks aren't going to take kindly—"

"I know that, judge. I've thought long and hard on it, but I'm raising my son. And to hell with folks. Besides, I've always...I've always been...as long as I can remember I've—"

"Been in love with Pearl. I understand, she's a lovely young lady." He gives me a tight smile, and nods...his approval, I believe. Then he continues, "I hear you've filed on a homestead as has Pearl, her brother Raymond, and Ian...and I understand it's a fine piece of land you've chosen. But it's only two miles downriver and you could be in town everyday should you desire. How would you like to read the law with me?"

I'm complimented he would ask.

"That's a fine compliment, Judge, but I only got through the eighth grade."

"That's quite aways farther than President Lincoln got."

That makes me laugh, and wonder if I couldn't do it.

"How long would it take?" I ask.

"Probably three or four years...maybe five, depending on how much time you can give it. You can work the farm at the same time."

"Hell, Judge, I'll be twenty-six or twenty-seven in four years, probably halfway through my life, if I study law with you."

"True, Braden. That's true. But let me ask, how old will you be in four years if you don't study law with me?"

I guess he's got a point.

THE END

About the Author

L. J. Martin is the author of over three dozen works of both fiction and non-fiction from Bantam, Avon, Pinnacle and his own Wolfpack Publishing. He lives in, and loves, Montana with his wife, NYT bestselling romantic suspense author Kat Martin. He's been a horse wrangler, cook as both avocation and vocation, volunteer firefighter, real estate broker, general contractor, appraiser, disaster evaluator for FEMA, and traveled a good part of the world, some in his own ketch. A hunter, fisherman, photographer, cook, father and grandfather, he's been car and plane wrecked, visited a number of jusgados and a road camp, and survived cancer twice. He carries a bail-enforcement, bounty hunter, shield. He knows about what he writes about, and tries to write about what he knows.

Other Works by L. J. Martin

Windfall. From the boardroom to the bedroom, David Drake has fought his way…nearly…to the top. From the jungles of Vietnam, to the vineyards of Napa, to the grit and grime of the California oil fields, he's clawed his way up. The only thing missing is the woman he's loved most of his life. Now, he's going to risk it all to win it all, or end up on the very bottom where he started. This business adventure-thriller will leave you breathless.

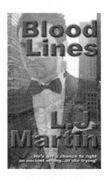

Bloodlines. When an ancient document is found deep under the streets of Manhattan, no one can anticipate the wild results. A businessman is forced to search deep into his past and reach back to those who once were wronged, and redeem for them what is right and just. There's a woman he's yearned for, and must have, but all is against them...and someone want him dead.

The Repairman. No. 1 on Amazon's crime list! Got a problem? Need it fixed? Call Mike Reardon, the repairman, just don't ask him how he'll get it done. Trained as a Recon Marine to search and destroy, he brings those skills to the tough streets of America's cities. If you like your stories spiced with fists, guns, and beautiful women, this is the fast paced novel for you.

<u>The Bakken</u> No. 1 on Amazon's crime list! The stand alone sequel to The Repairman. Mike Reardon gets a call from his old CO in Iraq, who's now a VP at an oil well service company in North America's hottest boomtown, and dope and prostitution is running wild and costing the company millions, and the cops are overwhelmed. If you have a problem, and want it fixed, call the repairman…just don't ask him what he's gonna do.

G5, Gee Whiz When a fifty million dollar G5 is stolen and flown out of the country, who you gonna call? If you have a problem, and want it fixed, call the repairman…just don't ask him what he's gonna do.

Who's On Top   Mike Reardon thinks his new gig, finding an errant daughter of a NY billionaire will be a laydown...how wrong can one guy be? She's tied up with an eco-terrorist group, who proves to be much more than that. And this time, the group he's up against may be bad guys, or kids with their heart in the right place. Who gets lead and who gets a kick in the backside. And if things go wrong, the whole country may be at risk! Another kick-ass Repairman Mike Reardon thriller from acclaimed author L. J. Martin.

<u>Target Shy & Sexy</u> What's easier for a search and destroy guy than a simple bodyguard gig, particularly when the body being guarded is on of America's premiere country singers and the body is knockdown beautiful...until she's abducted while he's on his way to report for his new assignment. Who'd have guessed that the hunt for his employer would lead him into a nest of hard ass Albanians and he'd find himself between them and some bent nose boys from Vegas! Another in the highly acclaimed The Repairman Series...Mike Reardon is at it again.

Judge, Jury, Desert Fury. Back in the fray, only this time it's as a private contractor. Mike

Reardon and his buddies are hired to free a couple of American's held captive by a Taliban mullah, and, as usual, it's duck, dodge and kick ass when everyone in the country wants a piece of you. Don't miss this high action adventure by renowned author L. J. Martin. No. 6 in The Repairman series, each book stands alone.

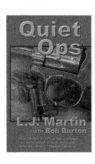

Quiet Ops. "…knows crime and how to write about it…you won't put this one down." Elmore Leonard

L. J. Martin with America's No. 1 bounty hunter, Bob Burton, brings action-adventure in double doses. From Malibu to West Palm Beach, Brad Benedick hooks 'em up and haul 'em in…in chains.

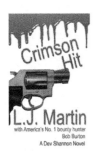

Crimson Hit. Dev Shannon loves his job, travels, makes good money, meets interesting

people…then hauls them in cuffs and chains to justice. Only this time it's personal.

Bullet Blues. Shannon normally doesn't work in his hometown, but this time it's a friend who's gone missing, and he's got to help…if he can stay alive long enough. Tracking down a stolen yacht, which takes him all the way to Jamaica, he finds himself deep in the dirty underbelly of the drug trade.

The Clint Ryan Series:

El Lazo. John Clinton Ryan, young, fresh to the sea from Mystic, Connecticut, is shipwrecked on the California coast…and blamed for the catastrophe. Hunted by the hide, horn and tallow captains, he escapes into the world of the vaquero, and soon gains the name El Lazo, for his skill with the lasso. A classic western tale of action and adventure, and the start of the John Clinton Ryan, the Clint Ryan series.

Against the 7th Flag. Clint Ryan, now skilled with horse and reata, finds himself caught up in the war of California revolution, Manifest Destiny is on the march, and he's in the middle of the fray, with friends on one side and countrymen on the other…it's fight or be killed, but for whom?

The Devil's Bounty. On a trip to buy horses for his new ranch in the wilds of swampy Central California, Clint finds himself compelled to help a rich Californio don who's beautiful daughter has been kidnapped and hauled to the barracoons of the Barbary Coast. Thrown in among the Chinese tongs, Australian Sidney Ducks, and the dredges of the gold rush failures, he soon finds an ally in a slave, now a newly freedman, and it's gunsmoke and flashing blades to fight his way to free the senorita.

[The Benicia Belle](). Clint signs on as master-at-arms on a paddle wheeler plying the Sacramento from San Francisco to the gold fields. He's soon blackmailed by the boats owner and drawn to a woman as dangerous and beautiful as the sea he left behind. Framed for a crime he didn't commit, he has only one chance to exact a measure of justice and…revenge.

[Shadow of the Grizzly](). "Martin has produced a landlocked, Old West version of Peter Benchley's *Jaws*," Publisher's Weekly. When the Stokes brothers, the worst kind of meat hunters, stumble on Clint's horse ranch, they are looking to take what he has. A wounded griz is only trying to stay alive, but he's a horrible danger to man and beast. And it's Clint, and his crew, including a young boy, who face hell together.

Condor Canyon. On his way to Los Angeles, a pueblo of only one thousand, Clint is ambushed by a posse after the abductor of a young woman. Soon he finds himself trading his Colt and his skill for the horses he seeks…now if he can only stay alive to claim them.

The Montana Series – The Clan:

Stranahan. "A good solid fish-slinging gunslinging read," William W. Johnstone. Sam Stranahan's an honest man who finds himself on the wrong side of the law, and the law has their own version of right and wrong. He's on his way to find his brother, and walks into an explosive case of murder. He has to make sure justice is done…with or without the law.

McCreed's Law. Gone…a shipment of gold and a handful of passengers from the Transcontinental Railroad. Found…a man who knows the owlhoots and the Indians who are holding the passengers for ransom. When you want to catch outlaws, hire an outlaw…and get the hell out of the way.

Wolf Mountain. The McQuades are running cattle, while running from the tribes who are fresh from killing Custer, and they know no fear. They have a rare opportunity, to get a herd to Mile's and his troops at the mouth of the Tongue…or to die trying. And a beautiful woman and her father, of questionable background, who wander into camp look like a blessing, but trouble is close on their trail…as if the McQuades don't have trouble enough.

O'Rourke's Revenge. Surviving the notorious Yuma Prison should be enough trouble for any man…but Ryan O'Rourke is not just any man. He wants blood, the blood of those who framed him for a crime he didn't commit. He plans to extract revenge, if it costs him all he has left, which is less than nothing…except his very life.

McKeag's Mountain. Old Bertoldus Prager has long wanted McKeag's Mountain, the Lucky Seven Ranch his father had built, and seven hired guns tried to take it the hard way, leaving Dan McKeag for dead...but he's a McKeag, and clings to life. They should have made sure...for now it will cost them all, or he'll die trying, and Prager's in his sights as well.

The Nemesis Series:

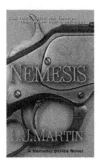

Nemesis. The fools killed his family...then made him a lawman! There are times when it pays not to be known, for if they had, they'd have killed him on the spot. He hadn't seen his sister since before the war, and never met her husband and two young daughters...but when he heard they'd been murdered, it was time to come down out of the high country and scatter the country with blood and guts.

<u>Mr. Pettigrew</u>. Beau Boone, starving, half a left leg, at the end of his rope, falls off the train in the hell-on-wheels town of Nemesis. But Mr. Pettigrew intervenes. Beau owes him, but does he owe him his very life? Can a one-legged man sit shotgun in one of the toughest saloons on the Transcontinental. He can, if he doesn't have anything to lose.

The Ned Cody Series:

<u>Buckshot</u>. Young Ned Cody takes the job as City Marshal…after all, he's from a long line of lawmen. But they didn't face a corrupt sheriff and his half-dozen hard deputies, a half-Mexican half-Indian killer, and a town who thinks he could never do the job.

<u>Mojave Showdown</u>. Ned Cody goes far out of his jurisdiction when one of his deputies is hauled into the hell's fire of the Mojave Desert by a tattooed Indian who could track a deer fly and live on his leavings. He's the toughest of the tough, and the Mojave has produced the worst. It's ride into the jaws of hell, and don't worry about coming back.

Made in United States
Orlando, FL
18 April 2022

16959488R10192